MW01488124

BETSEY ANNE

Diana Buckley

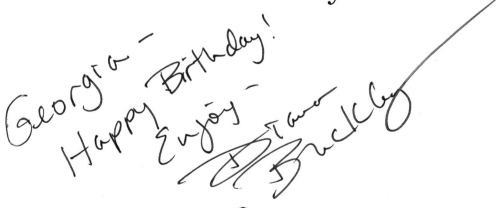

Georgia –
Happy Birthday!
Enjoy –
Diana Buckley

author HOUSE®

AuthorHouse™
1663 Liberty Drive
Bloomington, IN 47403
www.authorhouse.com
Phone: 1-800-839-8640

First published by AuthorHouse 10/20/2010

ISBN: 978-1-4520-5615-9 (sc)
ISBN: 978-1-4520-5616-6 (hc)
ISBN: 978-1-4520-5617-3 (e)

Printed in the United States of America

This book is printed on acid-free paper.

1858

CHAPTER ONE

Flossie Cline had a way of getting you up before dawn no matter what time of year it was, eliminating one of the few pleasures Betsey Anne had ever really known. She reflected on this fact as she stumbled over dirt clods in the already muggy half-light, with two wooden buckets dangling from her fingers.

If she had her own house, she'd lie in bed on summer mornings until the birds began to sing. It was really just a few minutes longer; not enough to hurt anything. Not enough to make the work lag behind. Just enough to make waking a pleasure.

"But I ain't much likely to ever have a house of my own," she grumbled to herself. "More likely I'll live and die right here, just Flossie Cline's girl, working my fingers to the bone."

With both the buckets full of cool, sweet-smelling water, she headed back toward the house, stepping carefully so as not to slosh the water out. Flossie couldn't abide wasted water **or** wet shoes in the kitchen, and it would only make for a long day to start off with a scolding.

Flossie was in the kitchen with her apron on and her sleeves rolled up, already measuring out the starter for the sourdough bread.

She looked up with a smile that made Betsey feel a twinge of guilt. She really ought not to think hateful thoughts about Flossie. One thing you could certainly say for Flossie was she worked as hard as anyone did.

Only five years older than Betsey, Flossie was plain without being homely, taller than the average woman, with straight, mouse-colored hair and hazel eyes. Most considered her remarkably fortunate to have married George Cline, ten years her senior, and already owner of the biggest farm in the county. But George was a demanding man, requiring as much of Flossie as he did of the hired help, even though her third child was on the way.

Betsey glanced toward the corner of the kitchen where the other two slept: Little Florence, four years old, her brown curls damp from the heat of the stove, and George, three, at his sweetest when fast asleep.

The two women worked beside each other with a rhythm that came from experience, both knowing without speaking what to do, how, and when. The bread filled the hot room with its heavy, sweet smell as it lay rising under a damp towel, the promise of its goodness reserved for the evening meal. Potatoes and onions simmered together on the back of the stove while bacon snapped and sizzled nearer the front.

Betsey tucked a mixing bowl up in the crook of her left arm and whipped the cornbread batter until it was foamy and ready to bake. Flossie's first words came as Betsey spooned the batter into the cast-iron skillet that waited on the front corner of the hot stove.

"Betsey, my new dress -- I, I need you to finish it," she straightened her back and looked as if she couldn't decide whether to be cross or supplicating. "I know I said *I'd* do the sewing, but well, you're faster at it and **this** dress is too tight already. If George sees it…" Her voice trailed off as her eyes met Betsey's and she involuntarily placed a hand on her round abdomen.

"No, that's alright, Floss," Betsey said. "You were right to have said it. Sewing's the lighter work and you in the condition you're in. But I **am** faster at it – besides it's nigh done." She splashed cold water over her hands and dried them on her apron before sitting down with the sewing basket, glad of the slight reprieve.

Ever since she was four years old, Betsey had loved to sew. She smiled as she stitched, remembering how she'd hounded her mother to let her try. "I'm big enough, I *am!*" she had begged. Her mother had a pillowcase to finish and gave it to little Betsey, who was sitting on a stool at her side. "Anything worth doing is worth doing right," she'd said, making Betsey take out the crooked stitches and try them again and again until they were right.

Flossie's new dress was nearly finished, needing only the hem, which they had marked and pinned the day before. Flossie was careful with her sewing, as with everything, but she labored over it almost painfully. Often Betsey shook her head as she went about the other work of the house while Flossie plodded along with her sewing only to turn out garments that were plain as plain, lacking any shred of imagination. Betsey offered, of course, to take a hand in the sewing, but Flossie had flown into a tirade.

"I'm the mistress of this house," she screamed, "I'll choose my own chores and line yours out besides!"

Betsey looked up from her reverie at Flossie, seated at the table with the two toddlers. She was sweet with them when she had the time, Betsey realized, but now she snapped angrily at them to eat their breakfasts quickly, glancing frequently at the door. George and the farm hands were due in from the milking soon, and they never wanted to wait on their breakfast. It wouldn't do for the children to be sitting at the table when the men came in.

Nor for Flossie to be wearing that over-tight dress she had on, Betsey realized with a start. Her fingers flew as the needle went in and out of the coarse, black homespun hem. Yards and yards around, it was, to accommodate Flossie's increasing girth as the child within her grew. Betsey focused on her stitches, scarcely aware of the activity around her. When she looked up again, the children were clean and seated on the mat in the corner with their dolls. With a quick snip of her scissors, she said,

"Floss – here's the dress, and just in time, I'm guessing. Why don't you go ahead on and change while I get the food set out?"

Flossie snatched the dress with a look that said she didn't need to be told what to do and disappeared into the bedroom with a slam of the door. Betsey Anne laid out the large pottery plates for the men with a practiced eye, tucking a folded napkin under one side and a fork under the other side as she went. Heavy earthenware coffee cups were set out next, and tin cups for milk or apple cider.

Betsey Anne heard the men at the pump outside as she threw the hot pads out on the middle of the solid plank table. Quickly, she grabbed the serving bowls and scraped the potatoes and scrambled eggs into them, depositing both on the table just as George stepped into the doorway.

The bacon was already draining on a large platter. Betsey slipped that on the table next and then cut the cornbread in squares as the rest of the men shuffled into the kitchen and slid into their accustomed places on the benches around the table. Flossie came to the table with the milk pitcher in her left hand, the jug of apple cider in her right, looking a little flushed and no doubt hoping George hadn't noticed she wasn't in the kitchen when he came in.

The men didn't talk much while they ate – didn't **visit** at all. George, looking for all the world like a storybook giant in his chair at the head of the table, lined out the day's work for each man between bites; they nodded or grunted but didn't bother complaining. It would've done no good in any case; George ruled his farm with an iron hand. But he paid out the wages on time, and the men were all glad of the work.

Flossie sat silently beside her husband, eating with small bites, careful not to have too full a mouth in case he spoke directly to her. Betsey was stationed beside the stove, ready to fill empty coffee cups or pass a bowl for a second helping, not really taking the conversation in. Until she heard Flossie say, "Send Betsey Anne?" with a high-pitched incredulity in her voice.

"I don't want you seen around town in your condition, looking as big as a barn. It ain't seemly to my way of thinking." George buttered a piece of corn bread as he spoke, then put the whole thing in his mouth in one bite.

Betsey turned her back on the table, not wanting to meet Flossie's glance. Market day came but once a month and it was Flossie's greatest pleasure. To be sure, Betsey would savor the afternoon away from the work of the farmhouse, but it was likely to cost a price, and a dear one at that.

"I've always done my own marketing, George, expecting or no," Flossie said carefully. "And the girl, well, I dunno…" She looked up at her husband out from under her long, brown lashes, letting her voice trail off.

"I know you like to go to town, sweet, I do," George said with an uncharacteristic smile. "But things have changed a mite around here since the boy was born, and well, I'm in a different position now. It just won't look right, Floss. Write out your list and send the girl in with Amos right after dinner."

He pushed his chair back with a scrape on the wooden floor, touched the back of a work-hardened hand gently to Flossie's cheek and went out through the open door. The benches scraped and work boots bumped and scuffed as the men hurried to follow him.

Betsey peeked surreptitiously over her shoulder at Flossie, who sat at the table with her hands lying listlessly in her lap, staring straight ahead. Her new-found sense of charity towards her employer surfacing again, Betsey said, "I'm awful sorry, Flossie, I know …"

"You know nothing," snapped Flossie. "Nothing at all and that's why you're not fit to do my marketing. But I got no one else to send, so I expect I'll have to make do. Wouldn't be proper for **me** to go, this far along and all."

Flossie got up and started clearing the food from the table. "Fetch that water and set it to boiling so we can get this kitchen cleared up and get at the garden."

Betsey closed her mouth with a snap and sloshed some water into the reservoir on the side of the stove, wishing she'd done that earlier. If she had it would be already hot and ready to wash with -- and picking vegetables in the garden seemed much more preferable to the stuffy kitchen just then.

Flossie cleared the table, placing what food was left over onto a clean plate that she thumped down at the end of the table for Betsey Anne. Betsey checked the coffeepot but found it empty and had to settle for half a glass of lukewarm apple cider. And as usual, the men had not left much food behind. It was just as well, though, as there was seldom much time allotted for her to eat it, and this morning, less than usual.

Without saying another word, Flossie applied bonnets to the heads

5

of the children, whose quiet play had given way to argumentative shrieking the minute their father left the house. She pushed them out the door with her person as she tied on her own bonnet and left Betsey to the kitchen.

Betsey gulped down her food, washed it down with the cider and added her plate to the waiting pile. With straining muscles, she lugged a large stockpot full of navy beans to the door where she could drain off the soak water that had been added the night before. Placing the pot on the back of the stove, she added fresh water and two pieces of salt pork. She chopped a large onion and scraped it into the pot. Then before she plopped the iron lid into place, she poured in a little molasses, smiling to think poor Flossie would never know the secret that made Betsey's beans more popular with the men.

"You ask me, it's time to start cooking in the yard," she said to herself as she mopped the sweat from the back of her neck and dried her damp forehead. Rolling her sleeves above her elbows, she started in on the dishes. The water in the reservoir hot and ready, the washing process didn't take long for one as practiced as she, and the dishes were soon stacked neatly in their places on the sideboard shelves.

Betsey retrieved her own bonnet from the airless lean-to Flossie liked to call her "quarters" and rolled down her sleeves as she stepped out into the hot sunshine. The day was characteristically humid, but the clouds were too thin to block the heat of the sun. Betsey Anne walked quickly to the garden, knowing that the picking and weeding would have to be finished before noontime if she was to get that promised trip to town.

Flossie and the children were already in the garden. Flossie had her picking basket over her arm and almost half full of green beans. The children were on their haunches pulling weeds along the straight rows of vegetables with at least a semblance of industry.

There would also be cucumbers, beets and mustard greens to harvest this morning, so Betsey Anne set right to work.

In the garden, the hottest sun did not beat down until later in the afternoon, so with the slight breeze that stirred, Betsey found the work almost pleasant. She walked bent over at the waist moving her picking basket ahead with every second stride and swinging from side to side picking the produce that was ready. Years of repetition made the work almost involuntary and she allowed her mind to wander freely, focusing mostly on the hoped-for trip to town.

The hours passed so quickly it seemed only minutes before the bushel baskets full of vegetables were stacked in the cool cellar and the lunch dishes were set around the table. Betsey gave the beans a stir with a long wooden spoon and heaved the huge pot onto the trivet in the middle of the table, then dropped the serving ladle in. While Flossie fed the children on beans mashed to cool more quickly and chopped apples, Betsey Anne stirred up her second batch of cornbread for the day and poured it sizzling into the skillet just as the men began to splash out the water at the pump in the yard.

She filled the water reservoir with the last of the water from the buckets she'd brought in at daybreak with a sideways glance at Flossie. Sure enough, her employer noticed the action, but responded with a laugh instead of a scolding. "So that's it, is it girl? Takes the promise of a free afternoon to get you thinking ahead?" Betsey flashed her a sheepish smile as she set the apple cider on the table.

"Need a hand with the little ones here?" she asked. Without waiting for the obvious answer Betsey Anne swept the children's spills off the table and the bench. Flossie deposited the brother and sister on the mat in the corner with their toys just as George's hulking form filled the doorway.

"Them beans smell powerful good, Mrs. Cline," he bellowed in a cheerful voice. "Set on an extra bowl, here's my old friend come to join us today."

Betsey looked up from testing the cornbread for doneness as George clapped his old friend on the back by way of presenting him to Flossie. "Ol' Tom Jefferson Hawkins from back in Ohio – I expect you'll remember me making mention of him before."

Flossie smiled shyly at the imposing figure before her – over six feet tall with broad, square shoulders and a long flowing beard almost in the Amish style. "I'm pleased to meet you," she murmured. "Won't you sit down?"

Betsey shuffled the bowls on the table to make room for the extra place and laid out an extra tin cup and coffee mug. Spoons being in short supply, she slid over the one from Flossie's place and replaced that with a fork, hoping the stranger wouldn't notice. But when she looked up, she found he was looking directly at her.

For a moment she was frozen as if physically caught by his disconcerting stare. He was in his early thirties, dark brown hair with a tinge of gray where his hair formed a widow's peak on his forehead. His left eye was hooded slightly, which only served to make the other all the more piercing, and his mouth had an insolent half smile that seemed out of place above the square-cut beard. Betsey dropped her eyes with a sudden sense that she'd been locked in his gaze for hours. Hurrying back to her place by the stove, she kept her back turned.

Why, oh why, didn't they cook outside this time of year, Betsey thought as she pressed sweaty palms against her apron and blew air from her lower lip toward the beads of sweat on her brow. She busied herself with needless work, afraid to turn around, and straining to hear every word of the conversation.

Even so, she could hear only snatches. "…until he locates…" and "…help out in some way…" then something about "…fine looking team…" and "…be more'n happy to." The clanking of spoons, bowls and cups suddenly ceased, all activity suspended as if everyone inhaled at once, then George barked out the orders for the rest of the afternoon. Betsey bit her lower lip when she heard Amos assigned to muck the barn, thinking with remorse that she'd somehow lost her precious trip to town.

"And Betsey can ride in with old Tom J here for them things you need, Flossie," George finished as he pushed his chair back from the table.

With old Tom J! Betsey gasped and whirled around to face the table, her eyes wide with amazement. She was being sent into town with that insolent stranger! Almost involuntarily, she looked at the tall visitor: his eyes were once again locked with her own. Feeling as though she had to wrench free from his gaze, Betsey turned back to the stove and busied herself checking the fire that was obviously hot enough and sliding cast-iron skillets back and forth. She was aware that everyone left the room except Flossie and the dark-haired intruder from Ohio.

"Betsey, *girl*," said Flossie with a measured tone, "Let's not keep our guest waiting. Get yourself ready whilst I make out my list."

Not daring to speak, Betsey hung her apron on the hook by the back door and hastened out to her tiny room. Shedding her work dress, she struggled into her only other garment, exclaiming to herself over and over again as the sleeve twisted itself, the collar turned under, the hem caught itself on the lid of her trunk and the buttons refused utterly to cooperate with her stiff and sweaty fingers.

"Oh, I wish I had a mirror," she said out loud as she fumbled with her thick, wavy, auburn hair. Knowing there wasn't time to let it down and start over again without fear of a scolding, she tucked the loose tendrils up under the braided coil at the back or behind her ears then looked down at her scuffed boots with dismay. She splashed a little water on her hot cheeks and left it there to dry while she dabbed at her poor boots with a wet corner of the wash rag.

"A lot of good that did, you fool," she scolded, "And as if it matters what any old chum of George Cline has to think about your boots anyhow!"

When Betsey Anne entered the kitchen, Flossie and the stranger were standing by the door as if waiting impatiently for her arrival. Hawkins was smoothing his flowing brown beard with his left hand while using his right to sweep his dusty hat across his thigh. Giving the hat one last flick with the backs of his fingers, he set it carefully on his head, stepped back from the door with a half-bow and said, "After you, Miss Springer."

Feeling Flossie stiffen as she handed Betsey the shopping list, Betsey ducked her head down and gave a tug at the brim of her hat as she stepped through the door.

The ride into town was something Betsey Anne had always relished — seldom as it occurred — if only for the sheer idleness of it. But on this day it seemed as if the tall stranger at her side was intentionally guiding his team over the roughest sections of the road and at just that certain trot guaranteed to add discomfort to any ride.

Betsey alternated between grabbing her hat and clutching the narrow bar at the side of the seat, her feet braced against the floorboards in a very unladylike fashion. Steadfastly she turned her gaze away from that of the stranger, although she could not help but be aware of his fixed stare. He said nothing.

The general store was a welcome sight, indeed: until Betsey Anne realized that she would be forced to allow this Hawkins character to help her down from the high carriage. "Well, that's all for it then," she said to herself. Refusing to show any discomfiture, she tilted her chin a little higher and straightened her skirt and hat.

"Thank you, sir," she said in her most gracious tone when Hawkins came around to her side of the carriage to help her disembark. His hands went easily around her waist and he dropped her lightly to the ground a little too close to his own person in Betsey Anne's estimation. But keeping her chin high, she stepped back slightly and said, "What time should I meet you back here, then?"

"I got nothing to do today but help you with your marketing, little miss," came the unexpected and unwelcome reply. "Just lead the way!"

"Oh!" Betsey Anne hoped with all her heart that he didn't hear her gasp. She snapped her mouth shut and swallowed quickly. "Why, thank you, then."

With a rustle of heavy skirts, she stepped up onto the wooden porch and into the cool, dark interior of Henderson's general store. Stopping to allow her eyes to adjust to the dim lighting, she fumbled in her sleeve for Flossie's list and managed to produce it just as she was approached by Mr. Henderson.

"May I help you?" he said politely and then jerked his bald head back quickly and exclaimed, "Oh! Betsey Anne! I didn't recognize you!" He shot a suspicious glance in the direction of her bearded companion.

"Thomas Jefferson Hawkins," said that same fellow with his right hand stretched out and that intense, almost insulting glint in his eye. Mr. Henderson took the proffered hand and shook it timidly, waiting, apparently, for Hawkins to continue. But in that insolent way of his, he simply stared and gave out only half a smile besides.

"Well, well, then, shall we get to the list here?" said Mr. Henderson, involuntarily wiping his hand on his striped apron before reaching for the small piece of paper that Betsey offered him. "I'll have these things wrapped up right away. Please, please, look around. There's some nice new dress goods and I just got in one of them automatic sewing machines from New York!"

"A sewing machine!" Betsey Anne shrieked with delight before she could catch herself. "I've always wanted to see one! Where is it?"

"I'll show it to you, Betsey *girl*."

Betsey straightened her back and tilted her chin upward, then forced what she hoped was a fetching smile before turning around to face her cousin, Mary Jane Crabb.

"Why, Mary Jane! I ain't seen you in a month of Sundays! Where you been keeping yourself?"

"Right here in this general store, day n' night it seems. But I ain't complaining mind you, on account of its mighty nice work compared to some," she paused pointedly. "How **are** things out to Cline's these days?" The innuendo was not lost on Betsey Anne.

"Oh, fine, fine," she replied, turning her eyes toward Hawkins and reaching a hand to touch him on the arm as though she had somehow the right to do so. "Things are as right as ever out there, ain't they?"

Again, the room itself seemed to await Mr. Hawkins's reply – and again it did not come. He did, however, take Betsey's hand and tuck it possessively under his arm just as they stopped in front of the automatic sewing machine Mr. Henderson had spoken of so proudly.

The machine instantly claimed all of Betsey's attention. It stood in a corner by itself like some kind of wooden-and-wrought-iron soldier with its chest all puffed out. Its treadle was as ornate as any she'd seen in a magazine ad. Its wooden surfaces fairly gleamed, so smoothly polished were they. A large wooden spool of thread was perched atop its spindle, and behind it were draped the promised new-styled dress goods.

"Oh my," she murmured as she ran her fingertips gingerly over the soft wood. "What a beautiful thing. I ain't never seen the like. Couldn't I just turn out the loveliest dresses with such a machine?"

"Betsey Anne," called Mr. Henderson from the other end of the store, "Mrs. Cline's a-wanting a new tea kettle, and there's two to choose from. You'd best come and take a look."

Betsey went reluctantly, leaving Hawkins and Mary Jane by the beautiful sewing machine. She caught a glimpse of Mary Jane's best flirtatious smile as she was turning to go, and then scolded herself for even noticing.

"You're a fool Betsey Anne. It ain't as if you wanted him for yourself."

She chose the tea kettle and then obliged Mr. Henderson by looking over the other new items he had in stock so she could "tell Mrs. Cline" about the new modern conveniences that were so easily within her reach. Betsey focused studiously on the items Mr. Henderson was showing her, one by one, keeping her head carefully turned away from Mary Jane and the stranger. But when Mary Jane's high-pitched laughter rang out through the store and she exclaimed, "Oh, you wicked thing!" Betsey suddenly felt an intense need to leave the room.

"Mr. Henderson, I've just remembered I've a letter to mail to my ma," she said, hastily. "Just see that these things get loaded up and tell Mr. Hawkins I'll be back soon enough." She left without waiting for his reply and hurried out onto the porch and down the stairs before she even took a breath.

"Oh, what does it matter anyhow?" she asked herself. "You never laid eyes on Thomas Jefferson Hawkins till this very day, and he's insolent, besides, locking eyes with girls he's never even met before and refusing to answer people's polite questions." She held her skirts up as she crossed the dusty street and then took the wooden sidewalk on the other side down to the post office, a tiny building not much bigger than an outhouse.

She'd written the letter to her mother weeks earlier, sitting up late into one dark night thinking of all the things she would like to pour out: the heavy sense of poverty that accompanied going into service for another woman, her longing to control her own life, to run her own household, to marry and to mother, and the harshness of her daily reality. Instead, she'd written only that she was *enjoying good health, and hope you are all well. Give my love to Granny Wright and kiss the children for me. I want to see you and am saving my wages till I can come home -- I hope on my birthday."* She smiled to herself as she paid the penny for postage and went back out into the street. Ma would know what she meant, how she felt. Ma always knew.

Thomas Jefferson Hawkins was already sitting on the seat of his rig when she approached. He bounded down and tipped his hat to her, making even that gesture of gentlemanly courtesy seem forward with his hooded gaze, then helped her up into the seat. The bed of the wagon seemed quite full, the goods covered with a green woolen blanket. Betsey wondered briefly just what Hawkins had found it necessary to buy, rolled her eyes at herself for caring and braced herself for the uncomfortable ride ahead.

Again, Hawkins was overtly silent, giving off a sense of having some deliciously funny secret and staring at Betsey until she almost wanted to scream. "I can be just as stubborn as the next fellow," she thought to herself, and steadfastly refused to even glance in his direction, let alone smile or attempt to engage him in conversation. Not a single word was exchanged until they stopped in Cline's front yard and disembarked. "Thank you then, Mr. Hawkins," snipped Betsey haughtily as she gathered up her skirt and headed straight to her quarters.

She couldn't help but notice that he didn't bother to reply.

Shaking out her good dress before hanging it up, Betsey Anne slithered quickly into her work clothes and went about the evening's chores. She tended chickens, carried water, washed up dishes that Flossie had ignored through the afternoon, and then served the men their light evening meal of fresh sourdough bread with homemade cherry preserves and slices of cheese followed by plenty of fresh, cold milk. The tea was prepared with the new tea kettle that Flossie hated to admit had been the right choice.

Thomas Jefferson Hawkins was conspicuous in his absence from the table, making the normal slight hum of conversation seem somehow odd.

After cleaning the supper dishes, Betsey Anne set out the sourdough starter for the next morning, swept out the front room, and refilled the water reservoir on the side of the stove. She should have been describing all the new items Mr. Henderson had shown her, but found herself unable to summon the words.

Flossie cleaned the children up and tucked them into bed. She turned down the lantern and hung her apron on its nail by the back door just as Betsey Anne did the same.

"Goodnight, Betsey Anne," Flossie said without feeling before disappearing into the other room with her husband.

Betsey went quietly through the back door and into her private little closet. She closed her door behind her for a sense of personal space, even though the day's heat was still heavy in the little room. Reaching automatically for things placed in the same place every time they were used, she lit her lantern and turned it up to fill the room with light.

She unbuttoned her dress and slipped it off, giving it a shake and a slap with the back of her hand and turned around to hang it on its hook.

"Oh! Oh my!" The dress fell unheeded to the floor as both her hands flew to cover her mouth, her eyes wide and filled with sudden tears as she beheld the automatic sewing machine that stood in the corner of her room.

CHAPTER TWO

Before the appearance of Thomas Jefferson Hawkins, summer plodded along like an old horse on a familiar road, one cracked hoof in front of the other, no need or desire to look from side to side, feeling only the constant weight of its burden. The meals were cooked, the dishes were washed, the children were cared for, the garden was tended: all without variation, without choice.

But two things were different for Betsey Anne in the long, hot month of July: the promise of a trip to see her ma in August, and the sewing machine.

The machine itself was a wonderful thing, all shiny and new and smooth. She quietly bought a piece of muslin from the peddler when he came clanking through on a blistering morning, biting her lip at the expense of precious money she guarded so carefully. To Flossie she said only that she "needed a new shimey or two," having decided to confine her creations to undergarments for the sake of secrecy.

She could certainly never let it be known that she had accepted such a gift from the likes of Thomas Jefferson Hawkins, in spite of the fact that she'd had no opportunity to turn it down. He'd not been seen nor heard from since that market day. Betsey listened carefully at meal times, hoping George Cline would make some mention of "Ol' Tom J" but she heard nothing.

She wasn't even sure what she wanted to hear. After all, he was a strange and disconcerting man, insolent beyond words. She shuddered when she remembered how she'd feigned familiarity with him to get Mary Jane's goat and how he'd taken advantage of it, tucking her hand so tightly in the crook of his elbow. Perhaps that action alone had given him the idea that he had a right to bestow gifts on her – and a right to expect something in return. She hated the memory of the way he looked at her with his hooded stare and that straight-lipped smile that seemed to stand guard over thoughts locked tightly in his head.

What was he thinking? Why had he bought her such an expensive gift, and then left without so much as a word? Did Mary Jane know what he'd done? Was Betsey the topic of town gossip by now? And what would Hawkins himself expect on his return?

Betsey would go over and over the questions and doubts as her hands performed the duties required by her employer. Round and round the same problems, rehearsing in her mind the myriad speeches she might give when he would come to confront her. She grew so used to repeating things to herself that poor Flossie sometimes had to shout to break through the reverie.

"Betsey! What **are** you thinking about? I've said three times to get the child out of the bath water! I swear to goodness a more absent-minded girl I've never seen!"

But by the light of her lantern, in the close heat of her own little room, she pumped the treadle till she heard the soothing hum of that wonderful machine and forgot all else. She crafted fine, dainty undergarments from her precious piece of muslin, literally breathing in pleasure from the process. She had always loved to sew, always reveled in her own skill at it, but the machine was its own source of joy and wonder.

One thing she had to say for Hawkins: he knew what she wanted. How did he know? Did Mary Jane tell him? Did he just see it in the way she touched the machine that day? Did he have that extra intuition about people, like her ma had? Did he just buy the most expensive thing in the store by way of making an impression?

By day Betsey wondered, and dreaded his reappearance. What price might he expect of her? Would she somehow be forced to surrender the beautiful machine if she were unwilling to pay his price?

By night, Betsey sewed and forgot. And for this little piece of sanity she was thankful.

The fourth day of August was the day promised for her trip to see her family – her 17th birthday. Her mother's letter had arrived, saying they'd expect her. It also said they were glad she was saving her wages – if she'd saved enough perhaps she could remain at home, but not to get her hopes up too high. Granny Wright was in a bad way and pa's back wasn't much better than before. Ma had suffered with a stitch in her shoulder, but she'd worked all summer anyway, what with Betsey Anne and Fannie both working away. Lydia had been sick again; she wasn't able to help much around the house even though she was almost 11.

No, it didn't sound hopeful for staying at home. Betsey thought about it again as she lay on her bed that August morning. A few weeks earlier she wanted nothing more than to go home and never come back. But now – well, if she stayed home she'd have to leave that sewing machine behind. In a way, she was afraid ma would **ask** her to stay home and help with the work there.

Feeling suddenly hot and bothered, she kicked back her light quilt and lay arms and legs akimbo on top of the bed. One thing she most certainly would not do was rise before daylight on her birthday. Her one day off. It wasn't like Amos would shake himself to drive her into town before he'd had his breakfast anyway.

She lay with her toes stretched out and picked a strand of hair up from her forehead, stretching it out to its full auburn length and twisting it round and round before choosing another strand for exactly the same exercise, savoring the sheer idleness of the moment. Suddenly the door of her tiny apartment burst open and the room was filled with the hulking frame of George Cline, a look of terror on his face and sweat running down his neck.

"Get help – get the midwife – do it now!" He was gone again as swiftly as he arrived and Betsey was into her dress before she knew she had gotten to her feet. Shoving her toes into her boots and turning the tops to the inside so they wouldn't flap, she headed out the door on the run.

The midwife was at the next farm – about a mile down the road.

The midwife. It was far too early for Flossie to give birth. Far too early. A wild scream reached out from the house like the lash of a whip and goaded Betsey on. She pulled the back of her skirt up between her legs, drawing it up pantaloon style so she could run a little faster.

The next farm was awake and in motion as the sun was beginning to peek over the horizon. Betsey found Middie Watson at her well drawing her morning's water. It took Middie only one look at the disheveled girl to realize the problem. Wordlessly, she ran into the house and returned with her bag, her husband following her out the door pulling his suspenders over his shoulders as he ran toward the barn. He had the horse in its traces before Betsey Anne had fully caught her breath and they were on their way back to Cline's.

As soon as they arrived, Middie swung down from the wagon seat and disappeared into the house. Screams were still coming from the bedroom, but the quality of them was somehow different. Betsey Anne went to the kitchen and gathered up Little Florence and Georgy and hustled them out into the garden.

The children were scared, she could see, and at first they were just glad to have some attention, no matter whose it was. Before long, however, they began to cry for their mama and resist each thing she tried to do with them. The morning inched by as she struggled to employ or entertain their frightened energies, first picking hard, green pears to munch on in the orchard, then pulling weeds in the garden, then digging carrots and potatoes, and finally drawing pictures in the dirt. When that wore out, she considered venturing a little closer to the house where their father had built them a wooden swing, but that's when she saw Middie Watson sitting on the bench outside the front door with her arm around George Cline's slumped shoulders.

Betsey froze, unsure what to do, or what would be expected of her. Suddenly realizing that the children were clamoring at her skirts, she bent down and hugged them close, wondering just how bad it was at the house. Was Flossie gone? Or just the child?

"Come with me, girl, and bring those children alongside their mother." It was Middie, standing at the garden fence. "Who knows, maybe it'll help."

Betsey led the children to Middie, who took them matter-of-factly by the hand and said, "Come along then, your ma needs you right now, younguns, so mind your manners and hold your tongues."

Betsey hung back a few paces, not wanting to be forward, but not wanting to be out of reach if she were called. George had splashed his face with cold water from the pump in the yard, then wiped his huge sleeve across his chin and watched in silence as his children went through the front door.

"George?" Betsey used only his name to embody her question.

He looked at her dully for a moment, then growled out, "I reckon she'll live," and turned his back, heading toward the barn.

Betsey Anne went hesitantly into the kitchen to see what might need doing. The stuffy room was heavy with the smell of childbirth, so she opened the back door for a cross draft and started tidying up. A good pot of coffee brewing on the back of the stove would go a long way toward normalizing things, she thought, so that she tackled next, then started chopping potatoes and onions by way of a late noon meal.

She could hear Middie's deep, soothing voice in the next room, but no response from Flossie or the children. Finally, after what seemed like hours, the children emerged and went straight to their mat in the corner to fall into a tug-of-war over a favored doll. "Younguns, hush yourselves, or I'll be sending you to the barn," said Middie as she closed the bedroom door behind her.

"Them are nice smells you got going on the stove, girl." Middie clapped a work-worn hand on Betsey's shoulder. "Could you pour me a cup of that coffee?"

Betsey Anne retrieved a mug from the shelf and filled it with the steaming brew. Parking it on the table in front of the midwife, she sat down opposite, flashing a quick glance over her shoulder at the children. "Little pitchers have big ears," she offered as a way to open the conversation.

"Aye, that they do," was the only reply, followed by a deep slurping of hot coffee. Silence lingered heavily in the air for a few minutes. Middie didn't speak again until she'd finished her coffee and headed toward the door. "I'll send for the parson to take care of the burying and at least that'll be done. There'll be no more children born to that little mother, or I miss my guess. It's that pain that's the heaviest on her right now I think."

Betsey Anne didn't move from the bench until she smelled a

slight burning of potatoes and onions. No more children for Flossie. Betsey had followed her mother around dispensing herbs and teas and healing advice since she was big enough to walk. Between that and being the second of six children, she'd seen a lot of babies come into the world – and a lot of the associated complications. She tried to think back. One time her ma had said there'd be no more children. She called it a prolapse and she said the pain was great.

But that woman hadn't suffered any hysterics about it – she had ten children already and was very nearly 40 years old. It was different for Flossie. Flossie **wanted** ten children and she only had two. And she was given to hysterics to begin with.

Betsey Anne put the children down at the table with plates of potatoes and cups of cold milk in front of them then went to the sideboard for a piece of paper. She'd write a letter to ma. Had to be done no matter what to let her know why she hadn't made it home for her birthday. And maybe ma would send her a concoction or two to soothe poor Flossie's sorrow.

She made what she hoped was a cup of comforting tea and tiptoed into the bedroom to set it on the stand beside the bed. Flossie was not asleep. She lay on her side staring straight at the wall but it was apparent she saw nothing. She didn't even stir when Betsey Anne came in, nor again when she went out, carrying the soiled sheets with her.

The day inched by with its curious absence of work or routine. Standing in the doorway, Betsey could see there was no activity at all on the place. The tools and farm implements all stood untouched. Even the animals seemed subdued.

All Betsey could do was struggle with the unhappy children and check the fire in the stove where the fried potatoes rested unused. The sun went down and night began to gather in the corners, but still George did not reappear.

With a sigh, Betsey Anne got out the children's night things and readied them for bed. She tucked them in and listened to their prayers, shushing their cries for mama and reassuring them that mama was just tired and they'd see her in the morning.

In her own room at last, she sagged onto the bed where the quilt still lay in a rumpled heap since morning. Even the magical sewing machine held no interest to her fatigued mind. To be sure, she felt disappointed in the loss of her long-awaited birthday trip to see her ma. Oh, how she'd longed for the restfulness of idle afternoon hours. But in the face of Flossie's pain, it seemed ever so selfish to even consider her own loss, and so the day's idleness was awkward and had weighed heavy on her to the point of exhaustion.

"Tomorrow's another day, child," she recalled her mother's familiar words, whispering them to herself as she climbed under the quilt at last. "Everything seems worst in the dark of the night." Tomorrow would no doubt hold the usual routine of cooking, cleaning, gardening. The men would work and would need to be fed. Flossie would at least gather her wits about her and comfort her children, even if she didn't rise from her bed. Yes, tomorrow would be another day.

And she'd surely see her ma soon enough.

CHAPTER THREE

Flossie did not rise from her bed the next day – nor did she gather her wits or her children about her. In fact, it was fully three days before Betsey Anne could coax her to sit up and have her hair brushed and her gown changed. "She's worse to care for than Granny Wright," Betsey mumbled to herself after attending to some of Flossie's personal needs.

The parson had appeared and read a few words from the Bible over the spot where the lifeless child had been laid. Little Florence and Georgy clung to their father's trouser legs silently sucking their thumbs and staring wide-eyed at the parson. Betsey Anne listened with one ear as the words of the familiar twenty-third Psalm were intoned without depth or feeling. She glanced over her shoulder time and again, hoping that Flossie would come out of the house and join them. Pain or no, it was selfish to miss your own child's funeral.

Next morning, George Cline and the men returned to their normal schedule for meals, which Betsey struggled to prepare by herself. She juggled the children's needs in where she could, and bit her lip when she heard herself snapping angrily at them. After all, they wanted their mama and they couldn't understand why Flossie didn't come to them.

The days were over full. The farm clearly required more than one woman in the house: otherwise, Betsey Anne reasoned, she wouldn't be there in the first place. She rose well before dawn each day. She organized and planned, remembering to do the extra little things in advance that saved so much time and effort later in the day. She worked as hard as she could, never allowing herself an idle moment.

And she dropped into her bed at night with nothing more than a longing glance at her beloved sewing machine, too tired to even caress the smooth wooden surface of its cabinet before dropping off to sleep.

"Something has to be done," she murmured to herself as she pulled the second bucket of water from the well early in September. "Something. Something." But no ideas came to her as she trudged toward the house to begin the day's struggle anew.

Nothing came to her as she prepared the breakfast for the men. Nothing came to her as she shoveled food into the children's squabbling mouths. Nothing came to her as she cleaned them up and piled them in the corner with their toys. Nothing came to her as she set out the food and poured the coffee.

But when Georgy toddled over to the table and stood by his father's knee, looking up at him with big brown eyes and upchucked his breakfast in his father's lap, something came to her.

"Oh, for pity's sake!" she exclaimed. While George Cline scraped back his chair and made haste for the door amid a mixture of guffaws and gags from his men, Betsey Anne snatched up the pale-faced child and burst into Flossie's bedroom where she deposited him in the middle of his mother with force.

"Now there's the last straw, Florence Cline!" she said angrily. "I've done your mothering for you for long enough. If this farm can be run by one woman alone, then that woman's you and not me, and that's a certain fact. Hard work's the best remedy for a heavy heart anyway, my ma always said, and you're fixing to get yourself a strong dose. I ain't a'coming back in till you've cleaned up that child's spew and that's final."

She spun on her heel and went back through the kitchen to the back door and out. Once out, she ran as fast as she could to the orchard and dropped down, shaking, under the shade of a pear tree. Putting her hands to her burning face she began to cry. "Oh my, Betsey Anne, you've done it this time," she chided herself. "You've sure enough done it this time."

But after a while the tears subsided and she curled herself on her side on the mossy ground and slept, weary to the bone. It was the sun, directly overhead and twinkling through the leaves that woke her. Noon. At least.

She rose stiffly from the ground and dusted her skirts off, shaking the leaves out of her apron and picking a twig or two from her braided hair.

"Well, I guess you're not fired yet, girl," she said to herself and she started back to the house to see what the damages were. A few yards from the door, she began to hear voices, more jovial than she'd heard in a while. One speaker was Flossie!

And one was Thomas Jefferson Hawkins.

Betsey Anne hitched up her skirts and hurried around to the front of the house. There was his team! She rushed to her room, heart pounding, closed the door and leaned hard against it, as though to prevent someone from breaking in. She stared at the machine – the beloved sewing machine. So this was it. This was the day she'd been dreading. What price would he demand?

She shook herself and thought to tidy herself up a bit. Splashing water in her basin, she used it to freshen her tear-stained face and cool the back of her neck. She coiled her long braid up around her head in what she hoped was a more grown-up fashion then laughed at herself for caring. Licking her dry lips with a tongue that seemed swollen too big for her mouth, she laid her hand on the doorknob and said out loud, "Well, at least Flossie's finally stirred from her bed."

She opened the back door of the house with as much feigned confidence as she could muster and announced herself with a cheerful, "Flossie! It's so good to see you up and about! It truly is!"

Flossie turned from her conversation with Hawkins and surveyed Betsey Anne for a moment or two, her mouth partly open as if to speak. Finally, she closed her mouth with a snap and said, "You'd best snap to, girl, the men'll be here any minute now."

Betsey nodded a quick "Yes'm" and headed for the stove, feeling quite lucky to have retained her job and afraid to look at the guest. He was characteristically silent and she could feel that hooded stare of his boring into the space between her shoulders as she worked.

George Cline was struck momentarily speechless himself when he caught sight of his wife, dressed and seated demurely at the table as if nothing unusual had transpired.

"Well if it ain't Ol' Tom J himself!" he bellowed with a clap on the back and a shake of the visitor's hand. "Where you been keeping yourself?"

"I've located me a piece of land in section 12," said Hawkins, looking directly into Betsey Anne's upturned eyes.

There was a sudden buzzing in her ears and a flush came over her, a wave of heat that seemed to start in her toes and threatened to knock her to her knees. She had turned from the stove and was looking shamelessly up at him with her mouth open as though she had a right to listen! What would Flossie think? Had George noticed?

Thomas Jefferson Hawkins had most certainly not missed it. Her breath came in quick, short gulps and she burned her hand reaching absently for the cornbread skillet without benefit of a hot pad. Stifling an exclamation of pain, she shook the affected hand and used the other to remove the bread from the stove and deposit it in the middle of the plank table. She brought the apple cider and then the coffee while Flossie ladled navy beans into the upheld bowls around the table.

"Thank heavens," Betsey thought to herself as she reflected on how much more smoothly the serving of the meal went with two women in the kitchen. "Only imagine how things would've gone if *he* came whilst *she* was still a'lying in her bed."

She busied herself once again with needless tasks around the stove or in the corner where the children were playing. Again, she strained her ears to hear any part of the conversation with regard to the stranger.

"I think it's only fair, George," came that unfamiliar voice in a tone that seemed to have been raised up and heaved over his shoulder in her direction. "After all, she's had extra work on her shoulders whilst the missus was laid up so long."

"Yes, yes I agree," said Flossie.

Betsey stole a glance at the recently recovered Mrs. Cline just in time to catch her shooting a sharp glare at Hawkins across the table. They were obviously talking about her, Betsey knew. But she hadn't been able to hear what came before. She swallowed hard and hurried back over to the table with the coffeepot, her burned hand shaking as she filled George's mug.

"Well, I guess you're right on it, then," said the head of the household between bites of buttered cornbread. "You might as well take out right after dinner, I expect, but she'll have to be back here by Saturday night and no later." He wiped a thick hand across his mustache and scraped his chair back from the table, the men rising from their benches as one with him.

Take out after dinner. Back by Saturday. What in the world could they mean? Was she being sent somewhere with Hawkins? And where?

"Don't lollygag around, girl," came Flossie's sharp voice. "Mr. Hawkins'll have his team ready and you haven't even cleared the table yet, and him kind enough to fetch you all the way to your mother's and back."

"Ma!" Betsey bit her lip to stifle her excitement and caught herself just in time to avoid spilling the dish water. She was to go see her mother that very afternoon! And to be driven all the way!

By Thomas Jefferson Hawkins.

At that thought her mind seemed to lock itself into a panicky spin. *Hawkins. The sewing machine. Hawkins. The sewing machine. What would he want? What would he say? What would he think? Would he tell her mother? Hawkins. The sewing machine. The sewing machine. Her lovely machine...*

Suddenly, Flossie's startled shriek pierced Betsey's reverie. "Mr. Hawkins! You frightened me a'coming in that back door without a warning! Why, what in the world! Betsey, girl, you've kept our guest waiting long enough now – put down that apron and skedaddle!"

"My dress --," started Betsey, smoothing the front of her work dress with a still-damp hand.

"You look right as rain to me, little miss," said the usually silent Hawkins. "And my team's a'waiting by the door." He placed a proprietary hand in the middle of her back and urged her toward the front door as she gave a wide-eyed look to a surprised Flossie.

Flossie recovered first. "Here, girl, here – take my bonnet!" She sprang to the hook on the wall and offered her gardening bonnet to Betsey just before she headed out into the afternoon sun.

Betsey Anne already knew what kind of buggy ride to expect from "Ol' Tom J", so she positioned herself accordingly on the high seat, bracing her feet and taking a firm hold of the small railing at her side. Still feeling a little startled at the rush he gave her to get out the door and on the way, she offered him a watery little smile out from under the extra-wide brim of Flossie's bonnet. Hawkins responded just as she had expected him to: in silence and with his trademark "cat that swallowed a bird" smile and that annoying twinkle in his eye.

There was a quick snap of the reins and they were off, trotting almost violently down the rutted road toward town. Toward home and ma. Betsey couldn't help a little thrill of excitement that coursed through her. It had been over eight months since she'd seen her ma and pa. Lydia, Adam, Ransom and Baby Charles would all seem to have grown up overnight. Fannie would no doubt not be home, since Betsey wasn't expected that day. And Granny Wright would call out for "Little Bets" to sit beside her while she dropped off to sleep.

Even being rushed out the door in her work dress still damp from the dishwashing and a borrowed bonnet couldn't spoil the fun of surprising them all. It was almost better than the promised trip home for her birthday, given that element of fun. She smiled to herself thinking of the many jokes she'd lovingly played on her family over the years – egged on by her fun-loving pa. One morning she'd baked little bits of newly-carded cotton in the middles of their corn muffins; another she'd substituted raw eggs for hard-boiled at the dinner table. Betsey Anne laughed right out loud as she recalled the time she and her pa had kept the whole family in stitches all the way through breakfast by reporting to ma that young Ransom had "slumbered in his bed last night" and then sitting back quietly while the indignant child argued that he'd done "no such thing, mama, really I didn't!"

"What's so funny?" asked Hawkins suddenly.

"Oh!" cried Betsey, realizing she'd completely forgotten his presence until he spoke. "Oh – I was just thinking about seeing my family and all. It'll be good, that it will."

He flashed her a sudden mouthful of sparkling white teeth he'd never shown before and gave out a laugh of his own which Betsey couldn't help joining. "You're a mighty pretty girl when you get a smile on your face, little miss, and your laugh's like a little tin bell." That compliment delivered, he shut his mouth down again to that flat-lipped half-smile and went right back to staring at her out from under his hooded eyelid.

She looked away, but found that his stare drew her back again. She stared right back at him, full on, as though she had no shame. Then suddenly he winked his right eye at her and the effect made him appear so comical that she burst out laughing again. The laughter bubbled up from way down deep inside her, like so much pent-up emotion from all the hard months behind her. Feeling like a schoolgirl getting out for summer vacation, she threw her head back and laughed until the tears rolled down her cheeks and she had to fight for breath.

When she came to herself, she realized they were already beyond town, which meant she'd cackled like an old laying hen all the way down the middle of Main Street, right past Henderson's store and the Post Office both, and the thought of the townsfolk gathering around to discuss her bizarre behavior sent her off in another spasm of glee.

Hawkins said nothing more. He just drove in that pell-mell way of his and smiled like he'd swallowed his tongue.

"There's the house!" Betsey cried at last just as dusk began to fall. "And durned if that ain't Liddy dragging a bucket in from the well!"

She stood up in spite of the wildly bouncing carriage, maintaining her death-grip on the hand-rail with her right hand and waving her left arm over her head. "LIDDY!! LIDDY!!! Look who's a'coming home!" On the word "home" the wagon lurched over a great rut in the road and Hawkins had to put a quick, strong arm around her waist to keep her from tumbling headlong over the traces.

Lydia dropped her buckets of water and ran screaming toward the house. The heavy front door seemed to open up and spit out one family member after another. Ma, then Pa and a tumbling mass of arms and legs that had to be the boys. Even Granny Wright came tapping out, leaning heavy on her deceased husband's ornately carved cane.

Hawkins brought his team to a fighting halt next to the well and Betsey Anne literally fell into the arms of her waiting family. There were hugs all around and a cacophony of laughing and talking that carried the group right into the house where Betsey Anne and Hawkins were stationed at the table and plates were brought and filled for them from the supper that had already been eaten.

It wasn't till Ma poured Hawkins his second cup of coffee that she actually noticed his presence. He looked her in the eye and noticed her realization and paused for a moment before saying, "Thomas Jefferson Hawkins, ma'am," in answer to her unspoken question.

Ann Springer turned her questioning gaze toward her daughter then, and Betsey stammered, looking back and forth from her mother's face to her bearded benefactor's tight-lipped smile and finally managed to murmur, "He's a -- friend of mine."

The answer seemed to suddenly turn the focus of the impromptu celebration toward Hawkins and he displayed the jovial attitude he had always displayed in the presence of his old friend George Cline. He held forth on his long-time friendship with both George and Flossie, and on his newly-located homestead and his many plans for a prosperous future in the area. He never let Betsey's gaze out of his own for very long, and he peppered his soliloquy with numerous compliments of her appearance, her sewing skill, and her delicious navy beans.

The laughter and the talk continued far into the night, long after the lanterns had been lit and the little ones had dropped off to sleep on the rag rug underneath the table. Finally, Granny Wright let out with a loud, prolonged snore from her rocker in the corner and the startled group hushed and turned to see her fast asleep with her head thrown back and her arms hanging loose over the sides of the chair, which was still in motion.

Turning back toward each other with sheepish grins, they passed smiles around the table in lieu of pleasantries and separated at last for the night, with Pa taking Hawkins by the arm and leading him out to the barn where the two would bunk in the hay loft for the night.

Betsey drifted off to sleep in the big bed beside her ma, wondering where she'd ever gotten the idea that Thomas Jefferson Hawkins was anything but charming.

CHAPTER FOUR

Hawkins spent the next day being nothing but charming.

He toweled the dishes dry after breakfast. He helped Pa with the chores. He helped Ransom fetch in the cows. Showed Adam how to whittle a whistle out of a hollow stick. Carried Charles piggyback for hours. Called Ma "ma'am" and pulled out her chair at the supper table. Sat silently beside Granny Wright while she told the same story over and over again.

Called Betsey Anne "little miss" and caught her in that penetrating gaze of his every chance he got, smiling that cat-bird smile and locking eyes with hers until it bordered on indecent.

Saturday came all too soon. The noon meal over and the dishes done, Ma began pressing gifts into Betsey's arms one by one as it neared time for them to go.

Betsey gave her mother the money she had earned and watched her hide quick tears as she accepted it.

"You know I hate to send you off to work for another woman thisaway, Betsey sweet," she said with her back turned. "You know I do. But with your Pa still down in the back and Granny needing a square on her chest and with that swollen leg – Liddy ain't strong neither and the boys..."

"That's alright, Ma, I don't mind going," said Betsey, thinking for the first time in three days of her sewing machine. She caught her breath and realized that Hawkins had not mentioned it either.

Perhaps it was just a generous gift with no expectations behind it. She had read him wrong before. He was charming and perhaps a bit shy... She realized with a start that her mother was standing there looking at her while she daydreamed about Thomas Jefferson Hawkins and the automatic sewing machine.

"Here, Ma, let's get a piece of string to tie up these here things, so's nothing gets broke along the way."

"I got one more thing, girl," said her mother, producing a heavy piece of hand-woven dress goods from the wooden box at the foot of her bed.

"Oh Ma!" cried Betsey with genuine delight. Then catching herself, she said, "No, I can't take it, Ma. You'll be needing it for yourself or Liddy soon enough. I can buy a piece for myself when I need it."

"No – at your age you're much more likely to need a new dress than I am, and that's for certain," Ma tucked the dress goods firmly under the other gifts and folded wrinkled brown paper up neatly over the top, a tear glinting in the corner of her eye.

Betsey got one last glimpse of the gifts, stacked neatly together as they were there, just before her mother closed the paper around them. Two jars of preserves, a packet of beef jerky, a burlap pouch full of iris bulbs, a bar of scented lye soap, and a new piece of dress goods. It struck her that this was no random package.

Her mother suspected that marriage was in the offing.

Was it? Betsey Anne bit her lower lip and turned back to the tiny mirror on the dresser to fiddle with her hair. She had to admit to herself that she had been considering it. Especially the last two days. But before that, even. When he'd given her the sewing machine and she wondered what he wanted in exchange. Perhaps he *did* give it to her as a courting gift. She had considered other, less admirable, motives. But here, at her parents' home, her opinion of him had undergone a transformation, and her thoughts had circled back to marriage.

Yet he'd said nothing. "That's hardly unusual for him, you fool," she thought to herself with a snort. The only indication she had of his feelings was the way he stared at her, and that was hard to read.

Impossible to read.

He could be thinking anything at all.

Betsey blinked and realized there were two faces in the mirror: her own and Lydia's.

"Whatcha thinking, Betsey Anne?" said the latter.

Betsey studied her sister's pale pink skin, stretched thinly over prominent cheekbones, and her deep-set, dark blue eyes and soft blond hair. "Little enough, child," she answered, giving her sister a quick tickle under the arm. "Little enough, and that's for certain."

They wrestled each other out into the front room, laughing and trying to trip one another in a very unladylike fashion. The rest of the family was assembled there, Ma holding six-year old Ransom as though her life depended on it. And Hawkins holding the brown paper package and smiling that flat-lipped smile.

Betsey flashed her best devil-may-care smile and said, "Well, I suppose I'll be seeing you for Thanksgiving next, and I'll be expecting some mighty fine eating, too." She hugged her Granny Wright, kissed her father, punched her brother Adam in the arm, pulled Lydia's braid, ruffled Ransom's hair, fished Charles out from under Ma's skirts for a kiss, and hugged him right in with her mother, then pulled up her borrowed bonnet and stepped out the door, not daring to look at Hawkins at all.

She noticed the care with which he tucked the brown paper bundle into the back of the wagon. She noticed the very placement of his hands around her waist as he helped her up into the high seat. She noticed the shape of his fingers as he gathered up the reigns and with a flick of the wrist started the horses down the road. She turned to wave to her family, gathered in the front yard, and noticed the gray hairs in his beard and at his temple. She even noticed the fragrance of him.

Overcome with a sudden nervous sickness in the pit of her stomach, she turned to her right and braced herself in her now-accustomed fashion for the roughness of the ride. "What're you thinking, you fool," she admonished herself with an inward groan. "Two days ago you couldn't stand the man, and now you're thinking of marrying him."

What was she thinking, indeed? What did she know about him? Really? Nothing. Nothing at all. He was a friend of George Cline. What did that tell her? That he must be at least 30, maybe more. He had located land in section 12. Why? Why not locate nearer his own family? What made a man in his 30's move off on his own that way? And why was he interested in her? **Was** he interested in her?

As if in answer to her unspoken questions, he suddenly began to talk, more to the horses than to her it seemed. He talked of life on his father's farm in Ohio, where he had lived right up until the time he came to Michigan. He talked of his brothers: William, hard-working with a farm of his own and James Madison, studying at University. He talked of his sisters: Frances Maria Garnier, Elisabeth Rolph, and Analisa Laughton. Frances was closest to his own age: they had picked apples together, eating more than they carried home, and pelting each other mercilessly with the mushy cores. Elisabeth was full of herself, he said. She'd married well and had a disdainful attitude about all her siblings. Analisa – well, she was his baby sister. The youngest of the family, married only a year.

Betsey Anne reminded him of Analisa, he said.

"My pa left me the farm when he died – lock, stock and barrel. But it weighed me down, it surely did. I just wanted me a place of my own. So here I am."

Betsey had been so engrossed in his story that she had not noticed the passing countryside until he stopped talking. Suddenly she realized that she had no idea where they were.

"Are you lost?" she blurted out, then tried to recover her dignity by finishing with, "Or is it just me? 'Cause I don't see nothing familiar at all!"

He cut his eyes to the side till the hooded lid seemed to cover his left eye completely in a sort of sideways wink and chuckled low in his throat. "Naw, we ain't lost, little miss."

Betsey waited a moment expecting him to explain. But he just kept smiling and chuckling, as if he were enjoying some hugely private joke.

She felt a familiar annoyance rising up in her throat. He could be so insolent! The one minute he was talking on till she lost track of the time completely, then suddenly, he clamped his lips together till you needed a pry bar to get anything out of him.

"Well, where **are** we, then, Mr. Hawkins?" she asked with sharp sarcasm in her voice.

"Almost to my place."

Betsey could think of no reply. ***His*** place? What in the world could he be thinking? What in the world could he be planning? She straightened her back and tilted her chin up defiantly. Insolent. That's all there was to say for him.

He tucked his head down as if studying the toes of his boots, then suddenly pulled his horses to a halt. "The circuit rider's at the neighbor's house tonight. We could go there – I thought – well, it would be – well, blame it, Betsey Anne, will you marry me?"

"Marry you!" Betsey exclaimed as if she hadn't been thinking of it herself. As if her mother hadn't given her a pile of wedding gifts that very morning! "My sewing machine…" she said, and then realized how that must have sounded to him, how insulting. He proposed marriage and she answered only "my sewing machine" as though she were perhaps already married to that article. As though his gift was more important than his proposal, than his feelings.

"I mean…, well, I…, it's still at Cline's and all."

He flashed a full grin and then, reaching behind the seat, he flipped up the ever-present wool blanket – and there was her sewing machine! And her quilt, folded carefully around a bundle of something Betsey could only assume was her clothing!

"Oh, my!" Betsey's hands flew to her face as she blushed deeply, imagining his hands folding her most intimate garments. "Oh, my!"

A moment's pause lingered heavily in the air between them. "Oh, my!"

Now it was her turn to feel insulted. Of all the insolent things! To have loaded up her things – to have gone in her room and loaded up all her things without asking! On the other hand, wasn't that how the machine had arrived in the first place?

"My word you're an insolent fool, Thomas Jefferson Hawkins."

"I know that. You ain't the first to tell me so. But will you marry me?" He saw that his gesture had not met with her approval, seemed to sense that perhaps his proposal was in line to be rejected, and with an air like a puppy come wagging up to the bearer of a bone, he began to lay out his appeal. "We'll be strong together, and that's a certain fact. We'll make our own way, on our own place – we'll show them all we can do it, and put them all to shame for wondering!"

There was no talk of love.

She stared at the sewing machine and calculated her answer. So this was it – this was indeed the price of that machine. Many a night she'd admitted to herself that she was willing to do almost anything if it meant keeping that wonderful machine. Many a time she'd considered this very idea. But could she really do it? Could she *marry* Thomas Jefferson Hawkins? Today?

She looked up at him and there was a certain something about the look on his face. That face of his with its hooded eye that expressed feelings and hid thoughts so cleverly that you never knew where you stood.

He beamed out a sudden smile – the charming one – and said softly, "I been planning this all week."

She smiled back and thought of clever little boys with mischief in their eyes and brown-haired girls with a knack for charming you past all reason all lined up around her own dinner table. Before she could change her mind, she said simply, "Well, alright then."

Ol' Tom J uttered a boyish whoop as he whipped his team up to that bone-jarring trot and then on into a full-out gallop that sent them flying over the very tops of the ruts in the road. Betsey had to throw her arms around his waist just to stay on the seat.

It was in this fashion that they careened into the yard of the house where the minister was passing the night. As if they weren't raising enough of a clatter, Hawkins hollered out at the top of his lungs, "There's a'gonna be a wedding here tonight!"

The door of the farmhouse burst open, light and warmth and smiling strangers pouring out into the gathering dusk. Their merry excitement caught hold of Betsey Anne as Hawkins swung her lightly down from the wagon and presented her to his neighbors with a flourish.

"This," he said, pushing her forward, "Is Betsey Anne Springer, soon to be Hawkins!"

There was another rush and flurry of talking and hugging and laughter that seemed to dance around them as they entered the house, where enough candles glowed to make one think it was much later in the evening than it was.

Apparently, Ol' Tom J wasn't the only one who had been planning a wedding all week.

Sarah Barnes, the mistress of that house, was as soft and sweet as any highbred lady might cultivate to be – but without any of the helplessness that might accompany such a practiced femininity. She wore a calico dress on which had been lavished many hours of patient stitchery, its workaday sturdiness thus transformed into grace, its soft navy-and-pink floral pattern complimenting her blond and blue-eyed beauty.

Her little hand-built kitchen with its plain plank flooring had been scrubbed till it shone and the dozen homemade candles that blazed from its corners filled the room with a dainty and welcoming perfume. She had set out a light and simple supper for her guests, much like any other supper in any other farmhouse – sourdough bread, cheese, butter and preserves. But she presided over the affair with such grace and enthusiasm that Betsey Anne began to feel she was the honored guest at the grandest reception in the county.

It took her fully half an hour to notice any of the others seated around the table.

The minister. Kind and tired looking in his Methodist collar and dusty suit. Charles Barnes. Looking round and well fed and enamored of his wife. Beth Barnes. Awkwardly fourteen, a woman one minute and a child the next, but a beauty through and through like her mother. Round, happy twin boys, Andrew and John. So named for the apostles of the Lord, which fact came out early in the meal.

And Thomas Jefferson Hawkins. Whom they all called Jefferson. Fondly, it seemed.

Betsey Anne looked at him with a jarring realization that she knew him not at all and had promised to marry him. Here. This night.

She hadn't even formed a habit of calling him by any name in particular – had in fact thought of him only as Thomas Jefferson Hawkins, or "Ol' Tom J" as George Cline was wont to call him.

"Jefferson," she said, as much to try out the sound of his name as to make a request of him. "Jefferson, please pass me another slice of bread."

She decided the name would do as well as any other and then continued through the rest of the meal in silence, feeling as though she were somehow separated from the gathering, separated even from herself.

Late that night, she lay staring into the darkness of a tiny bedroom – one of the two rooms in her new home. Beyond the uncovered doorway, in the cabin's main room, a single beam of moonlight illuminated the automatic sewing machine that she so greatly prized – and which looked so terribly incongruous against the rough-hewn wall that rose from the hard-packed dirt floor.

Feeling suddenly stifled by the closeness of the room, she crept out of bed and slipped into the night, trying to remember just where Jefferson had been pointing when he mentioned the location of the privy. Tenderness and a rip in her carefully crafted muslin gown reminded her that in one way, at least, she did now know Jefferson intimately. Try as she might, she could conjure up but precious little else to say she really knew about him.

But she'd married the man. Love, honor, and obey, she'd said. Till death do us part.

Yes, she'd married him alright. In front of God and a roomful of strangers.

And all the while wearing her oldest brown work dress.

1860

CHAPTER FIVE

"Why do you think I bought it in the first place?" he'd shouted, slamming the door behind him.

Betsey Anne sat staring at her beloved sewing machine through swollen eyes, her head throbbing from hours of crying. She pressed her fingers to her temples and sucked in a deep, jerky breath. The tears were gone; no more sobs grew up in her heart. Instead what she felt there was something cold, something hard, something that seemed to grow up from the sick feeling in the pit of her stomach.

Was it fear? Was it anger? Some kind of instinct for survival? Or just the unwelcome realization that she was a fool?

She could still see the look of – what, shame? -- on her mother's face when she'd first come after their marriage. Ma had tried to hide it – had tried to be glad – had helped her set up housekeeping in that tiny little two-room shack they still called home.

Betsey had pretended not to notice. She'd excused the size of the shack by the short time Jefferson had been on his place. She'd ignored the fact that the land wasn't much cleared. She'd told her father the garden wasn't planted on account of the time of year he'd located.

She'd talked of the adventure of spending the logging season "up in them woods" at the logging camp.

But that was two years ago and here she was in that same tiny shack with the dirt floor. A one year-old baby asleep at last in his cradle in the bedroom and a second child already growing in her belly and it took him saying it for her to realize the truth. There it was. Staring her right in the face all that time.

She was a fool. He'd bought her that sewing machine because he figured she could make a living out of making pretty things for other women. And then he'd married her to save himself the trouble of scratching a living out of the Michigan soil.

Well. What price material gain? She had to admit she'd known at the first there'd be a price to pay for that pretty machine and she'd outright decided to pay it. Then she pulled the wool over her own eyes pretending Hawkins held the key to her dreams.

She stood slowly, pressing a hand into the small of her back to help herself straighten up. She ladled some cold water out of the bucket by the door and drank deeply, then splashed the rest on her hot face and rubbed her tender eyelids. "So be it, then," she said out loud. She was married to the man; they had a child and the second was nothing but a temporary secret. So at least she had more than one thing from him that she'd dreamt of, and she'd do what she had to do.

And the first thing she had to do was talk to Sarah.

Taking up the red-and-white pinwheel quilt that had been Sarah's wedding present to her, she almost ran to the clothesline. The hanging of that quilt on the line – wet or dry – had become her signal to Sarah that she needed to talk.

Betsey Anne wiped away a few fresh tears that sprang to her eyes as she thought of the difference that Sarah had made in her life. Without her sunny friendship, Betsey realized, the last two years would have been nigh impossible.

Somehow Sarah's outlook always made things seem a little better. Bearable, at least. She'd say, "Things ain't never so bad they couldn't be worse!" And just like Betsey's mother, she'd say, "Hard work heals a heavy heart." And she'd never fail to suggest just such a job of work.

Like the time Betsey had complained that her newborn Samuel would have to play on the dirt floor and Jefferson seemed adamant in his refusal to plank it in. Sarah said, "Aw, you can make your own floor – you don't need a man for that!" And they had proceeded to do so, gathering up all the available rags of old clothes, useless ruffles on undergarments, even old wash rags, and then cutting them into long strips that could be braided and sewn together in a heavy coil. The work had occupied Betsey's hands and her heart, and in the end, she covered a section of her well-swept dirt floor for the baby to play on.

Having hung the quilt on the line, Betsey headed into the kitchen to start a pot of tea so at least she'd have something to offer when Sarah arrived. The kitchen was stuffy. Betsey remarked to herself that October had seemed to arrive while summer was still alive and well. She propped her little front door open with the water bucket and looked longingly at the paper window, wishing she had some way to open it.

She stopped to smile at the sleeping form of little Sammy. He was dressed in carefully crafted bloomers made out of the last of her precious muslin, bought in a time that now seemed so very long ago. He had so narrowly missed being born on her own eighteenth birthday that she would forever consider him God's birthday gift.

Tying back the calico curtain that served as the only separation between kitchen and bedroom, Betsey Anne crossed to the cabin's other window – of sorts. An opening covered only with a rough-hewn wooden shutter. But it would allow a cross draft, at least, and freshen up the house, so she eased it open and blocked it there with a stick that was kept on the ledge for that purpose.

Betsey checked out the front door to see if she could catch sight of Sarah yet. No sign of her. No sign of Jefferson anywhere on the place, either. With a sigh she realized that his absence, at least, was normal. When they'd had a row, he disappeared like that. Sometimes for hours. Sometimes for days. One thing she had learned early on was to make sure, if nothing else, that she was there when he returned, and life in the little shack was going along as usual.

The water was boiling, so she poured it into the teapot and

pinched in her prized best tea, the kind her mother cured with secret ingredients, "sure to make you feel calm inside your heart." She covered the little crockery pot with a towel to keep in the steam and sat down to wait, careful to sit with her back to the sewing machine.

She couldn't bear to look at it yet. She knew she'd have to, soon enough. She knew she'd have to do what he said. She wouldn't have minded, even, not really, except for the knowledge that he'd planned it all along. And the way that he said it. That flat-lipped know-it-all smile of his.

She shook herself, and with a swipe of a work-worn hand dashed new tears from her cheeks and scolded herself. "You're a fool, Betsey Anne. A bald fool. And you've always been one, far as I can see. That's a fact." It helped some to hear her own voice. She took up the broom from behind the door and pulled the table and benches to the side of the room, setting to work with a practiced swing. But sweeping the dirt floor only served to remind her of her present predicament, so she checked the road again, in search of any glimpse of her friend.

Seeing none, she turned back toward the stove and surveyed it as if to find the answer rising from its black iron surface. "Canning – that's the thing. I'll gather up them crabapples from out back and dig up some ginger root besides. Sarah gets here we'll work while we talk." The stove seemed to nod its assent, and behind the little calico curtain, Sammy snored as if to agree to the plan as well.

She took her largest stockpot off its hook on the wall and headed out to the scraggly old crabapple tree. Real apples would have been nicer, or cherries like Sarah had growing in her yard, but crabapples were all she had – all over the homestead – and she had learned by trial and error to cook them long with plenty of ginger root and a handful of dried mint leaves. Beans and potatoes were the only garden crops she'd been able to coax any production out of in her rocky, stump-filled garden through the summer, so it would be smart to put up all of those apples that she could. She resolved to gather them from all the trees – not just the one right there in the yard – and store them in the cool cellar that Charles Barnes had helped Jefferson dig last fall.

He'd called it his gift for the arrival of the baby.

The realization came fresh to Betsey Anne again – everybody else seemed to already know what she was only this morning admitting. Jefferson was not providing for his family. She had defended him – she had filled her own thoughts and her words with excuses for him: the land was rocky, the soil was poor, the trees were many, his tools were few, he was tired from logging all winter up at the camps. The list went on and on.

She'd given the excuses to her parents. She'd given the excuses to Sarah and Charles. She'd given the excuses to Flossie Cline when she chanced to be in Henderson's store on the same day last spring, juggling a crying Sammy while trying to negotiate a little more credit for supplies. She'd given the excuses to herself.

She'd even given them to Jefferson. What an abject fool he must think her to be. Must have thought all along, to have so elaborately laid a trap for her. How he must have laughed to himself after he'd taken her to bed, no doubt knowing she'd work all the harder with children to provide for.

How could she have ever thought he loved her?

Heaving the apple-filled stock pot up onto her hip she started for the house, wondering if she'd even stopped to ask herself that question once before.

She came around the front corner of the house to see Sarah coming, just a little beyond the red-and-white quilt where it flapped on the clothesline. She looked like an angel to Betsey, with her halo of blonde curls shining in the sun, a clear expanse of brown fields and blue sky behind her, the Barnes' tidy little house looking like a pen-and-ink drawing on the edge of the horizon.

Betsey Anne cast a disparaging glance around her at her own stumpy garden in the front yard – the only part of their homestead that had as yet been cleared of its ancient growth of trees. Depositing her pot full of sour crabapples by the door, she hurried out to greet her friend.

Sarah took her hand with a warm squeeze that acknowledged the clothesline's message, but then said only, "How is our little Sammy today?"

"Asleep at last," said Betsey with a shake of her head. "I swear that child'll get the best of me yet. Just don't seem to like sleeping in the night time like regular folks."

Sarah gave a laugh so robust that it hardly seemed to belong to one so delicate and replied, "Well, you just got your hard one first, that's all."

Betsey picked up the apples as they went through the door into the kitchen. She noticed with some sense of satisfaction that the stuffiness was gone and the warm fragrance of the tea was light in the air. Sarah's gaze was already on the sleeping child, a soft maternal smile permeating her features. "Ain't he an angel, just," she said softly.

"*Just* while he's sleeping, you mean?"

At that, both women laughed and turned back to the kitchen where the crabapples awaited them.

"I thought we'd just as well set some apples to cook for putting up while we have our tea and all," said Betsey, knowing without asking that her friend wouldn't hesitate to roll up her sleeves and peel crabapples till noon if that's what was needed.

"Sounds like a fine idea to me," came the ready answer.

Betsey poured the tea, apologized for not having any sugar even though she knew Sarah wouldn't expect it, and they set to work.

Talk rolled freely as the crabapples were quartered, cored, peeled and piled back into the waiting stockpot.

"So I reckon that's all for it then," Betsey finished, having poured out the whole argument for Sarah from start to finish. "He bought that machine and asked me to marry him just on a purpose so's he'd not have to work. What a fool he must think I am! And I'm just that inclined to agree with him."

"Now, Betsey," came the soft answer. "Don't you know that a body's like to say things he don't rightly mean in the heat of a fight? It ain't all that's between you, not really. He'd not have waited two years to say so if it were."

"Oh, yes it is!" Betsey transferred some of her emotion to the apples at hand, chopping them with a vengeance, stacking up a large pile of the quarters before picking up her paring knife to settle in to the more calm peeling and coring process for a few minutes. "I never heard him speak to me of love, Sarah, never once in all the time I've known him."

There was a thoughtful silence, followed by the strident cry of little Samuel as he awoke from his nap.

"I'll fetch him," said Sarah quickly, wiping her hands on her apron as she stood up. Carrying the baby back from the bedroom, she cooed to him like a mother dove and tickled his ribs, then chucked him under the chin and planted kisses on the top of his little bald head. "I'd much rather sit here on your mat with you, little man, than chop them old sour apples, and that's a fact," she said in her singsong voice.

Sammy laughed as if she'd said something very funny, then reached up and grabbed a handful of her hair, plopping down on his braided mat with a shriek of delight. Sarah teased him with his handkerchief doll and a little wooden dog that Jefferson had whittled for him at Christmas. The dog seemed to give her the answer she'd been searching for, and she returned to the work at hand with a smile and a sigh.

"That child – such a treasure."

Again the work continued, for a few minutes unimpeded by conversation.

"Jefferson talks on about him every time he's over at our place, you know," Sarah opened. "I remember when he was a'carving that little dog – he must have thrown away a hundred little dogs half finished before he got it just right."

"He **does** love that boy," Betsey had to concede. "And I guess I thought he loved **me** – well, at least I thought he wanted me, else why would he have gone to all the trouble he went to, buying that machine and hiding it in my room and all."

"You didn't know him much when you married him, did you?"

"I knew him hardly at all. One minute I'd be thinking he was nothing but insolent, the next I'd think he was the most charming man I'd ever met. Even now, I – well, I just can't tell what he's thinking, really. He looks out from under that hooded eye like he knows something I don't know and he won't tell. And then other times, well he stares straight into my soul with them eyes, or he'll talk on about plans for the place, here, or tell tales about his growing

up time, or traveling. I don't know. I either want to thrash him or I…"
She broke off as she put the last piece of apple in the pot and stood
abruptly. "I'll fetch in some more water for these apples if you'll be
so good as to get a little juice for Sammy."

Betsey Anne picked up her two buckets and headed out the door.
Returning from the well, she set the stockpot up on the stove and
poured the water slowly over the crabapples till they were covered.
Taking a heavy knit potholder from its hook on the wall, she opened
the front of the stove and put in some wood, using the end of a small
stick to stir up the embers.

"I reckon we'll have to go outside now, it'll be getting too hot in
here. But it'll smell good." With a swift, practiced hand she sliced a
knotty ginger root into paper-thin pieces and scraped them off the
board into the pot. Taking a jar down from the shelf, she pinched in
some dried mint leaves and clapped a lid on the pot.

Having given Sammy his apple juice, Sarah poured herself
another cup of the now lukewarm tea and asked Betsey if she'd like
some. They wandered out to the yard, settled Sammy on a patch of
green clover and sat down on low stumps, with their boots tucked
up under their dresses like schoolgirls, sipping silently at their
tea.

Finally, Sarah said, "Well, I expect you can't thrash him, so just set
about loving him. And perhaps he'll do the same."

Betsey looked at her reflection in her tea cup, thinking how much
older she looked than 19 and noticing the hard set of her eyes and
mouth. After a while she said, "I guess it ain't so bad, really. I mean,
I like to sew. I always have. I can do fine work, too. The ladies are
always asking me to do it for them. I can earn plenty enough to keep
us from having to spend the winter up in them woods, anyhow."

Sarah sipped on in silence.

"And Jefferson could likely girdle some trees and work on some
tools, and all like that if we're here, home, all winter. Then when
spring comes, well, he'll just be ready, that's all."

"Take time to show him love. Fit him a new shirt when you've
got some goods left over. Make his favorite supper once in a while.
Look for the good in him, too, and love will grow."

"You think love grows?"

45

"My ma always said, *'Love's the only plant you can grow without a seed.'*" Sarah stood up. "I best be getting home. That Beth – she still makes mess of cornbread sometimes, even if she is a-coming on sixteen next month. I can't quite figure what it is she's leaving out."

"Maybe it's something she's putting **in**!" said Betsey with a laugh. And then, softly, "Thanks for coming."

Sarah smiled and chucked Betsey Anne under the chin as she had done Sammy earlier, then hollered a farewell to the child where he played and started for home.

After a light noon meal, Betsey combed her hair and washed her face, then put on her better dress for going out. She gathered Sammy up, put a bonnet on his head, and started down the road that led to the next farm in the direction opposite Barnes's place. It was down the hill, fully three miles away, and behind the woods on the Hawkins place that had never been cleared, so Betsey didn't know the family well. But she did know that they had a daughter soon to be wed, so she presented herself at the door and made her request.

After a cold glass of apple cider and the barest sense of familiarity, she walked back home with Sammy on her right hip and her left hand swinging a beautiful piece of dress goods for Olga Jensen's wedding dress, tied neatly in a brown paper package.

In the mornings she picked more crabapples, storing bushels of them in the hand-dug cellar and canning the rest with ginger and mint, lining up the finished jars with their paraffin lids almost proudly on her kitchen shelf.

In the afternoons, she sewed, putting to the back of her mind the reason for the task and focusing instead on the perfection of the work. As she stitched, she talked to Sammy as though he could really understand her, and she laughed out loud when she heard him try to imitate the humming sound her sewing machine made as she pumped the treadle with her work-worn boot.

On the fourth day, Olga Jensen came by for a fitting and was delighted with the progress of her wedding dress, Betsey having carefully added all the stylish embellishments that any bride could want. The following day, after a trip into town, Olga and her mother deposited three more paper bundles on Betsey's kitchen table, with instructions for two more dresses and a dark-green woolen coat with a collar to be fashioned from furs the father of the bride had carefully prepared for just that purpose.

Betsey sat down to her work each afternoon with a certain sense of pleasure in the task itself; when with a twinge she remembered that she was again nothing more than hired help for another woman, she scolded the complaint away with the thought that at least it was pleasant work. She could still be scrubbing Flossie Cline's floor, minding Flossie's children instead of her own. Worse yet, she could be cleaning hotel rooms and emptying chamber pots like Prudie Richy in town.

It was two days more before Jefferson came home. He stumbled in to the bedroom in the early hours of the morning, tumbling into bed with his boots on. He nuzzled down beneath the red-and-white quilt with unmistakable intentions and smelling of a strange mixture of alcohol and feminine perfume.

CHAPTER SIX

There followed a time in which both of them worked.

Betsey stitched and stitched, word having gotten around quickly after Olga Jensen's trip to town that the talented Mrs. Hawkins was taking in dressmaking. The customers came to her. In their carriages and buckboards and on foot, bringing brown paper bundles holding all types of dress goods and woolens.

Thinking of the smell of liquor on Jefferson's breath the night he came home, Betsey Anne was careful to accept her pay in non-cash goods. Lars Jensen spent two days helping Jefferson build a chicken house. Mr. Watkins furnished the chickens. Mrs. Henderson brought a side of salt pork and a ten-pound sack of flour. Mary Jane Crabb, to be married a year hence, brought dress goods for Betsey to make a dress for her own increasing girth, with a baby due to arrive in May.

Jefferson was docile if not charming, and careful to acquiesce to Betsey's every request. He girdled trees to be cut in the spring, working even after the snow was on the ground. He played with Sammy while Betsey sewed, and even contributed a few awkwardly prepared suppers when deadlines loomed large.

The work occupied Betsey's fingers if not her thoughts, and the pay kept food on the table. The little house began to brighten up, with curtains made from leftover dress goods, a new muslin tablecloth, and new crockery. Sammy grew fat and happy fed on fresh eggs, hot bread, and beans cooked with salt pork. Several of the ladies brought him little sticks of peppermint candy for Christmas.

All in all, the winter months fluttered by in relative peace, in spite of the difficulties of October. But Betsey could not erase from her mind the things Jefferson had said. Nor could she forget that he'd been gone for a week and had come home smelling of liquor and another woman's perfume. Something in their relationship had changed forever. She looked at him in a different light; looked at herself in a different light. There was no trust, and little reliance. She felt in many ways that she was on her own, maybe even responsible for **him**.

And still, he'd never said he loved her.

Once or twice as he fumbled for her under the quilt, he mumbled, "Love me, Betsey, love me please." But there was something too piteous, too childishly helpless in his manner and her heart only hardened as he begged. Her sense of failure increased as she heard over and over in her head the things that Sarah had said, *"Just set about loving him." "Love's the only plant you can grow without a seed."*

Betsey Anne's parents came in May when the baby was born. Ma brought her some tea for peace of mind, some salve for "putting yourself back to rights" and a little rag doll for the baby. Annie. Round and red and full of cheerful smiles, hungry most all of the time, and sleepy the rest.

Sarah and Charles Barnes came on the third day to see her. Sammy seemed to grow up overnight – gently rocking "baby sifter" in the cradle Betsey's father had made for him at his birth, then stomping out to help the men with their chores.

It was decided that a sewing room would be built behind the kitchen while Pa was there. Charles Barnes pitched in a day's labor as well. The room was built of rough-hewn logs like the rest of the house, but it was to have a real glass window.

And a plank floor.

Jefferson became animated during the building of the room – he boasted that he was building it as a gift for her. That she deserved it. That she was such a good little wife, such a sweet little mother. He stopped in the kitchen to caress her cheek as she worked. He carried water in for her twice a day. He admonished her not to work so hard in the planting of her garden. He told her parents what a marvelous daughter they'd raised, praising her sewing skills while hammering in the plank floor.

He crinkled his nose at Annie and said, "You're almost as pretty as your mama, that you are," and Betsey nearly burned the bacon, so frozen was she with shock at hearing it.

On the first night after her parents had returned home, Jefferson cradled Betsey softly in his arms till he slept, pressing his cheek against her hair. Perhaps he even kissed the top of her head: she wasn't sure. But he made no advances, just drew her gently to him and drifted off to sleep.

She lay long into the night, feeling the deep rise and fall of his breathing and wondering at the working of his mind. In the dark hours before the dawn, she nursed little Annie till she went back to sleep and then finally closed her own eyes in sheer exhaustion.

The morning dawned bright and clear before she awoke. Betsey realized with a start that the baby was crying and jumped out of bed with sick rush of dizziness at being awakened in such a way. Her head was reeling and blackness pressed her vision momentarily into a tunnel. She stumbled and groped her way to the cradle and lurched to her knees, reaching for the baby through a haze.

There was no baby.

Instant panic gave way almost as quickly to the realization that Jefferson was in the kitchen with the children, clucking and singing in a hushed voice, in an utterly vain effort to silence Annie's expressions of hunger.

Betsey leaned back against the wall, her bare legs splayed out on the dirt floor in front of her and pressed her fingertips to her pounding temples. She'd been awakened with a start before, had experienced that sort of flush before, but this was worse than usual. Her lips were dry and cracked, her mouth felt full of cotton. But Annie's cries grew louder and louder, so she heaved herself up from the floor feeling as though she'd doubled in size overnight and plodded out to the kitchen.

"There's your mama, little girl," said Jefferson's unfamiliar singsong tone.

"Mama! Mama! Eat! Eat!" cried Sammy, apparently just as hungry as Annie.

Betsey Anne shuffled over to the stove, still feeling the effects of her rude awakening. "I'll boil some water for your coffee, Jefferson, if you'll just fetch up some potatoes while I feed that girl."

The coffeepot seemed excessively heavy to her, but she filled it up and planted it noisily on the back of the stove, then clanked the cast-iron skillet for the potatoes into its accustomed place and bent down to stoke up the fire. Darkness closed in around her eyes in circles, one upon the other, spinning first one direction and then the other. Leaving the door of the stove open, she stumbled backward till she found the bench with her hands and then sat with her head between her knees breathing deeply.

Somewhere a baby cried loudly and a child chattered incessant little nothings. A door scraped open and heavy boots shuffled past, seeming only inches from her hot, red face.

"Jefferson, Jefferson!" Her voice was raspy, scarcely more than a whisper.

The sound of him placing the potatoes on the table was a deafening thump and crash and rumble like a violent summer thunderstorm. He turned toward her, reaching out to touch her forehead, and the clothing he wore made a loud rasping sound that sent a shiver up her back.

"Fever!" he exclaimed and she cried with the pain that his voice inflicted on her ears and then weakly slid to the floor in a heap.

Beth Barnes took the children home with her, little Annie crying all the way in hunger. Sarah sat beside the bed silently piecing a patchwork square after she carefully and tightly wrapped Betsey in the red-and-white pinwheel quilt. Every few minutes, she wiped the feverish brow with a soft, warm cloth and whispered the simple prayer, "Lord bless you, sweet girl."

Sarah sent Jefferson out the front door to work, reminding him that "Hard work heals a heavy heart," and that there was nothing he could do in the sick room. He worked listlessly, first at this thing and then at that, sticking his sun-reddened face through the calico curtain from time to time to check on the patient. Late in the afternoon of the second day, his resolve broke.

He came to the foot of the bed and stared at his wife where she lay as though in a world all her own, suffering alone and completely unaware of their presence, it seemed. He ran his long fingers through his heavy, graying hair and tugged at his beard, then thumped his hat against his thigh almost absently.

"I'm going for her ma," he finally said. "She's got herbs and such – I know it's a long way -- "

Sarah stopped him, "It's alright, Jefferson. I understand. I'm guessing that's a good idea. If she can't come, seeing as she just left here, and all, well maybe she can send along some herbs or tea."

He gave another look at Betsey Anne and paused a moment as if he were thinking hard, then turned and left the room without another word.

In Betsey's blistered mind, everything was sharply focused and greatly enlarged. Things close were so loud as to cause her physical pain, while things a few feet away seemed lost in a distant tunnel. She heard their words in pounding staccato like the beating of a wooden spoon on an overturned tin bucket. And somehow she knew what they meant to say and didn't.

"Say it! Say it!" she fairly screamed past her swollen tongue and cracked lips. "Say that you love me, Jefferson! In case I'm not here when you get back! Please say it, Jefferson, say that you love me!"

But her world was liquid, encased in some sort of clear, warm syrup from which no sound could escape, so the calico curtain swallowed him up and his far-off footsteps carried him out the front door.

Sarah shook her head and wondered at Betsey's tears as she mopped them away with her soft, warm cloth. Then she settled down again on the kitchen bench that had been placed beside the bed and quietly, patiently, stitched and watched.

Jefferson hitched the team and set out at a gallop for the Springer farm, arriving there in the middle of the night with his awful news.

"No use setting out in the night, thisaway," said the ever-sensible Ann. "We'll just end by making our ownselves sick, and then we'll be no help to her."

In the morning, the medicines were packed along with a packet of biscuits and jerked beef before Jefferson awoke. When he rose, they set out immediately, trotting up to the tiny house in the early part of the hot afternoon.

And then Ma was gently covering Betsey Anne's chest and throat, forehead and feet, with onion poultices and other mixtures, strong smelling but comforting for their sweet remembrance of childhood and mother's care. The fragrances and the memories combined with her mother's strong voice called her back so she began to fight the fever. In the wee-small hours of the next morning the fever broke and she slept, the first genuine sleep since the sickness had taken her.

With relief, the household began to bustle, as if all of its own accord.

The front door was thrown open wide, the window in the bedroom propped just a crack, to let in the warmth of the June sun. The braid rug was taken out and pounded on the clothesline, the hard-packed floor swept till it nearly glowed. Pots of water were boiled over a fire in the yard and every surface in the little house was washed as though to purge both the fever and the fear from its humble corners.

Betsey slept on.

Sarah's nimble fingers having pieced many a square while she sat beside the sickbed, there were plenty of Betsey's favorite red-and-white pinwheels from which to fashion curtains for the window in the bright new sewing room.

Betsey roused but slightly, seeing things clearly at last, but strong enough only to sip warm broth so filled with Ma's concoctions that it fairly tasted of earth.

Jefferson hitched his wagon for a trip to town, armed with a list in Ann Springer's unskilled cursive and Betsey's assurance that there was credit at Henderson's store, payment for the new spring dress Mrs. Henderson had ordered for her daughter. Betsey drifted off to sleep again with a smile on her face listening to the familiar click-clack of the peculiar gait at which he drove his team.

It was the half-light of early summer morning when Betsey Anne next awoke. Sarah had at last been able to return to her own family and her own bed, but Ma lay on a fresh straw ticking in the corner, snoring like a full grown man. Betsey had the sensation that she'd heard something and decided it must just have been Ma's snoring.

For a moment she considered a trip to the privy, then decided it could wait while the others slept. She turned her feather pillow over and plumped it up, then sank against it, still tired and weak, but not particularly sleepy.

Having nothing to do but listen, she chuckled to herself at the almost musical cadence of her mother's deep, noisy breathing. As the sun crept slowly out of its bunk, she reveled in the awakening sounds of the birds and the chattering of the squirrels as they hurried here and there. The chickens began their morning cluck-clucking and feather-ruffling as they stumbled from their roosting places.

Eggs. Eggs would taste so good. Eggs. With bacon. Yes, bacon and potatoes cooked with lots of onion and black pepper. Suddenly overpowered with the craving, she decided to take herself to the privy before waking Ma and Jefferson and requesting the meal. Her feet looked small and very white as she slid them into her boots. Her brown calico work dress had been washed during the cleaning frenzy and was neatly hung on its hook beside the bedroom curtain of the same material. She slipped it over her head feeling the soft coolness of it against her skin and remarked to herself that it hung on her form like a sack. She put a hand to her hair – it had been kept combed and braided throughout her illness. She smiled, thankful for the loving care of Sarah and Ma.

Finding it necessary to support herself by grasping the doorpost and then the table, then the handle of the little front door, she made her way out into the muggy morning. At the door, she paused and gasped with delight, for there beneath a paper-wrapped bundle of supplies stood a gleaming new rocking chair, the same blond-oak, store-bought finish as her sewing machine.

"Oh! Oh, my!" she exclaimed in her timorous, just-recovered voice as she sank into it, clutching the supplies to her chest as though they were a treasure. She closed her eyes with sheer joy as the smooth arms of the chair wrapped their glistening comfort around her and she rocked back and forth right there in the yard, thinking that she knew at last that Jefferson loved her.

For he couldn't have bought a rocking chair as a means of earning money. Never mind that it had been bought with the earnings from her labor, he had picked it out, had carried it home, had arranged for this surprise. It was surely a gift of love, this beautiful chair for her to rest in as she slowly, slowly built up her strength and went about the work of house and home.

"Look for the good in things, and you're just as apt to find it." "Love's the only plant you can grow without a seed." The creaking of the rocker seemed to sing out Sarah's oft-repeated words.

Ma stepped out the front door and without asking knew that her girl needed to be helped to the privy, so she assisted Betsey Anne up from the rocker and supported her with a loving arm as she tripped lightly down the path knowing at last that Jefferson loved her.

No, he had not spoken the words. Perhaps he would soon, but no matter. The chair was there to clearly tell it. She hummed a little to herself thinking only of his love, and the chair that would forever sing of it, and of eggs with bacon and potatoes cooked with lots of onion and black pepper.

She did not stop to notice, nor think it strange as Ma did, that Jefferson was washing at the pump in the yard at this early hour. She did not cast a second glance to see, as Ma did, that the shirt hanging by its tails from his waist as he washed was the good shirt he'd worn in to town yesterday.

Nor when he leaned down to kiss her in that beautiful chair where it languidly rocked on her own plank floor, her children at last back in her loving lap, did she catch any lingering fragrance of another woman's perfume. For that had been washed from his skin at the pump and was even now evaporating from the shirt as it flapped gaily on the line in the yard.

CHAPTER SEVEN

Betsey Anne's recovery was hastened by her high spirits. When her strength gave way, she had only to rock a while in the wonderful chair and listen to the sound of it against her own plank floor and she was ready to work again.

Everything suddenly appeared more beautiful to her. The sun seemed brighter than ever before, the sky more blue. She swore she'd never seen stars so huge, or a moon so yellow. Rain clouds, even, became to her things of utter beauty and majesty. She relished the feel and smell of the soil in her stumpy garden, even cultivated the tiny wildflowers that sprang up at the bases of the stumps.

Her two small children were nothing but a delight to her, Sammy's antics sure proof of his superior qualities, and Annie's round smiling face a constant source of joy through the summer days.

She gloried once again in the beauty of her sewing machine, drank in deep satisfaction in the task of sewing itself, pouring happy creativity into each and every garment.

Betsey Anne's customers reaped the benefits of her improved disposition: they were constantly amazed that she could produce ever more stylish results from even the most ordinary goods, and so soon after her illness. Perhaps, they thought, she'd come so near death that she appreciated life all the more.

Sarah wondered this same thing. In early August, she thought perhaps the time had come to talk to Betsey about life *and* death and her plans for the hereafter. She approached the Hawkins homestead with a basket of baked goods on her arm and unfamiliar trepidation in her heart. It was easy enough to give advice when one was invited to do so, another thing to set out to offer it.

"Oh! Come in, Sarah, come in!" called Betsey as soon as she saw her friend coming up the road. "I've just put the tea to steep. I'll set it out in the sewing room."

Betsey pulled the kitchen bench up beside the rocker and laid the tea things on one end of it. With a beaming smile, she motioned Sarah to the rocker. "Go ahead on and sit in it! You'll like it, I know."

"No, you're still getting better after your fever and all, you'd best sit there yourself."

But Betsey insisted and so at last Sarah settled into the prized rocker and accepted the cup of steaming tea she was offered.

"Lovely, ain't it?" asked the younger woman.

"That's a fact," came Sarah's answer as she rocked. Then with a nervous grin, she blurted out, "But I must say, you're sure seeing things in a different light these days."

"He loves me, Sarah – for certain, he does. I ain't sure if he always did, but you're sitting in the proof of it right now!"

"The chair?"

"The chair – don't you see? He couldn't have bought *that* for any purpose other'n just loving me. And this room – well, he planked in the floor."

"So you saw his love in the things that he did for you, and that's what's changed you?"

"Am I so different then?" Betsey asked with a twinkle in her eye.

"I had to bring along some baked goods this morning to welcome my new neighbor!" came the mischievous answer.

Both women laughed, and Betsey poked Sarah in the knee with the toe of her boot before they lapsed into a comfortable silence filled only with the sipping of Ma's special tea.

Suddenly Sarah planted both her feet to stop the rocking of the chair and said, "Where's the babies? And how could I have waited so long to even ask!"

"*You* must be the new neighbor, then" said Betsey. "Sarah *Barnes* always asks after that Sammy the minute she comes through my door, and she'll nigh wake the baby up just to see her smile!" She paused for effect and then added as if forced to continue, "Alright then, Sammy's gone a'fishing with his pa, and Annie's asleep. I swear, she's either asleep or she's eating! Even on cow's milk she's as fat and happy as ever a baby was."

Sarah sat back and began to rock again, taking up her tea. They visited a while about the many small, seemingly unimportant details of which life is truly made, inspecting some of Betsey's stitch work, talking over new recipes for canning and for bread and for stew, smiling wistfully at the baby's plump sleeping form and remarking how swiftly children grow.

The dinner hour drew near and Sarah reluctantly prepared to go, since Beth was away at her aunt's for the summer "and them men folk of mine are plum spoiled out of knowing how to cook a thing!" As she tied on her bonnet before stepping out into the sun, Sarah brought the conversation back around to Betsey's change in attitude.

"I'm glad to see you doing so well, Betsey Anne, and I pray the change runs deep. I thought perhaps in that fever, well, you might have had a glimpse of the hereafter."

Betsey looked down at the floor, somehow a trifle embarrassed by the frankness of what she wanted to say, even before her closest friend. "Jefferson's a hard man to know, and this here's a hard life. It ain't much what I was ever hoping for, and it seems like the load is mine to carry still. But now, well I thought I saw something on his face once when I was down sick, and then he brought the chair and all, and it's just like you said, Sarah, about love, and it being a plant that you can grow..."

Sarah reached over and pulled her chin up, leaning in close, eye to eye. "Don't forget to water it, then."

She stood a long while, searching Betsey's face, reading down into her eyes for a deeper understanding. No, it was not time for more serious talk about God, something told her. Betsey had much to learn about love, and that's where her thoughts were held. Sarah flashed a brilliant smile and surrounded Betsey with a friendly hug, then she was out the door and gone, her compact legs carrying her swiftly down the road with an almost childlike skip.

Don't forget to water it, then. Betsey stood watching until Sarah's gingham bonnet had disappeared in the fields below, then she roused herself from her reverie and went in to ready some milk for Annie who was sure to wake up soon.

"I'm right here, child, I'm right here," she called when Annie's cries reached her ears. "Tch, tch, tch," Betsey clicked her tongue against the roof of her mouth while she fed the plump baby, then deposited her on a little cotton blanket next to a stump in the front yard.

A pot of chicken stew was buried in the fire pit outside the front door, August's heat rendering indoor cooking an unpleasant thing. Betsey hummed to herself as she went back and forth between the kitchen and the fire, happily preparing the noon meal for Jefferson and Sammy who would certainly return soon from their fishing trip.

She stirred up some coals in one corner of the rock-ringed pit and tossed on a few more sticks before setting out the coffeepot. Then with the mixing bowl resting firmly on her hip, she deftly cracked eggs and measured corn meal with the other hand and stirred up the cornbread batter. Having poured the thick mixture into her cast-iron skillet, she tossed on one more slightly larger log and balanced the cornbread atop it to cook.

She was just making plans to smoke the day's fresh catch and put it up in the cellar in jars when she heard the bumping and creaking of a wagon coming up the road. Catching little Annie up into a protective arm, she tucked wisps of her gold-red hair behind her ears and tried in vain to smooth her soot-stained apron. George Cline was driving the wagon up the rutted road in his usual careful manner. Flossie was seated beside him in her Sunday finest, which Betsey had been commissioned to create late in April. The dress was a dark gray organdy with a fashionable high waist, voluminous skirt hemmed to sweep the ground as she walked, and sleeves fitted ever so carefully to the elbow before they drooped down in graceful bells that emphasized the petite size of her feminine wrist. Flossie's clean white collar was painstakingly tatted in a pattern to match the fashionable snood into which her otherwise unremarkable hair had been pinned.

In the back of the wagon, a stranger in a long, square coat and a brown silk vest with a yellowed but heavily starched shirt beneath it was wrestling with a squealing pig.

"What in the world!" Betsey couldn't help calling out as they approached, feeling too familiar with Flossie to be put off by her newly-assumed lady-of-leisure snootiness. She approached the wagon from the side opposite the squirming sow to see little Florence, a curly-haired beauty at seven, and Georgy, a capable boy of six, sitting primly behind their mother with eyes carefully pinned to the stranger.

As Cline reined in his team, the stranger with his long beard and graying mustache, hopped lithely down from the open back, then grappled the pig down on to the ground. It was an odd way to transport a sow: indeed odd to transport one such a distance at all, and for all his pains to do so the man could not prevent looking foolish in the process of removing the animal from the wagon.

As soon as its hooves touched the soil, the sow squeaked and squealed and ran as fast as its stubby legs could carry it, taking cover just beyond the timber line.

George Cline had assisted Flossie from the wagon with a great rustling of fabric, the hoops of her skirt sailing high into the air as he swung her lightly down. Georgy and Little Florence scrambled down by the same route the pig had taken, and departed almost as quickly as she had, only in the opposite direction, instantly falling into a characteristic disagreement over possession of a certain supple hickory switch.

Flossie moved as if to go after them, then turned back, suddenly remembering that introductions were to be made. But just as she opened her mouth to make them, Jefferson and Sammy entered the clearing. Coming around the corner of the barn, Jefferson broke into a run and fell upon the stranger as if he were, of all mankind, dearest to his heart.

Betsey, surprised at such a display from Jefferson, only stood gaping as the two clapped one another on the back, shook one another by the shoulders, shouted and guffawed and whispered with their heads close together like a pair of school boys. Flossie stood primly beside her husband, her expression saying clearly that she disapproved. But George's bushy mustache was stretched from one side of his face to the other, so wide was his smile.

Finally, as if it had only just occurred to him that Betsey Anne didn't know the guest, Jefferson thrust the man bodily toward her and said with the sense of finishing a conversation, "And *that's* the little woman, there."

"And a right fine little doll she is," said the man in an oily voice, doffing his hat as he approached her. "Betsey Anne." This came as an appraisal of sorts, a statement of value it seemed, followed up by a visual appraisal that started with her scarcely-tamed crown of curly hair and followed downward to her dusty, work-worn boots. Betsey's hand flew to her throat as his eyes crossed there, where her collar had not been pinned on that day and the button had been loosened to accommodate the hot work above the fire. She squirmed as though caught in a misdeed when his eyebrows were raised, she thought, at the condition of the apron she wore, soiled as it was and made from the least faded part of last year's work dress.

A gasp escaped her mouth and she would literally have run away, but her feet were trapped by a knee-high hug from little Sammy. Suddenly, the stranger bowed, from the waist, his hat held out in front of him, displaying a long, thin tail of graying brown hair tied at the back of his neck with a piece of grimy string and tucked down inside the collar of his stiff shirt.

"John H. Bernard, *Esq*uire, at your service, mistress," he said, sending Jefferson and George Cline both into another paroxysm of laughter. After a moment, Flossie joined them, her forced and affected cackling leaving Betsey feeling like the joke was somehow on her.

Hot embarrassment so flooded her face that her lips burned and she felt a little dizzy. Though it took the last of her breath, she somehow stammered, "Well, you've all come at the right time, at least, as the dinner's just ready this minute." Holding her eyes wide open and her head tilted back lest any tears should escape, Betsey Anne started toward the house, fairly dragging poor Sammy along as she went.

The meal was one long trial for Betsey Anne. John H. Bernard, she decided, was for some reason cruelly bent on humiliating her.

His remarks either belittled her as being childish and backwoods or else they referred to her baldly as a mere possession, peppered with purely indecent references – "She's a shapely thing, and that's for certain, Tom J. And seems to be right at hand to produce a fine offspring to boot!"

Betsey Anne alternately picked Annie up and put her down again, offered more coffee, poured apple juice, all with a shaking hand and a lump in her throat that would not allow her to speak. She looked in desperation to Flossie, hoping at least for a word of shocked disapproval at the too-frank discussion of her motherhood. She found Flossie smiling smugly while dipping her spoon carefully into the hot chicken stew.

"Yes, shapely indeed," said Bernard again. Betsey turned in shock to Jefferson for support, but found him instead staring at her with that old flat-lipped smile, his hooded gaze too personal for mixed company.

At long last, the meal was over, and the little party strolled out to the yard to survey the sow. Bernard said "Alice's mother" had sent her to Jefferson. Then with a sideways glance at Betsey, he added, "As a token of her esteem." George burst out with another loud guffaw, pounding Jefferson on the back and almost choking on his own words. "Shows just what she thinks of you, Tom J!"

Bernard volunteered that "Alice being nigh grown and all, that fine gift there" had "erased any obligation" felt by that individual toward Jefferson, and everyone laughed again, then looked all at once at Betsey and spluttered in some feigned effort to suppress their mirth.

If Jefferson was in any way embarrassed, he did not show it, only laughed right along with them. Betsey had the sinking sensation that this joke, too, was at her expense, in spite of the fact that she was entirely ignorant of the person or the circumstances they found so hilarious.

Flossie indicated her intentions by merely herding her noisy children into the wagon and then stationing herself beside the tall front wheel with her right hand held aloft. As George sprang forward to lift her onto the wagon, she said coolly, "Thank you for a –" she paused as words seemed to fail her, "--- a **wholesome** meal, Betsey-*girl*."

Betsey winced at the belittling term, but managed to stammer out, "You're welcome, I'm certain," and the visitors were off, creaking and rumbling down over the rocky hillside in the direction from which they had come.

Betsey turned slowly toward Jefferson, almost fearful, so broken with humiliation that she expected to be scolded for her dismal failure as a hostess.

But Jefferson merely flashed a smile – the charming one – and said, "Got a big mess of fish here and I'll cut some apple wood for smoking it."

They worked side by side all that afternoon, Betsey feeling awkward and jumpy, waiting for the next rebuke that must surely be forthcoming. Her mind was so bruised that she struggled with each ordinary decision: Which knife was best to clean the fish? Was it time for Annie to eat? Was that enough wood for the fire? Would she like Jefferson to carry a bucket of water to the house?

The light evening supper of cheese and day-old bread also passed as if in a haze, and the children were tucked into bed, Annie with fatherly kisses, and Sammy with one of Jefferson's coveted tall tales.

Betsey filled her best wash basin with cold water thinking with remorse that it only looked out of place amid her other things, all old and worn or crude to begin with. She scrubbed at her face and hands with some of Ma's creamy soap. She wished she could wash away the signs of work she saw on her hands, the freckles that dotted her nose and cheeks from carelessly venturing out of doors without a bonnet.

She stood there peering into her tiny round mirror at a person who only that morning had seemed beautiful and capable to her, had known with certainty that she was loved.

Jefferson stepped into the room and hung his shirt on its hook. He stopped behind her and bent to kiss her neck, taking the mirror out of her hand and laying it almost tenderly down on the bureau. He pulled the long pins out of her hair and shook it down with both his hands, then drew her down beside him on the bed.

Long after he was spent and lay sleeping soundly, his breathing deep and regular, she stared into the night and searched for answers to ill-defined questions.

She had told Sarah that Jefferson was a hard man to read, that she wasn't sure he'd always loved her. Love had grown, though, she'd said. Like a plant you could grow without a seed, she'd said. She'd had the proof of it in that rocking chair – a present bought without regard for cost, without motive other than to see her happy. She'd had proof of his love in the planked-in floor of the sewing room.

She'd had proof of his love in his arms after the lights had been turned down.

Hadn't she?

But what about that horrible noon meal? What had he proven when he laughed at Bernard's brazen torture, appraising her figure and her ability to produce "offspring," right there at the dinner table? What of that familiar flat-lipped smile and the secrets it hid from her?

Never mind – she'd had proof of his love in the work they had done, shoulder to shoulder, all through the hot afternoon. She'd had proof of his love in his desire to accomplish all the household tasks – to do them the way she wanted them done.

She'd had proof of his love in the care he'd shown for the children, in the uncomplaining quiet in which he ate the simple meal of leftover bread.

Hadn't she?

But what of the sow and the ribald jokes about someone referred to only as "Alice's mother?" Who was Alice? And why did her mother think of Jefferson as swine? What possible obligation could she have had toward him?

What was it that Sarah said – "You saw his love in the things that he did for you, and that's what changed you?" Had she sounded surprised? Didn't she see it, too? The proof?

Or didn't she think that proof was what Betsey should be looking for?

Sarah had talked about a "glimpse of the hereafter" and then left that subject behind when Betsey rattled on about rocking chairs and planked-in floors. She had searched Betsey's face for a long time as though on the brink of saying something, and then turned aside from it, saying only, "Don't forget to water it."

Don't forget to water it. That love plant, she meant, no doubt.

Perhaps she meant that a love that grew only on the surface was sure to wither and die. It was water that caused the plants in the garden to put down their roots, curving, diving, snaking through the rocky soil in search of nourishment.

What, then, was the nourishment for love?

Perhaps, she thought, it was knowledge. If only she could truly *know* Jefferson. If she could understand him, know his thoughts, his feelings. If she could plumb the mysterious depths of his past, the secrets he seemed forever shading behind that half-closed eye.

Or would that knowledge prove to be a poison that would kill this fledgling love? Were his secrets terrible and humiliating like Bernard's verbal barbs?

Perhaps she had to nourish the love with something that came from inside her*self.* If only he could truly know her, come to understand her. Or would he be reviled? Would he only discover that she had married him for the sewing machine? That she all but considered her acquiescence to his proposal her payment for the machine? That she had only wanted to escape from servitude in Flossie Cline's kitchen, had only thought of him as a provider for the things that she dreamt of?

As the night grew deeper, even the crickets hushed their repetitive racket, but still Betsey struggled on with her questions, her doubts, her empty longing for – for what?

She'd had proof of his love – or had she? She *need*ed proof of his love – or did she? She loved him, at least – or did she? Only that morning, she'd been happy, singing while she worked – now she wallowed in self-inflicted misery.

As she descended at last into a fitful sleep, it occurred to her for a brief moment that the date was August 4.

Her birthday.

CHAPTER EIGHT

In the morning it was discovered that the sow had rooted up a large portion of the garden, feeling perhaps that she had both a need and a right to round up her own breakfast. Jefferson chose to butcher her rather than build a pen for her and Betsey didn't argue. Nor did she help with the butchering, spending the morning instead on her hands and knees in a vain attempt to repair some of the damage to the garden.

Silently, she wondered if she'd even be able to swallow the meat, or if it would bring up bile by evoking memories of John H. Bernard's horrible visit.

Mary Jane Crabb's impending marriage to a well-to-do salesman from Detroit required many hours of Betsey Anne's able assistance as the trousseau was to be all but extravagant. Mary Jane, apparently reveling in her ability to employ her less fortunate cousin, made numerous trips to the little house, holding her skirts daintily up as she tiptoed through the kitchen, not letting them down until she safely reached the plank floor of the sewing room. The wedding dress was to be made from fifteen yards of stiff yellow silk, dotted all over with tiny blue nosegays with bright green leaves. Betsey fit and measured, fit and measured, time and time again until she feared she would soil the frivolous gown beyond repair.

"Did you ever see such a useless piece of goods?" she complained to Sarah one morning over tea. "She calls it a ***morning*** dress, and

I guess that's about as long as she can wear it before it's ruined, so light a color and all."

There were two sets of pantaloons, three petticoats, a night dress, a robe, two ordinary plaid dresses and a wine-colored traveling dress and matching woolen coat with heavy braid trim that was ordered specially and brought on the train. Each garment required fitting after fitting, with Mary Jane never seeming quite satisfied with the result. Betsey Anne worked at the sewing every evening until the light gave out, then carried water for the morning, set out her sourdough, tucked in the children and dropped into bed exhausted.

When she awoke in the mornings, she was tired still and every day began with a claustrophobic dash for fresh air and a rush to the privy to heave up nothing while sweat poured off her brow. She scolded that she had no stomach for "that wretched pork" until Jefferson took it to set a trap for bear.

But it was not until Sarah said, "You're expecting," in her soft, matter-of-fact way that Betsey Anne admitted it was true.

Coming as it did so closely on the heels of Annie's birth and the fever that followed, the pregnancy took a high toll on her strength, making the morning's chores seem pure drudgery, the children's smallest whimperings seem overwhelming, and Jefferson's accustomed silence intentionally designed to perturb. Her sewing, always her link to sanity, was instead a burden to be endured, due in part to her condition and in part to Mary Jane's incessant faultfinding and conceited prattle about her intended's wealth and status.

Gradually, happenings of the summer faded into the background, hovering behind her consciousness like a long-healed injury.

But in one way, Mr. Bernard's visit changed their lives forever, opening a door that had been locked if not completely hidden. Letters began to arrive from Jefferson's family. It was odd to Betsey that they had not written before – none of them, not even once. But after Bernard's visit, epistles were penned by the dainty hands of Frances Garnier, Elisabeth Rolph, and even Analisa Laughton.

The letters opened a window on another world for Betsey. She began to feel as though she had been living in ignorance, locked away somehow in her tiny little cabin in its hilltop clearing. She wondered at herself that **she** had not written to his family, had never even inquired where to address them. She pondered long over the letters with their news of a world she had not known existed and their clues to a past she could never decipher.

Frances wrote:

Betsey, I am glad for your sake that your boys is not old enough to go to war, although I consider it an honor to them that is old enough to fight for their country. Arthur seemed to think it was his duty to enlist. It is almost four months since he enlisted. We have not heard from him in over a week. I expect to hear he is wounded or killed, although I hope for the better. We have lost three of our men neighbors. They was killed in the battle of the 20th of September. They was in the same company that Arthur is in. He was fighting by their side when they fell. Should like to see you all very much. It seems to me that Thomas might get a living easier out of them woods, where folks live, although if you are all contented it is just as well. I hope you will not neglect writing as I have. Excuse all mistakes. Write as soon as you can. My best respects, F.M. Garnier to Betsey A. Hawkins

Jefferson left the house in silence after the reading of the letter, hitched up the team and went, Betsey assumed, into town. She had until the following day at noontime to wonder to herself about this sister of his. Why did she write to Betsey, and not to Jefferson? Why had she not written before? Wasn't it odd that Jefferson was called "Thomas" or "Tom J" by those who knew him "before"?

She didn't even know who Arthur was, and as Jefferson did not enlighten her, had to hazard a guess on her own that Arthur was perhaps Frances' son, or maybe even her husband.

Jefferson returned in time for the noon meal the next day, bringing her a letter from her own sister with another brief mention of a war she had not even recognized before Frances' letter: *"Highwalker came here the 22nd of September and took Owen Wilson away. We have not heard anything in particular since he left home, only we heard that he enlisted."*

In his usual fashion, Jefferson said nothing about his absence, and Betsey had long since learned not to ask. Instead she made sure the daily activities of the house were quietly normal and meals of his favorite foods were efficiently laid on the table. The time of her morning sickness having passed, she found herself better able to "keep a civil tongue" as the days marched monotonously through November.

Still, she was weary with the heavy burden of sewing and the care of Annie and Sammy as well as the daily chores of the house. Cooking was a special drudgery as winter drug on, since most of the potatoes had been destroyed by Bernard's sow and the pork had all been left to rot in a trap that never enticed a bear, or any other edible game.

By late November, Betsey Anne began to wish for any break in the normal routine, telling herself that she didn't care what form it took. Just anything. Any lightening of the load. Any alteration in the steady drone of work.

Only a week before her wedding was to take place, while Mary Jane Crabb stood on the kitchen bench in the middle of the sewing room posing for yet another minute adjustment to the hem of her sun-colored wedding gown, the kitchen door burst open. There stood Betsey's brother Adam, at sixteen years old all of six feet tall and long used to doing the lion's share of work due to their father's infirmity.

No words were needed to tell Betsey Anne that something was wrong. Rising from her chair, she absently replaced her scissors and pins in their accustomed places before she found the strength to whisper, "What is it, Adam?"

"It's Granny Wright. Ma says she's calling you and to hurry up about bringing you on."

"I'll get my things and bundle the children if you'll fetch Jefferson from the barn so's I can tell him."

Adam disappeared into the snow-covered cold, pulling the door firmly behind him and Betsey hung her apron on the hook by the door and stood staring at her sleeping children and trying to collect her thoughts. She had quite literally forgotten Mary Jane's presence until she called out from the sewing room where she was still marooned atop the wobbly bench with pins in the hem of her dress.

"Surely you ain't a'planning to go off without finishing my dress, Betsey girl!"

"Oh, Mary Jane!" Betsey's tone was sharp with frustration.

"You're such a child, so all-fired certain that you're the only person in the world what matters a lick!"

Mary Jane suddenly found the ability to help herself down from the bench and swept her silken pleats and gathers right up close to Betsey's faded work dress with a pointed raising of carefully groomed eyebrows. "I'll say I **ought** to matter to you, Betsey Anne, since I certain won't pay for the dress without you finish it. And Jefferson don't waste much of his time in working to feed your little flock, does he?" She turned back to the sewing room, unbuttoning the dress in question and slipping the bodice down over her shoulders. Then placing one hand at her bosom in feigned modesty, she faced Betsey again with a knowing smirk.

"And I'll say one more thing you ought to do, Betsey, is take that husband of yours along with you, or he'll be certain to make Prudie Richy ride the old stag's back whilst you're gone. Then again," she continued, with a twist of her mouth and a sideways jerk of her chin, "Maybe that doesn't matter to you either, or you'd have had something to say about it long before now!"

Betsey didn't wait for Mary Jane to close the sewing room door, but instead dodged behind the calico curtain into the bedroom and took a deep breath, her nostrils suddenly filled with the memory of a strange perfume mixed with liquor. She shook herself and pulled Jefferson's worn out carpetbag out from under the bed. "You ain't got time to waste worrying about what Mary Jane Crabb has to say about things," she chided herself as she stuffed a few necessities into the bag and tossed it with a thump onto the floor by the kitchen door. Waking Sammy, she bundled him up in all of his clothing, layer upon layer, with a knit cap pulled down hard over his ears.

Adam returned and she sent him immediately out again with Sammy waddling close behind him and the sturdy braided mat to separate the children from the chill in the back of the wagon tucked under his arm. "Tch, tch, tch," she clucked under her breath to Annie as she began the bundling-up process a second time. Picking the stiffly wrapped baby up from the corner of the kitchen floor she went into the bedroom for one last quilt – the red and white pinwheel pattern from Sarah.

"I'm sorry."

70

The words startled her, though spoken softly and with genuine feeling behind them.

"About your Granny, I mean." It was Jefferson. Standing in the doorway with the curtain caught on his rough winter coat.

She passed the bundled baby to him wordlessly and reached for her own wraps, stuffing her boots into large felt overshoes, buttoning on a thick sheepskin coat and pinning a woolen shawl over her bonnet. Suddenly she whirled around and said, "Come with us, Jefferson," then bit her lip. Was she asking that because she wanted him along or because she was afraid what Mary Jane said was true? "Come with us," it spilled uninvited from her lips a second time.

"I'll come fetch you, later on."

Betsey could only nod, her throat constricted with sudden emotion. Jefferson carried Annie out to the wagon where Adam and Sammy were already waiting. Settling herself onto the rag rug in the floor of the wagon, Betsey pulled her two well-wrapped offspring into her lap and drew the pinwheel quilt over them all before giving the nod to Adam to drive on.

She stared at Jefferson where he stood in the yard, wanting desperately to call out to him but not knowing what to say.

The ride was interminable. The children were stiff and miserable in their heavy layers of clothing and struggled incessantly to climb out from under the quilt. The cold air seemed to hover in front of Betsey's eyes, making them smart and causing her breath to produce little clouds of moisture. Adam drove at a steady jogging pace in a straight line without regard for the deep frozen ruts or rock-hard clumps of horse manure that jolted the wagon until it seemed the sideboards would fall right off.

Nor did he hold forth with any cheering conversation. And his silence served well to remind her of her silent husband with his mysterious ways and his dubious love.

Betsey Anne shook herself time and again in an effort to force her mind to other avenues, away from Mary Jane's taunts, but the only other thought she could conjure up was the imminent passing of Granny Wright, which was worse still. So always after a few minutes she found herself again picturing a dark pre-dawn hour filled with the almost tangible odors of perfume and alcohol. Over and over in her head she heard Mary Jane's grating voice repeat, "make Prudie Richy ride the old stag's back."

Eventually the rough, cold drive was over, and Betsey climbed stiffly down over the sideboards only to read in her ma's eyes that they were too late. Granny Wright was gone.

Suddenly her emotions boiled over, the pent-up mixture of overwork, loneliness, self-doubt and grief rolling off her tongue sounding strangely like anger. "Why didn't you send for me sooner, Ma, why? Granny calling for me and all!"

She scolded Sammy for stumbling in the crusty week-old snow, heavily bundled as he was. She wiped hot tears from her cheeks with the back of a chapped hand as she struggled to unbutton the extra layers of clothing from a screaming Annie. She sniffed and snapped throughout the process of settling the children into the corner with some toys, wishing that she'd stopped to remove her own wraps before starting on theirs.

"Alright then, the top's *fine*, Sammy," she blurted out in frustration, yanking hard at a lock of her own hair that had fallen into her face for the third time. Clawing at the pin that held her scarf in place and kicking one heavy boot off with the toe of the other, she turned to face her family, lined around the room staring at her. She knew she was making a scene, but found herself unable to stop. She stripped her heavy winter coat off her shoulders and deposited it in a heap atop her boots and scarf, giving them a push with her foot. Still struggling with the wayward hair, she stabbed her hairpins almost viciously into the bun at the back of her head and took another swipe at the unbidden tears.

Finally her mother came to her rescue, taking her gently by the arm and leading her into Granny's bedroom where the body lay, ready for the burying that must soon take place.

Betsey Anne stood a long time looking down at the ancient face, calm in its final repose. "Granny had a hard life," she said softly.

"There was hard in it, that's true," came the answer. "And she was given to looking for the bad and not the good, I guess. But Granny had a good, long life with children to love her."

Another period of silence passed as Betsey stood contemplating her grandmother's visage, marked with lines of sternness, and her folded hands, gnarled from years of hard work.

Suddenly Ma chuckled, "I expect she's found something to correct about heaven itself, by this time!"

Betsey started to laugh, softly at first. But the laughter grew until it seemed to fill up her lungs and, rising up into her throat, threatened to choke her as it turned into a loud, stricken wail. She dropped to her knees with her head on Granny Wright's bed, her hands gripping the familiar coverlet as if her own life depended on it. And she cried.

On and on she cried. Not tearfully from the eyes, but howlingly from the heart, from the pit of her stomach.

On and on she cried. Not only for the loss of her grandmother. No, it was more, much more.

On and on she cried. For loss and for waste. For girlhood as lost to her as the stern grandmother who represented it.

On and on she cried. For want of a future and a hope. For desperate need of love and happiness that seemed destined to elude her.

On and on she cried. For knowing what she'd long pretended not to know.

CHAPTER NINE

On the morrow friends and family began to gather, bringing with them such as they had to offer by way of good cheer. Smoked meat, jerked meat, kettles of stew, pitchers of milk balanced carefully in laps as wagons jolted over rutted roads. And baked goods. Soon the Springer's spacious kitchen was filled to the brim with well-wishers, and its shelves lined with all manner of muffins and cakes and bread.

Betsey's stomach was churning; the mere sight of the food sickened her. She was loath to greet the comers as well. Why couldn't they go away and let the family mourn in peace? Anger formed a hard rock in her chest as she watched her mother flitting from guest to guest like a young girl at a barn dance, smiling and laughing and telling jokes about Granny Wright.

"That's enough, Betsey Anne," her mother had said, shaking her shoulder as she'd cried by Granny's bed. "That's enough. Shake yourself, girl. Dust yourself off and get on with it. Granny would want you to celebrate her passing to the next life, into the presence of God."

But Betsey didn't feel like a celebration. She stood in the corner near the children and glowered at the guests, pressing her lips tightly together and giving a stiff shake of her head whenever any of them approached her. "Stop that!" she snapped at Sammy if he clutched at her skirt. "Just wait, you," she clipped out at Annie when she whimpered for her meal.

And every time the cabin door opened to let in another gust of winter and another gift of food, she jumped and held her breath until the face behind the wraps would become visible. Would it be Jefferson? He said he would come for her. Would he?

She knew she wanted him to come – knew she wanted to see him. But she only wished it were because he would come to her and enfold her in his arms and stroke her hair and coo comforting nothings in her ear. In truth it was because she just wanted to know that he was there, with her, and not with Prudie Richy.

The child within her began to kick and stir, making her finally so uncomfortable that she went into Ma's bedroom in search of a chair. It was quite a tussle to extract it and then to move it through the sea of skirts and homespun breeches back to her corner with the children. Countless hands reached out to help, but she stubbornly brushed them off, murmuring, "No, no, I can get it, I'm just fine." By the time she dropped heavily into its waiting comfort, Annie's tone had become strident and she had to wend her way back across the kitchen to retrieve some milk. Filling two tin mugs half full, she plucked two corn muffins from the nearest basket and crumbled them in on top, then tucked two spoons and a soft rag under her arm and began ducking her way back to the opposite corner.

Sammy could eat his own, of course, but Annie had to be fed, and hungry as she was it still seemed to Betsey that she took time to savor each tasty mouthful. By the time the cup was empty, Betsey's back was aching from bending over and her temper was even shorter. Turning back toward the roomful of guests, she pressed her back against the smooth, straight slats of the chair and stretched her shoulders up and back, closing her eyes tightly and rolling her head on her neck.

"Betsey **Anne**." It was more of a taunt than a greeting.

Betsey's eyes flew open. There stood Mary Jane Crabb, a smug smile on her lips and a hard glint in her eye. Though she knew it placed her at a disadvantage to remain seated, she gripped the bottom of her chair tightly and glared up at the intruder. "Mary Jane."

"I'm sorry about your granny – I expect you're missing her." There was a long pause as their eyes locked together. "*And* Jefferson, I'm certain."

Betsey bit her tongue inside her mouth. "Well, you're right about that, Mary Jane. I sure do miss my Granny. She lived with us ever since I was an infant child, like Annie here, after grandfather was killed by the train in New York State."

"Oh that train!" cried James Springer, coming into the conversation entirely unconscious of the rescue he was performing. "That miserable train – run that track right through the middle of the pasture, they did, and then proceeded to run down more cows than we could count! And left me with this stitch in my back besides. But we couldn't get Pa Wright to move off there for any amount a' begging and we just stood right there till it took him, too. I'll wager your Granny's a scolding him right now, and I reckon it's his turn!"

Other guests had been drawn into the tale, a familiar old standard tale that gave a certain measure of comfort to the mourners, and in this way Mary Jane was gently jostled away. Betsey Anne fell back into her previous pattern of anxious idleness feeling cheated that the only relief she'd had came in the form of the querulous Mary Jane.

At last, word came that the grave was dug and the parson had arrived. By some unanimous consent, the gathering began collectively to bundle up and load into the motley array of wagons and sleighs tethered in the frozen front yard. Ma told Lydia to help Betsey Anne bundle up the youngsters, but it was the gangling Adam who actually helped the most, giving his sisters an exasperated look as he tied the children into his own coat, using the sleeves to fasten them there, and headed out the door into the cold brightness.

Betsey Anne avoided meeting anyone's gaze but took care not to allow herself to be handed up into the wagon that contained Mary Jane. "Crabb," she thought in an attempt to humor herself, "Such a fitting name and all, it's a pity she's soon to marry out of it."

She stood stoically beside the yawning grave, hacked so laboriously out of the frozen sod, and saw Granny Wright's wooden coffin lowered into it, hearing only snatches of what the minister was saying. *"I will fear no evil." "Thy rod and thy staff, they comfort me." "Forever."*

Could one really find comfort in God? she wondered. Or was all that just for the dead? Certainly, Granny Wright would find comfort now, having passed into the next life. But just as certainly she'd never found comfort on earth.

But Sarah – Sarah seemed to somehow **know** God. *"I thought you* *might have had a glimpse of the hereafter,"* Sarah had said. What could she have meant?

Betsey was stricken with a sudden desire to turn and look over her shoulder, to search the crowd for a certain tall, bearded stranger. Yes, stranger, for she knew him hardly at all, even with the third of his children growing within her. She scolded herself for thinking of her own troubles while Granny Wright was being laid to rest.

"Dust thou art, to dust thou shalt return." She followed the others in prying an already-frozen clod of dirt from the pile beside the grave and dropped it in, impulsively ripping a button from her sleeve and throwing it in after. *"Oh God, our help in ages past, our hope for years to come, be Thou our guide while life shall last, and our eternal home."* She intoned the words of the hymn without thinking, so familiar were they, and yet, for her, devoid of meaning.

It was time to go; the guests loaded into their own carriages and sleighs for their own homeward journeys. The Springers packed tightly into the flat farm wagon and both Sammy and Annie began to put up a fuss about their continued confinement in Adam's coat and the nip of the cold air about their faces.

"Oh hush up, you," Betsey Anne scolded. "You're not any colder than anybody else, and we'll be home soon enough."

"Come here to your Old Pa," came a soft comforting voice that instantly brought stinging tears to Betsey's eyes. "Come here and I'll sing you a song – tch, tch, tch – leave off your crying now."

Betsey buried her face in her scarf and smothered her own sobs with tightly closed eyes, pretending that Pa was singing to her and not to her children.

"Oh God, our help in ages past, our hope for years to come, be Thou our guide while life shall last, and our eternal home."

She had sung the song a thousand times, she knew. Had heard her father's sweet baritone voice ring it clearly out at least that many times besides. Why had she never listened to it before?

God, our help. Our guide while life shall last. Certainly God was not guiding her. How did you get Him to do that? she wondered.

The wagon lurched to a halt in front of the house and the singing stopped. For the first time she noticed that the singing had, indeed, quieted the children. Annie was asleep, exhausted no doubt. Ma remarked how early dusk would gather at this time of the year. Pa and the boys went straight to the chores. Fannie lit the lamps while Ma loudly stirred up the fire in the stove and Lydia was sent, grumbling, out the door with buckets in her hands. Betsey Anne tucked Annie between two pillows on Granny's bed and settled Sammy in the corner with a sharp, "Hush – dinner'll be ready soon enough." Then, woodenly, she joined the others in laying a meal on the table.

"Well, there's plenty to choose from for dinner, and little enough work to setting it out." Fannie sounded cheerful and quick resentment sprang into Betsey's throat.

"I reckon it's a good thing Granny died, then," she snapped, "So's you wouldn't have too much work to do!" She slammed a plate down onto the heavy table and pretended not to notice the startled look on Fannie's face, nor the "keep your tongue" glance Ma shot her.

Why did they have to be so matter-of-fact all the time? Couldn't they cry? Didn't it matter that Granny's whole life had passed, and all that had filled it was the daily parade of duty and work? Didn't it matter that Granny never really had anything her heart longed for? That the unfulfilled longing had turned her into a cranky old woman long years before?

The meal was gotten through somehow, and Sammy bathed and nestled down for the night. Annie was moved to the mat in the corner beside her brother, and Betsey went to bed in Granny's room beside Fannie, whose deep, even breathing quickly told Betsey that she was sleeping the sleep of the innocent.

Betsey Anne ran her fingers over the seams in the coverlet in the darkness, marking out in her mind the familiar duck-and-geese pattern pieced from countless dresses and shirts and jackets that had been turned to one last use after seeming to have given their all. Granny could remember them all. "Wore that poor dress to meeting two years running, week in and week out, because the crops was poor." "Had that new the year your ma was married." "Bought that piece of goods off of a peddler that come through, and he used the money to run off with my sister!"

Granny had married young and worked hard under a mother-in-law that ruled the farm with an iron fist. She'd lost three babies and raised three children, but Ann was the only one left. She'd buried a husband who wouldn't leave the family farm even when the railroad cut right through the middle of it because of his devotion to his mother. And then she'd left him there, where he was buried, and come with Ann and James to the Michigan wilderness with hope in her heart. But life hadn't been much better here. There was enough, but never more, what with six children to feed and James having been injured in the same accident that claimed Grandfather's life.

Betsey turned on her side and eased closer to her sister's sleeping form for warmth. How did Fannie do it? She always seemed so easily satisfied. Like Ma. Never dreaming about "pie in the sky" as Ma would accuse Betsey of doing. Never striving, but never shirking. Just working, working. Day after day. Never rising, and never falling, just flat. Always flat.

No, perhaps that wouldn't be so pleasant after all. Just accepting sameness with no desire for more. What was the use of thinking about it, anyway? She'd never be like that.

No, she wanted to be like Sarah. Sweet, sunny Sarah. Always working, but with a song on her lips. Always thinking up some improvement, working toward some future hope, and yet, still content with what she had.

What was there that Sarah had and Betsey didn't?

"She ain't married to Thomas Jefferson Hawkins, that's one thing," she told herself in a whisper. No, Sarah was married to Charles. Charles, who was home nights, no matter what. Charles, who worked cheerfully dawn to dusk clearing his fields and planting them, tending the crops with constant care. Charles, who saw to it that the house was warm and well-built, the garden was fenced, and the chickens were housed.

Charles, who never came home smelling of liquor and strange perfume.

As she drifted off to sleep enumerating the differences between Charles and Jefferson, the differences between herself and Sarah, she almost missed the repetition of a soft, sweet melody that seemed to be floating somewhere in her head. Faintly, faintly it echoed in her heart.

"Oh God, our help in ages past, our hope for years to come. Be Thou our guide while life shall last, and our eternal home."

CHAPTER TEN

It was three days more before Jefferson came.

She heard his wagon rattling over the frozen ground as she was cleaning the children up after the noon meal. She kept her head down and forced herself to finish the task, every movement studied and deliberate, not wanting to let her mother see how anxious she was.

Sammy heard the wagon, too, and ran to the window shouting "Pa's back! Pa's back!" and Betsey Anne couldn't help but think to herself, "Back – back from where? Where has he been?"

And then Jefferson was bursting through the door with her father and the boys, all stamping from the cold and chattering like magpies. All except Jefferson, of course, who searched her out with his eyes and gave her that knowing stare she remembered so well. Then he flashed out with a charming smile for her mother, bending over her work-worn hand as though greeting a member of royalty.

Then with Sammy clinging to his leg and Annie squawking in the corner for her own share of his attention, Lydia led him to the table and pressed him onto the bench. "…a mite of dinner." It was the end of Lydia's sentence, Betsey knew, but she heard it with a start, feeling as if she'd been caught napping at school, suddenly aware that everyone was looking at her.

"Yes, yes – let me get you a plate." She smoothed her apron and licked her dry lips as she hurried to the stove to see what might still be warm.

No one seemed to notice her discomfiture. They all gathered around Jefferson as though they'd been counting the hours till his arrival and he treated them each to a private glance that seemed to say, "You're the only one I came to see, and the only one that knows it." Lydia was fluttering around helping him off with his wraps and bringing him steaming coffee. Ransom was showing off a bit of carving, and Adam was talking farming as if he were the biggest landowner in the district. Pa had launched into dire reports of the war, though Betsey'd never heard him mention it before, and Ma was apologizing to Jefferson for having "kept your wife whilst you had to fend for yourself all this while."

Sammy had clambered up on his pa's lap and someone had carried Annie to him to be cuddled and bounced, her bubbling laughter indicating that she thought indeed *she* was the only one he'd come to see and the only one that knew it. Betsey had filled a bowl with heavy beef stew and then burned her fingers toasting a three-day-old bun that someone had brought for Granny's funeral. She bit her lip to keep from crying out, sticking the offended digit into the water bucket to ease the pain.

"...this feller some food," she heard her pa say as the room became momentarily quiet.

"I'm coming, here I come," she said, turning toward the table with the stew in one hand and a plate of hot buns in the other.

It was one of Sammy's toys, left unheeded on the floor in the excitement of Jefferson's arrival, that she stumbled over. She wasn't sure if it was the food in her hands or her maternal girth that made it invisible to her, but the result was the same either way and she landed in a heap on the floor with stew in her hair watching the buns skitter across the floor like startled mice.

There was a general uproar – laughter from her brothers, shrieking from Lydia as though she herself had fallen, efficient attention from her ma. But Jefferson was all solicitation. Handing Annie to her Old Pa and sliding Sammy quickly to the bench, he bent and lifted Betsey gently from the floor, a tender hand straightening her dress and smoothing her apron over her waist with an understanding pause, while a strong arm caught her close to him.

She felt the warmth of his breath in her hair as he soothed her, "There now, come sit beside me here – no, better in this chair what has a back on it." She allowed him to lead her like a child, to a straight-backed chair by the wall. The bustle was all about her now

– was she hurt? Was that a burn on her hand? Oh, my! The stew was in her hair! Would she like a little coffee or milk?

Betsey Anne couldn't seem to rally – her senses were numbed, her thoughts in a fog. It was only a stumble, simple enough. "It ain't like you're hurt, you fool," she heard her own voice say, somewhere deep inside her head. But she allowed herself to be petted and coddled without saying a word until she heard someone say "fever" and another "bed" and she realized if she went to bed her ma'd know soon enough that she was only sick at heart.

Not to mention that Jefferson would most likely go on back home without her.

"Ginger tea, please, Ma," she said, finally. "My head's swimming just a bit."

"Swimming in *stew*," lamented Lydia, who'd been given the job of combing the food out of Betsey's thick, curly mane.

Laughter followed and soon the family seemed all back to normal, the children napping in the corner, the boys working on tools or pieces of harness in front of the fire, Pa in the rocking chair with one of Ma's poultices on his always-aching back, Ma scolding Lydia gently about the quality of her sewing, Jefferson and Betsey Anne on the kitchen bench, he eating stew and she sipping hot ginger tea.

Jefferson pushed back his bowl with a scrape and stood up, laying a hand on Betsey's shoulder. "Well, wife, I reckon its time we pushed off if we aim to make it home before nightfall."

"Why don't you stay till morning, then," said Pa without turning his head toward them. "The children are asleep, and all."

But Betsey Anne shook her head. "I've been away long enough as it is," she said. "I've still got to finish them things for Mary Jane, and her wedding's on Saturday."

"Oh, my, you'll be hard pressed to do that," said the ever-practical Ann. "And you in the condition you're in. I'd best keep them younguns here with me. You can come on back down here for Christmas and take them home then."

The offer was like a lifeline to Betsey Anne, drowning as it were in a sea of tumultuous emotions. Two less people to worry about – two fewer to make strident demands on her time and her strength.

"Oh, Ma, thank you. That'll be such a help to me."

"Let's get going then," said Jefferson, shooting her a look that was hard to read. He grabbed his hat and donned his coat, buttoning it up the front as he headed toward the barn with young Adam to help hitch the team.

There was another quick flurry of activity, stuffing Betsey Anne's things into the carpetbag along with a few jars of preserves, a loaf of hard bread, and some jerked venison from the supplies the neighbors had brought in for the burial.

"Your Granny would want you to have this," Ann said, pressing a small bundle into her daughter's hands.

Betsey Anne knew what lay wrapped in the yellowing muslin, tied with a faded satin ribbon. It was Granny Wright's treasured Bible, with its soft leather cover and gilt-edged pages as thin as the skin of an onion. Granny had shown it to her time and again over the years, but never before had she been allowed to touch it.

Tears started from Betsey's eyes as she kissed her sleeping children and she wavered. Could she really live without them for almost three weeks? Would they cry when they saw that she was gone?

Straightening up, she saw the look of devotion shining in her father's eyes as he gazed at the two little bundles, and she wiped her tears away with a quick flick of a gloved hand and turned away.

There was little time for tender farewells with the team stomping in the cold and everyone's breath freezing into little clouds before them. But Betsey's mother uttered a stern, "Be good" as she tucked her grown girl into the wagon under the pinwheel quilt with a look that made Betsey feel as if she were off to a school dance again. Then they were jolting over the frozen road at that bone-jarring gait Jefferson took so much delight in inflicting upon her.

It was too cold to talk. Betsey could only huddle close to Jefferson on the seat of the wagon with her face tucked deep within her wraps and her gloved hands clinging stiffly to the railing. When she could remember to do so, she stamped her feet to warm them.

But if it was too cold to talk, it was not too cold to think, and Betsey found herself once again immersed in self-doubt and uncertainty about Jefferson. Was Mary Jane right? Had he taken Prudie Richy for a mistress? If he had, was it her own fault? Did he love her? Did she love him? Had she tried hard enough? Had she been a good wife?

With effort, she turned her head to an angle that allowed her to peer out at Jefferson and was startled when she saw the twinkle in his eye. His look was so familiar that it brought memory to her mind in a flash of another ride, along this same road, on a summer day that now seemed so very long ago. Suddenly she could remember every detail of that day, how charming she'd thought Jefferson, how they'd laughed.

Their eyes met and she smiled. Even though he couldn't see her mouth, her smile reached up into her eyes and he leaned toward her, wrinkling up his nose and giving his head a shake that caused a little bell-like tinkling from the tiny icicles formed by his breath on his beard. Betsey Anne laughed and settled incrementally closer to him on the bench as the cold and the rattling rhythm of the wagon served to end their interlude of communication.

"Look for the good in things and you're just as apt to find it." That's what Sarah would say. *"Love's the only plant you can grow without a seed."* Betsey hung on to the wagon railing and stared straight ahead, the white of the country side rolling past in an unconscious blur, hearing Sarah's words of advice over and over again in her head. "Betsey. Betsey. Betsey **Anne**."

She came to herself with a start. It really was Sarah's voice, repeating her name. And Sarah's hands in heavy leather gloves reaching up to her. "Betsey, get down here so's Jefferson can stable them horses. There's a good girl."

They were home, and Sarah was there, with the stove lit and the coffee hot, and Charles waiting to take her back home. There wasn't time for chatter, and Betsey was still too cold anyway. But she resolved she would get down to the Barnes farm as soon as she could, with a loaf of bread or a jar of preserves by way of thanks.

Hanging her coat on a hook by the door, she stamped her feet up and down, forcing warmth up through her tingling legs, and looked around. It was fully dark outside, but in her little rough-hewn kitchen the lamps were blazing and the coffee was filling the air with its inviting aroma. A simple supper of bread and cheese had been laid out on the table with a clean tea towel over the plates. That Sarah, she always seemed to know just what to do.

Jefferson came stamping in, closing the door behind him with a thump, making loud sound effects as he shook himself out of his coat and hung it on the hook. He removed his hat, flicking imaginary contaminants from its top with tender care, and then thumping it against his leg like an old dust rag before tossing it to the hook beside his coat. His big hand came down across his beard and he jumped in mock surprise. "Woman, I do believe I'm beginning to melt!"

Laughter filled the little room and carried them through their meal. Betsey twinkled shyly on her bench, picking daintily at her meal and offering the better part of it to Jefferson. He ate heartily while regaling her with tales of his boyhood – working with Frances, fighting with William, cooking up schemes with James Madison to trick Elisabeth into some hilarious misdeed, all of them together doting on the fair Analisa.

Still laughing, they banked down the fire and crept into bed, tired from the cold more than the trip. Betsey drifted off to a deep and restful sleep with her back pressed tightly to his solid form.

In the morning, almost without being bidden, Jefferson hitched up the team and fetched Mary Jane from town for her final fitting. She stayed all day, simpering at Jefferson and drinking cup after cup of coffee while Betsey pinned and tucked and stitched. But with Jefferson in the room, at least, Mary Jane couldn't, or wouldn't, say anything ugly. And so the day passed in relative pleasantry.

Betsey, as always, found joy in her sewing, and the garments all were so nearly completed that each time she snipped off her threads she was able to say, "There's *that*, now!" with a sense of finality and accomplishment. One by one, the garments were folded and wrapped carefully in brown paper, tied gently with stiff twine.

Jefferson hovered solicitously, pouring coffee, making more, stoking the fire, cutting the paper for wrapping. And listening to Mary Jane brag endlessly about her fiancé and his prospects for the future. When the dinner-hour approached, he browned some bacon, pan-scrambled some eggs and opened a jar of Betsey's gingered crabapples.

"My, ain't these delicious," Mary Jane crooned, with a kittenish glance at Betsey Anne. "You can certain put your hand to making something out of nothing, Betsey girl."

Betsey felt a flush rising in her cheeks at the implied insult, but when she looked up from her plate, she caught Jefferson's secretive smile just before he said, "It's a good thing you won't be called on to do that sort of thing yourself, ain't it Mary Jane?"

Mary Jane gave a close-mouthed smile and cocked her head to one side, with a forced laugh deep in her throat, waving her hand before her face to indicate that she couldn't speak until she'd had a chance to swallow.

"I believe I'm ready to get back to that stitching," Betsey said, turning quickly from the table to hide a wide smile and hunching her shoulders to smother a laugh.

Betsey made speedy work of the dishes, having filled the reservoir with water after breakfast. Jefferson hauled in a few armloads of wood to stoke up the fire in the stove as well as in the fireplace out in the sewing room while Mary Jane bundled herself up and made a trip out to the privy.

Late in the afternoon, the work was finally finished, the yellow silk with its sprigs of blue flowers having received its last readjustment. Betsey arranged its yards and yards of flowing skirt carefully, folding it over pieces of muslin to keep it from crushing, and smoothing its rows and rows of ramrod-straight pleats down the front of the bodice one last time. The twine had only just been knotted over the voluminous package when the soon-to-be husband arrived to return Mary Jane to town.

He proved to be a roundish, florid-faced Pole, with the practiced charm of a salesman and an obvious appreciation of Mary Jane as a woman who could help him attain his goals. His advent produced a visible change in Mary Jane's manner; she gazed upon him with studied adoration and fairly bubbled over with graciousness, introducing him as "Mr. Podinsky". They were bundled up and loaded into his waiting wagon amid Betsey's admonitions to "let that silk hang out" and Mary Jane's sugar-sweet reminders to "be at the church come Saturday."

Betsey Anne could scarcely believe that Mary Jane's interminable trousseau was finally completed and had rumbled off down the rutted road forever. But since it was true, warm relief settled down around her, a sense of utter leisure augmented by the absence of the children.

And the realization that they would not go anywhere near the church on Saturday.

Jefferson was charming and devoted to her every need. He presented her with a length of soft blue wool for a new dress of her own and hovered about the sewing room while she sewed. They laughed like children over his butterfingered attempts to help her pin and fit and shared a tender interlude when she explained that her system of adjustable pleats would allow for the needed expansion in the coming months of her pregnancy.

One peaceful day drifted into another, tucked neatly away in a solitary little house in the woods.

From time to time, Betsey would glance toward the Barnes farm as she journeyed to the privy or carried a basket of eggs back from the hen house. With a twinge, she would remember that she had intended to visit Sarah long before now. That she had intended to ask Sarah some important questions.

But her mind would shy away from the thought – pushing it figuratively behind some wall and focusing instead on the pleasure and the restfulness of these weeks. This was all they needed, she would tell herself. A time of respite, she and Jefferson. When there were no demands and no worries. A time to care for only each other. And there was little enough of it – the days were fleeting past.

Sarah would understand.

And so Betsey Anne and Jefferson drifted on.

One day when the sun was out long enough to feel almost warm, they hitched up the wagon and drove into town. Mr. Henderson expressed surprise that they had not attended Mary Jane's wedding and spent half an hour describing its every detail for them. Once the packages were wrapped and ready to load, Betsey excused herself and walked down to the post office to dispatch her ever-ready letter home, this one thanking her ma for keeping the children and promising to bring pie for Christmas dinner.

A letter from her ma was waiting for her:

Dear children, Jefferson and Betsey Anne, Sammy has been a pretty good boy if you take the time together. He wants to see you real bad. Annie is good, too. Betsey Anne, again I wish to speak a word to you, and I hope you won't be offended. It is about the management of your children. I know how it is, with you fatigued and tired a good deal of the time, almost sick. You haven't the patience with your children that you ought to have. I know by my own experience that it is for your own happiness and the happiness of your children that you change your course now while they are young, if you wish to have them love you and trust in you and have confidence in you. You know your children's temper and you can cultivate their tempers for better or for worse in the way you train them up. Perhaps I shall tire your patience. I will say a little more upon this subject. Any time when I speak kind and pleasant to Sammy to do anything, he will always do it. But if I speak out of patience and cross, his temper is touched and he won't stir. Betsey, now do try to speak pleasant and kind to your children. If you feel cross yourself, never try to govern them until you feel good natured. And never tell them you will punish them without you do it, but do it in a pleasant way and reason with them and they will learn to love you and fear you in love. Forgive your mother for what she has said. Remember that Bible is for reading and may God help you to do right, Betsey Anne. For this time good-bye, your Mother

Betsey read the letter in the kitchen while Jefferson put the horses up. Hot shame flushed her cheeks and she rushed into the bedroom to hide the letter in the little wooden box she kept under the bed.

Stirring the cornbread for supper, she tried not to think about the letter, but it kept popping into her mind. "It's just the fatigue," she rationalized. "Ma said it was – and she was right. Now I've had a rest, I'll be better. I'm better already."

Throughout supper, phrases from the letter spun round and round in her head. *Sammy wants to see you real bad. May God help you to do right.* Over and over like a familiar song, the words spun and danced in her head. *Betsey, now do try to speak pleasant and kind to your children.*

"Jefferson!" She heard it before she knew that she said it and they stared at one another in surprise for a moment. "Jefferson," she continued, unsure of what to say, her mouth dry, her throat tight. "Might be we should go and get the children whilst the weather holds."

She waited, conscious only of a feeling of sacrifice, of having given up something wonderful she could never get back.

"Might be," he said. And suddenly the conversation was over.

The meal was finished in that all-too-familiar silence she had come to hate so. She tidied up the dishes while he whittled by the fire in the sewing room. Wordlessly, she retrieved her workbasket and turned her needle to some of the every-day mending. At length, Jefferson banked down the fire for the night, and she followed him to the bedroom.

She lay stiffly under the red-and-white pinwheel quilt listening for his breathing, aching to reach across the gap that separated them. But she could not.

Perhaps the man who lay there was the same man she'd laughed with these weeks. But the woman beside him was different. She was mother of two, with new life stirring within her yet again. No, she could no more reach across the gap between them than she could return to carefree girlhood.

You had your burdens in life, and it was up to you to shoulder them.

May God help you to do right, Betsey Anne.

CHAPTER ELEVEN

Duty.

And some small, dim vision of what was right before God.

These were the predominant motions and emotions of Betsey Anne's existence from that time.

Duty. She gave herself to it. As though by so doing she might gain, or perchance regain, the favor of God. In the night, if wakefulness beset her, she uttered the Lord's Prayer over and over under her breath, more to keep from thinking than because she thought God heard her.

Duty. She provided for everyone's needs as best she could. She rose before first light to begin it. She labored with dogged determination and methodical precision the day long. So carefully did she practice speaking in a tone *"pleasant and kind"* to the children, refraining from trying to govern them whenever she might *" feel cross"*, that eventually she almost forgot to feel.

Duty.

There were, of course, moments of joy. Like the birth of the twins, Douglas and Herbert, early in May of 1862. Though the carrying of them had been hard on her and the care of them would produce new challenges, her heart was filled with the joy and wonder of their coming.

And there were times of sadness. Too long in the birthing, Betsey's ma said. That's why Herbert wasn't right. They knew it – had to admit it – before his first birthday. When Duga was walking, even climbing, babbling unintelligible words with the clearest of meanings, and Herbert was not. He lay on the old rag rug in the corner of the sewing room contented just to hear the humming of the machine and to gaze at a shaft of sunlight from the window.

But his demands were few and his love for Betsey Anne apparent in its own way, and genuine. So she gave him a special place in her heart with the fleeting thought that he, at least, would always be with her, and she pressed on under the constant burden – duty.

Oh, God our help... Sometimes the words of the hymn they'd sung at Granny Wright's burying came back to her. Would God really help? Sarah said He would. She said you had only to take your troubles to Him and He would always hear your prayers. He would **sustain** you, Sarah said.

"There you have it," Betsey said to herself as she watched Sarah trip lightly off and over the hill toward her own home that day. "He'll sustain you. He didn't promise nothing more. I reckon you'll take it and be glad."

Jefferson seemed somehow peripheral to her existence. She provided for his needs in every way a wife should, dutifully if not gladly. His meals were on the table, tasty, nourishing, and timely. The house was clean. The children were respectful. There was no nagging. There was no resistance when he came to her beneath the covers at night. If he detected a change in her, he never said so.

There was not much change in him. He was just as impossible to predict, as impossible to understand, as he had ever been. Now smiling that flat-lipped, insolent smile as though he alone knew something the world would love to know and he would never tell; now flashing his pearly whites in a grin that spread from ear to ear and seemed to bring light into the room. One morning taking Sammy down to the creek to catch some fish; another hitching up the wagon and driving away without a word. One evening helping to set out the supper and telling tall tales till the children sat staring in open-mouthed wonder with their spoons poised full above their plates; another evening not coming home at all.

There were long days and weeks of silence, short days and weeks of laughter. Jefferson whittled endlessly, sometimes presenting the children with intricate toys that brought smiles to both their faces and his. But sometimes, he dropped flawed baubles to the floor where he stomped them with a heavy boot, yelling epithets that hung in the air long after he stormed out and disappeared into the woods.

The farm was not a farm, not really. The stumps in the front yard put up new shoots and started their progress toward becoming trees again. Occasional trees were girdled and cut, their stumps glistening with fresh sap in the sunlight, their fragrance sharp on the breeze. The water pump grew rusty for lack of care, and when Betsey Anne ordered its replacement, the rusted one was thrown in a heap beside the stable with other things that met the same ends.

So Betsey sewed. She'd long known there was no sense in wishing otherwise. Occasionally, when she unwrapped a treasured piece of French lace, or fingered a new length of stiff silk or soft wool, when she stretched out a rope of heavy braid or locked eyes in the mirror with a bride who saw herself lovely for the first time in one of Betsey's creations, there was a stirring of the old joy in her art. But mostly it was provender to her and to her children.

She took care to send for fashion magazines from Henderson's store, to pore over them, noting the details and the changes – pleats here or there, buttons large or small, lace or braid or ruffles, hoops and gathers and bustles and bows. She took care to include these embellishments in the garments that she sewed, never duplicating anything exactly from one client to another, but always adding a touch here or there that each woman could wear proudly. This, she knew, was the real reason they came to her, bumping out over that long road from town or neighboring farms, or even other towns.

The rebellion, however distant, occasionally reached its bloody fingers into their lives. Mary Jane Crabb Podinsky's husband had enlisted, they heard. Betsey Anne's mother wrote, *"the destroyer of man is at his work"* the same week that Frances wrote, *"Arthur seemed to think it was his duty to enlist again. He took Bradford with him this time."* Owen Wilson was missing; Sarah's brother was dead.

Weeks drifted into months; months added up to years.

A letter came from Betsey's ma late in December of 1863:

I was very much disappointed, for it had seemed to me all day that you was a coming down. I will tell you what we had for Christmas supper. We had a roasted spare rib, some cranberries and peaches for sauce, and Lydia made three apple pies and some craut. If you and Jefferson had only been here to help us eat it! I want to see you all real bad. I don't think we can come up there this winter, but I think of you although you are a way off for you don't take care of yourself. You must dress warm for I do believe half of the consumptions that are made are made by going dressed too cold. Take care of your health. Health is of great value and when it is thoroughly broken it is hard to restore it again. I have not been to meeting much lately for I have not been able and we have all been sick. But we are all as well as is common except colds and headache this evening. David Collins is here for he has got a furlough and come home a recruiting. His arm is real crooked. Charles Stafford has deserted again and the same we hear with Owen Wilson. He has not been here yet, and he is a dunce if he comes to see Lydia. They are after him. Read your Bible and be a good girl. Kiss the baby and the children for me and I will come and see you as soon as I can. I send my love to you all. Good night, from your Mother.

Betsey gazed for a while at Herbert, whom her mother called "the baby", before she folded the letter and took it in the bedroom to tuck it into her letterbox. She laid it in atop the other treasured missives with a pat and a promise to herself to read them all again, sometime. Then she put the box back into its hiding place knowing full well that time would not be soon.

The children grew, and Betsey Anne cared for them and taught them the things she thought they ought to know – dutifully if not lovingly, kindly if not patiently. Sammy was a hard worker already at four, never wanting to be idle, always wanting to help. He herded Annie and Duga through the daily activities like a diminutive military man, while Betsey kept Herbert safe on his rug beside her, his cooing voice a melody, blending with the hum and buzz of the sewing machine.

Sammy would dig potatoes with vigor, while Annie would arrange them in rows pretending to teach them a song and Duga would bury them again. Sammy would collect the eggs from the hen house, holding the basket out carefully in front of him all the long way back to the house, while Annie petted the hens and Duga stalked about the yard in imitation of them. Sammy would fill the wooden bucket half full and spend the better part of half an hour laboring to bring it to the kitchen, while Annie drew pictures in the dirt and Duga patted mud into cakes.

In the afternoons, while she sewed, Betsey Anne could hear them in the yard, calling to one another in their games, always with Sammy in the lead and the other two following *him* if not his instructions.

When Jefferson was silent, the children didn't seem to notice. When he raged, they stood stock-still against the wall, with Sammy in the middle, small hands clasped, eyes averted. But when Jefferson was happy, the children were happy, and happy to accept what he had to give them, be it tiny wooden farm animals, acorn doll dishes, or stories of giants he'd happened to fight -- just there, inside the darkness that lurked beneath the trees at the edge of the woods. And Betsey, too, took whatever he had to give her – whether it be a look of merry mischief, an afternoon of solicitous assistance, a threatening tirade, or a heavy silence – in return giving him whatever he demanded of her.

And so it was that just when she was beginning to think that her family was complete, she discovered that her fifth child was on its way.

"It seems I've spent my whole life expecting a child," she lamented to Sarah over tea. But she agreed when Sarah answered that "Children are a blessing from the Lord."

For months on end Betsey Anne stayed at home -- there was no need to venture out, really. The ladies came to her for their orders and their fittings, although their orders were smaller and fewer between with the war on, and sometimes their payments were slow. Sarah came from time to time to take a cup of tea or help with canning or quilting. Jefferson made the trips to town alone – he mailed her letters to her ma and carried back others, presented her market lists to Mr. Henderson, and carried back the supplies. Betsey kept at home, with her own simple house, her own simple clothes, her own children, and her own thoughts.

So much so that when she ventured at last down to the Barnes's farm on the day of Beth's wedding, with Herbert balanced on her hip, she felt strange. It was like going on a trip to a place she'd never been before.

The children dodged each other in a game of tag, catching up her skirts like a shield against the others, jumping, and running and shouting. So often had they tripped down over the field to Sarah's well-stocked cookie jar that they didn't even need to watch for the path.

From the door of her kitchen, or for that matter, from anywhere in her stumpy front yard, Betsey could see the Barnes's straightly plowed north field, Sarah's little white house, and the barn just beyond. But as she came down over the crest of the hill that day, to the right and to the left were suddenly in view two or three more houses that she felt she'd never seen before – and miles upon miles, it seemed, of land turned from forest into field.

Producing farms. To the west and to the east and to the south, as far as the eye could see.

Betsey stopped and turned to face her own farm. There it was. A forest. Isolated. Perched upon a hill in the midst of all that waving grain, its rocky two-track disappearing between the trees where they stretched their limbs above the underbrush, reaching for the sky. Oh, to be sure, there was a clearing there, around the house, replete with stumps surrounded by the bright green of new growth and with the children's clothing dancing on the clothesline, startlingly gay in color against the weathered gray of the house.

Betsey clutched Herbert closely to her side as she stared at it. There was a choking feeling in her throat, a heavy pounding in her chest. She widened her stance to keep from falling down as the children bumped and jostled in their play. "Mama, Mama!" They bumped and tugged. They shook her elbow. "Mama!"

Suddenly she realized that they were no longer playing, but were indeed trying to get her attention. "Mama? We still going to the wedding?"

"Yes, Sammy, yes," she answered softly, reaching for Duga's hand and turning toward Sarah's again. A shiver went up her spine and she looked about for the cloud she thought must have passed before the sun. But there was none. It was a bright, sunny June day, with a soft breeze wafting up the fragrance of the soil and the grain from all around her. The whole world, it seemed, had been going along without her.

Sarah saw them coming, and greeted them on the front stoop with outstretched hands and an excited smile. Inside, the house was sparkling clean, brightly decorated with wildflowers, the windows all flung wide open to embrace the sweetness of the day. On a table against the back wall were the gifts brought to the young couple: canned pears, jars of sourdough starter, sacks of flour, muffins, loaves of bread, wooden spoons, shiny new cooking pots, hand-made crockery bowls. To these, Betsey Anne added her own offering of three intricately embroidered aprons for the bride.

It seemed a long time since she'd been in Sarah's house, Betsey thought. Her mind immediately went back to the first time she'd been there – her own wedding. Sarah smiling, candles glowing, strangers laughing. She looked across the room and saw that even the Methodist circuit rider was the same as that long-ago day.

"Thank you, Betsey Anne," said Beth sweetly, reaching slender fingers to caress the pattern of the aprons. "These are lovely – I'll be afraid to soil them!"

My, how grown-up she looks, Betsey thought. Then she bit her lip with the remorseful realization that Beth was only three years younger than she was.

What might have been different if she had waited to marry? Betsey wondered. Then she looked down at Herbert in the crook of her arm, his pudgy two-year-old face alight with enjoyment of the myriad sights and sounds that greeted him, and she shrugged off the thought. "You're welcome, Beth, you're welcome."

"Jefferson Hawkins! In the flesh!" It was Charles Barnes's booming voice that reached her ears next.

Jefferson. He'd come!

Her children were clamoring around their papa, Sammy and Annie and Duga, as if he'd been long out to sea instead of out cutting firewood. He swept Duga up onto his shoulder and gave Annie a quick tickle under the chin, nodding to the almost five-year-old Sammy as though he were a grown man. And then, across the room, above the other heads as it were, he caught Betsey's eye.

And flashed his most charming smile.

She smiled back and pressed her cheek against the soft clean top of Herbert's head, warming within, just as ready to accept whatever Jefferson had to give as the children were.

And so the day began. It was filled to the brim with laughter and chatter, storytelling and singing, dancing and eating, preaching and marrying, hugging and waving, packing up and sending off, reliving and dreaming, sharing and helping.

And then Betsey loaded her four tired children in the back of the wagon and sat smiling up at Jefferson and holding onto the rail as they jogged recklessly up the road toward home.

And duty.

CHAPTER TWELVE

But in the morning, Betsey Anne's head was aching and she was down in the back. There were extra chores to do since they'd been left undone on the day of the wedding. The children were tired, and consequently cranky. Even Herbert was whiny and his nose had started to run.

Jefferson sat whittling in the sunshine, leaned comfortably against a stump, oblivious to all. He whittled while Betsey gathered the eggs and fed the chickens. He whittled while Betsey carried in water and made coffee and breakfast. He whittled while Betsey swept out the house. He whittled while Betsey built a fire in the pit and while she prepared the stew to bury there in its heavy iron pot.

And Betsey smoldered.

She hated the sight of the wind-beaten wood of her house, never graced by so much as a single coat of paint. She hated the sound of his knife against the wood in his hands. She hated the sight of the children gathered expectantly around him, anxious to see what new delight his hands would produce.

"All they are is cranking at me," she mumbled to herself as she worked. "Cranking at me, who's slaving around here to keep them fed and washed. But for **him** it's all smiles." She twisted a shirt of Sammy's to wring out the sudsy water, grimacing at the sight of her reddened knuckles and how nearly her hands resembled those of her Granny Wright.

"Granny had a hard life," she'd said the last time she looked at Granny's hands.

"There was hard in it, that's true, and she was given to looking for the

bad and not the good, I guess," her mother had replied. *"But Granny had a good, long life with children to love her."*

"Well, you have plenty of children, that's for certain," she remarked under her breath, smoothing the front of her dress over the bulk that was the next-to-arrive addition to her family. Laboriously, she stood, going first onto her knees, then propping herself on one foot and pushing off with her hands. She picked up the heavy basket full of wet clothes and trudged to the clothesline to hang them out, feeling every bend and every stretch in her tired arms and aching back.

Jefferson whittled.

She gathered the children and sent them, whining all the way, to pull a few weeds and dig a few potatoes from the garden. Hunkered down on her heels, pushing and pulling with all of her strength, she overturned the wash pot and emptied out the dirty water. Righting it, she stood for a minute pressing a hand to her back and blowing a wisp of hair off her forehead with an audible sigh. She heard the children arguing. A crow scolded the children, hoping, no doubt, to scare them from the garden. Shrieking with mock terror, they abandoned their task and scampered away down the hill.

Jefferson whittled.

Betsey refilled the wash pot, bucketful by bucketful, tramping as loudly as she could from the pump to the fire pit, her cheeks tingling from contact with her sharpened tongue. "Don't he see nothing?" she asked her angry self. "Don't he see the work all around him, just begging for a hand to turn it under?"

The pot full, she poked another stick on the fire beneath it and brought an arm across her sweating brow.

"I believe I'll take them children fishing a spell." It was the first thing he'd said all morning.

Fishing. "Well, if that don't just beat all," she thought. But she said nothing. There was nothing to say, and no need to say it, for Jefferson had gone already, winding his way through the stumps toward the creek, whistling a summons to the children who were whooping for joy as they bounded after him.

"Well," she said to Herbert with a regretful smile, "At least we'll have us a mess of fish. Though I expect I'll have to smoke them myself. That I will, child. That I will."

She picked him up from the grassy spot where he'd been playing, bouncing him above her head and nuzzling the soft spot beside his ear. Yes, Herbert, at least, was with her, no matter what, and there was a certain amount of comfort in that.

She ought to get right to the sewing, she knew, while the fresh wash water was heating, but the quiet of the house was inviting, with the children and Jefferson gone.

She decided a little time spent washing herself up could scarcely pass for lazy, and she poured some water from the kitchen bucket into her basin. She dipped her hands into its freshness and splashed it up over her face and neck with relish. She thought of the work still to be done and hesitated for a moment, but eventually yielded to the need for respite of any sort.

She untied her soot-stained apron and stepped out of her dress, piling them in a heap by the bedroom door to be added to the next wash load. Taking a soft cloth from the ragbag, she gave herself and little Herbert a quick "once over" with the tepid water, letting it evaporate into coolness on their hot skin.

"There now, ain't that a sight better?" she asked Herbert, who answered only with a smile. She slipped into her other work dress and tied on a clean apron. Then she gathered Herbert up and headed out to the garden to complete the task the children had left undone.

Weeds left drying in the unrelenting sun and potatoes nestled in a basket by the front door, Betsey determined the wash water was hot and returned to the house for an armload of dirty clothing. With a huff and a puff, she retrieved her own soiled work dress and apron from the floor, wishing she'd placed them on a bench instead, and stepped behind the calico curtain to gather Jefferson's things. His best white shirt and black gabardine trousers hung on their hooks next to the window, and she tossed them over her arm, snapping the suspenders off with a practiced hand as she walked.

Deeming the dress and apron to be the dirtier of the garments to be washed, she wadded them up atop a stump near the fire and dropped Jefferson's shirt in first, giving it a thorough scrubbing on the glass ridges of the washboard and ringing it out before plopping it into the waiting basket. Taking up the black dress trousers, she heard the rattle of paper and paused to check the pockets.

There was a letter, its little brown envelope postmarked Toledo and addressed in a shaky scrawl to "Mr. Thomas J. Hawkins Esquire, sir". Such an address could only be from J.H. Bernard, of whom the smallest recollection brought a sick feeling to the pit of Betsey's stomach. She wondered briefly why Jefferson hadn't shown her the letter and whether she should look at it at all. But then she decided he had merely forgotten, in the excitement of the wedding and all, and she took the folded missive out and opened it to read.

Your letter of the 16th of May was received on the 29th of May 1864, the letter began. Betsey bit her lip. Jefferson had written a letter to Bernard? He had not made mention of it. Again, he must have forgotten, she scolded herself, or perhaps it just seemed unimportant to him.

Give my best respects to Cline and all that inquires after me. Tell them that I am in them woods and I shall come out there in a year or two and see what you are all about. What has become of Halls farm and what can we sell that land on the corners for? If I can find a chance to sell I will sell for ready pay if I can, if not as good as we can and I will send your share. In reply to your inquiry I cannot answer as to Lorne Rugles, but I received a letter from his wife some two or three months ago. She said that she lived near Hasting in Barry County, Michigan and thought that Lorne had gone to Pikes Peak to dig for gold and that is the last I have heard from them. I saw a comely woman tending bar down near the depot some months ago who said to send you her regards but she offered me no swine. She shared a drop or two with me but angered easily and said you was twice the man as I am. She did not like it when I offered to show her how to ride better than Old Abe shows his big fat...

"Oh, my!" Betsey lost her balance and sat with a plop in the dirt. Clapping her hand over her mouth, she could feel hot embarrassment flooding into her cheeks. She could not bring herself to read the rest of the letter, having seen with a sweep of her eyes that it was filled with innuendo and epithets and political charges of utter depravity against the president and his cabinet.

She folded the letter with shaking hands and stuffed it quickly back into its envelope, shoving it deep into the pocket from which she had removed it. "Oh, my," she repeated to herself as she cast about in her mind, wondering what she ought to do next.

It was clear she ought not to have read the letter. What a filthy epistle! From a filthy person! No contact with Bernard could possibly be good – she was now, if not before, thoroughly convinced.

A babbled word from Herbert startled Betsey into action. She struggled up from the ground and almost ran back into the house, where she pegged the trousers back on their hook. Turning aside, she glimpsed the suspenders she had removed, and with a guilty lurch she grabbed them and fumblingly reattached them to the trousers.

"Oh, my," she whispered to herself over and over again. She felt hotter and hotter and bile rose up in her throat. She should not have read the letter. Stumbling out again into the sunlight, she burst into tears.

"Oh, sweet baby," she crooned, taking Herbert up and cradling him close, pressing her tear-stained cheek against his soft pink one. "Oh, sweet baby."

How she cursed Jefferson's silent, secret past. How she lamented that she knew him not at all. Oh, what should she do? What **could** she do?

Herbert began to struggle, tired of being squeezed and eager to play with his dandelions and blades of grass. She plopped him down with one last kiss and then said to herself, "A job of work, that's what you'll do, Betsey Anne!"

Dropping her soiled work dress and apron into the hot water, she seized her wooden paddle and went after them with a vengeance while her thoughts ran wildly this way and that.

What land was this that Bernard spoke of, that Jefferson would have a share in? And what *"comely woman"* would be sending her regards to Jefferson? *"But offered me no swine..."* He was surely recalling the sow he brought as "a token of regard" from someone called "Alice's mother." Betsey's stomach turned anew as she recalled that horrid visit. She had not known that Jefferson was still in contact with the oily and obnoxious John H. Bernard – but clearly he had written to him. *"Your letter of the 16th of May was received on the 29th of May 1864,"* the letter said. Yes, Jefferson had written to Bernard, had known where to address the letter. Why had he written? She searched her mind almost gingerly, wanting to remember part of the letter, but wanting to forget most of it. *"In reply to your inquiry, I cannot answer as to Lorne Rugles..."*

That was it – Jefferson had just wanted to find someone, some mutual friend, like George Cline. Someone they both knew and Jefferson had not seen for some time.

Betsey scrubbed and scrubbed – first at the dress and then at the apron and back to the dress again. Back and forth over the ridges of the washboard she worked the garments, and back and forth over the letter she worked her thoughts. Surely Jefferson had written for this simple reason. But who was Lorne Rugles? If Jefferson was interested enough in his whereabouts to write Bernard a letter, why had she never heard his name before?

She switched from the dress to the apron again. Perhaps Jefferson had only written to answer a letter from Bernard, and while doing so had casually inquired of an old friend, brought to mind by Bernard's letter. Yes, that must surely be it. She dropped the apron and attacked the dress anew.

But if that were true, why had she not seen a letter from Bernard before? Was there any danger in corresponding with a man who wrote such treasonous things about the president in time of war? What suspicions would it raise should someone else read the letter?

"Oh, you're a fool, Betsey Anne," she scolded herself aloud at last. She fished the apron out of the water and wrung it tightly, twisting it first this way and then that. No self-respecting man would show his wife a filthy letter like the one she'd just read – and where there was smoke, there was fire.

There was no mystery here, she decided finally, as she pegged the garments onto the line. Jefferson had not mentioned this, or any other letter from J.H. Bernard Esquire, because his letters were not fit to mention.

"Come on, Herbert," she said, figuratively. "Let's see if that stew is ready for dinner."

She pushed the letter to the back of her mind, where it hovered like a black storm cloud, reaching an occasional chill finger to cause a shiver down her back. Jefferson and the children returned from fishing – Sammy with a string of fine trout, Annie with a pine-bough doll, and Duga with pockets full of rocks and mud.

All through dinner, Jefferson stared at her till she began to fancy that he knew she'd read the letter. He caught her from behind while she washed up the dishes and looked deep into her eyes until she squirmed, then he pressed on her lips a kiss heavy with intent and turned from her, drawing the children into the yard.

Flustered, she settled Herbert on his mat with his favorite wooden doll. She noticed that his nose was still dripping, so she mixed some of ma's herbs with a little applesauce and coaxed him to eat it before she turned to the sewing.

She longed to hang out the red-and-white pinwheel quilt to summon Sarah so they could talk. Sarah would surely make her feel better. Sarah was always ready to listen – she'd harbor no treasonous suspicions about Jefferson.

Suspicions.

The word stuck in her mind. What exactly did she suspect Jefferson of? she asked herself. Of treason? No, she did not suspect any such thing. But still, the chill wind blew at the back of her mind.

Perhaps the cause of it was the depravity she'd read of in the letter – even to think on such things was sure to cloud one's mind. Perhaps it was naught but the contact with Bernard –

Her foot on the treadle slowed to a stop, her fingers lay idle against the fabric. She stared straight ahead, lost completely to the memory of her first contact with the foul man…

Laughter. Pointed, intimate jokes. Jefferson's inscrutable smile. *"She's a shapely thing, and that's for certain, Tom J. And seems to be right at hand to produce a fine offspring to boot!"* The pig, snorting, squealing, rooting in Betsey's garden. *"Shows just what she thinks of you, Tom J!"* Alice's' mother. *"Alice being nigh grown and all, that fine gift there… erased any obligation…"*

Betsey's head began to spin. Laughing, jeering faces flashed before her eyes. Bernard: *"and a right shapely specimen she is, too!"* Flossie Cline: *"Betsey-**girl**."* Mary Jane: *"make Prudie Richy ride the old stag's back."*

Jefferson: silent, silent, silent.

"Aaaahhhh!!!" Betsey started up with a shriek as Jefferson's hands gripped her shoulders. He clapped one hand over her mouth and when she was quiet he took that hand to point toward Herbert, fast asleep, cherub-like, in the corner. Still gripping her shoulder, Jefferson guided her to the kitchen. Through the open door she had a glimpse of the other three children, skipping through Sarah's north field with the wind in their hair.

She hesitated as Jefferson drew her behind the calico curtain that served as their bedroom door. She felt faintly nauseated and wanted to scream at him, "No! No! Not now – not after what I read! Not while I feel like this!" But she did not dare, so she kept silent.

Jefferson was also silent as he pressed her onto the bed, urgency in his movements, his body strong and insistent against her. Her mind reeled, her head swam. She struggled to hold down a feeling of nausea, forced her mind physically away from the visions created by Bernard's letter. She closed her eyes tightly and wrestled with her thoughts, reality dim and distant, until at last it was over.

She waited, afraid to move, even to open her eyes lest she betray her emotions, until he left the room. Even then, she lay unmoving, silent tears slipping down her cheek and onto her pillow.

"A comely woman… who said to send you her regards… and said you was twice the man as I am…"

Suspicions, yes. But no, not treason.

CHAPTER THIRTEEN

July 13 1864
Dear Brother —
I take this opportunity to write a few lines to you and yours. I can say
we are all well at present, and hoping this will find you all the same.
Brother, it is with a heavy heart that I write to you of the death of
Analisa Laughton. She died the 4ᵗʰ of July. She had the consumption on
the lungs. Mother said she could never feel reconciled to her death, for
they did not send for a doctor until she was ready to die. She was sick
eight days. She left four children. Mother was there when I came home.
Smith wanted her to stay this winter. She was not very well. Thomas,
you have but two sisters left. Elisabeth was well. William was not very
well. The rest was all well, but William has had very bad luck. He has
lost his right arm in the thrasher. It was taken off just below the elbow.
We have had very pleasant weather. I often think of the time when you
and I used to pick apples. I think now it was the happiest time I ever
saw. How I should like to see you. If you will come out here, I will give
you all the apples you can eat. Write as soon as you get this. No more
at present. Yours truly, F.M. Garnier.
PS I will send you a piece of Analisa's shroud.

And there it was — a piece of the shroud, lying on Betsey Anne's
kitchen table. Not a piece of the shroud itself, really, Betsey reminded
herself. Rather, a corner of the cloth left over when the shroud was
cut. Trimmed into a neat little rectangle.

Jefferson was silent, staring with unseeing eyes at the letter.
Betsey stared at the letter, too, concentrating on every little detail.
It was written on blue paper, mailed in a blue envelope, the color of

the sky. The ink was brown, Frances's penmanship flowery, and the sad news delivered with a peculiar lack of feeling and an even more peculiar memento of the loss.

Betsey sat until her back ached and her neck stiffened. Then pushing the bench away from the table with a scrape she stood up and ambled woodenly to the door to look out at the children. They were happily engaged in their various pursuits – Sammy industriously moving rocks away from the plants in the garden, Annie lining them up so she could 'have a school', and Duga throwing them, with most landing right back in the garden. They were always together that way, each doing a separate thing, but never far from the other two.

She cast a glance to the grassy spot where Herbert lay, happily watching a parade of tiny black ants. She thought briefly of all that he missed, his world was so small; then she reminded herself that his needs were also small, his wants always met. More than you could say for many.

"So Analisa is dead," she said out loud. She looked back at the three in the garden and tried to imagine Jefferson at that age, picking apples with Frances and watching over little Analisa with tender protectiveness. "Your favorite sister."

Betsey turned back toward the table, where Jefferson sat unmoving.

"Baby sister," he said, softly.

"And William – his arm – bad luck indeed." She rubbed her hand in the small of her back and went absently to the stove to pour out a cup of lukewarm coffee. She set the cup before Jefferson.

"I'm sorry," she said. She reached past his shoulder for the letter, leaning forward and stretching her fingers out, her motherly belly seeming quite in her way. Snagging a corner of the blue paper with the tips of her fingers, she straightened back up and pulled it to her. The action sent the three-inch rectangle of muslin aloft. It seemed to catch a breeze from the open door, and hung strangely suspended in the air for a moment, then flipped and tumbled and turned in a dance of its own as it drifted slowly to the floor.

Jefferson made a dive, suddenly, forcefully pushing the bench out behind him, knocking Betsey's stiff knees out from under her and sending her staggering backward toward the stove. He snatched the remnant of Analisa's shroud off the hard-packed dirt, swinging around in the same motion and grabbing the letter from Betsey's hand. She backed another step away from him, bumping into the stove, momentarily thankful that it was not hot.

She'd seen many looks on Jefferson's face – indeed she had studied that face by the hour, searching it for feelings, for answers, for knowledge. But this look was one she had never seen before.

His right eye was opened widely, making the left one, with its drooping lid, seem nearly shut. His mouth hung open from the jaw, slack and loose, his tongue lolling forward. He looked alternately from Betsey to the letter and the cloth, held gingerly in trembling hands.

"I'm sorry," she said. "I, I didn't mean…" her voice trailed off as he let out a deep, guttural moan, rubbing his thumb up and down over the fabric in his right hand.

"I'm sorry." She could think of nothing else to say.

They stood for a long time that way, until finally she noticed that he closed his mouth and his shoulders began to droop. "Sit down, Jefferson," she said. Taking his arm she guided him back to the bench where he resumed his staring.

Betsey went out to the yard to see after the children, scolding Duga about stealing Annie's rock dolls, praising Sammy for his hard work, admiring Annie's skills as a teacher, carrying Herbert along with her as she went. She pulled the laundry down from the clothesline and stacked it in a basket which she deposited just inside the open door. She pumped a bucket of water for the children to wash up in, and uncovered the ever-present pot of chicken stew in the fire pit.

Going back into the kitchen for cornbread fixings, she saw that Jefferson had not moved.

The children gathered around her as she stirred up the corn meal, each wanting a turn at stirring the yellow batter, each wanting to share in scraping the batter from the bowl into the skillet. She stirred up the embers of the morning's fire and set the children to blowing on it while she gathered a few more sticks to throw on top.

"Now you watch right there till the sides begin to pull away from the pan," she instructed them. Sammy and Annie crouched dutifully down to watch the cornbread cook, but Duga skipped away and threw himself down on his belly beside Herbert to exchange loud, unintelligible sounds and sprinkle hands full of grass over one another's heads.

Betsey returned to the kitchen to lay out the dishes and pour the cider and milk.

Jefferson had not moved.

Irritated, she sighed audibly and said, "You'd best put that – letter – up now. Dinner's ready."

But he didn't move.

In fact, he continued to sit that way all through dinner, his meal untouched in front of him, while the children laughed and chattered and ate.

He continued to sit when the children returned to their games out of doors, Herbert entranced this time with the workings of a family of stinkbugs.

He did not move while Betsey washed the dishes, nor while she kneaded down the bread to set it for its second rising, though she made as much huffing and puffing about it as she could.

She left him, still motionless, when it was time to begin the day's sewing.

Some long while passed before she again heard the scraping of the bench on the hard-packed dirt floor of the kitchen, and the clumping of his boots as he came toward her.

"I'll be going then," he said.

"Going?" She could not think what he might mean.

"Back – home, I mean – to see them – to help."

She stared at him stupidly, astonished beyond words.

"They need my help."

"*They* need your help?" Her voice was harsh, angry, unfamiliar. "*Your* help?"

"They need my help," he repeated.

"Jefferson!" She fairly shrieked in exasperation, rising to her feet. "You can't just pick up and go – you'll be gone for weeks, no doubt, all the way to Ohio!"

He only stared, his lips thin and straight, his eyes beginning to harden.

"And what'll you do when you get there, anyhow?" she asked. "What? Just how do you think you can help? Analisa is **dead**!"

"William..." he said, his voice trailing off, almost helplessly, his eyes dropping toward the floor. "William – his arm – his right arm..."

"William!" Her voice was high, sharp, cutting him off mid-sentence. "William ain't got but one child, Jefferson. One child! And he's no doubt got hired help besides. He don't need **your** help!"

"Mother," he brought his eyes up to hers again. "There's mother – and Analisa's children – four of them Frances says."

"Think of your own four children!" Betsey bellowed. "And a fifth on the way!"

He didn't blink. Didn't shuffle – didn't move at all.

Betsey was breathing hard. Her cheeks were glowing, her mouth dry, her eyes burning in their sockets and blazing with anger. "Go on then, if you're of a mind to, you **fool**." She spat out the last word. "And you are that, Jefferson – a fool, if you think they need you. Look at you! You've barely kept **us** from starving!"

She stepped closer to him, the bulk of her pregnant form seeming to grow in her anger, her jaw clenched, her fists clenched, her eyes as hard as her voice. "I take that back," she said in a near-whisper. "I take that back. You ain't kept us from starving – I've done that my own self. Slaving around here, doing my duty, day in and day out. Washing, and cooking, and cleaning and **sewing**."

Something had broken, something had shattered within her and she could not stop her tongue. She stood toe to toe with him, her face raised to look deep into his unbelieving eyes.

"You think they need you? Well, they don't! They've got along fine without you all these years. Is it apples you're pining for? Them apples Frances says she'll give you? Well go on then! For certain there ain't no real apples on **this** farm!"

She saw tears welling up in the bottoms of his eyes, and she might have taken pity. In fact she considered it for a moment, hesitated as visions flashed before her eyes – the way he looked when he proposed, when Granny Wright died, when he gave her the rocking chair. She heard Sarah's voice somewhere in her head, saying *"Love's the only plant you can grow without a seed,"* and she swallowed hard. Tears formed in her own eyes and she bowed her head. Dropping it forward onto his chest, she pressed her face against the roughness of his shirt and took a deep breath.

And in that breath she thought she smelled the faintest lingering of a woman's perfume.

"Aaahh!" she turned away and pushed him from her. "Go on then, you fool, just go on then – I'll tell you what they need, they need to feed you for a while! Lord knows *I'm* tired of doing it! I'm tired, Jefferson. Tired, tired, tired!"

She sank down in front of the sewing machine with her head on her arm and gave herself over to sobbing. She heard him leave the room and her ears strained to hear where he would go, what he would do. She wanted to get up, wanted to stop him, wanted to tell him that she needed him, she needed his love. But she couldn't move.

She heard him whistle for the children, heard their excited clamor as they ran to him, bit her lip when she thought she heard Sammy say, "fishing." She forced herself up, hurried to the front door, and saw them, Duga on his shoulders, Annie holding his hand, Sammy leading the way – into the shelter of the trees they went, headed for the creek.

Suddenly ashamed of her tirade, Betsey Anne attacked her sewing with vigor, rushing to finish it so as to have time to prepare for their return – his return – at evening. She swept the kitchen floor twice over and set the table with a bouquet of wildflowers, preserved with boiling water so they'd hold their heads up high. She kneaded down the bread the last time and pressed it out flat, sprinkling it with cinnamon and precious sugar before rolling it up into a log for baking.

She washed her face and loosened her heavy auburn hair so it hung in gentle waves about her face and then sat on a stump in the front yard, jiggling Herbert on her knee, breathlessly crooning little nothings to him in the gathering dusk.

Panic had set in and she was just about to decide that he'd taken the children with him and set out walking to Ohio when she finally heard their happy voices rising on the evening air.

"Oh, oh, they're home, Herbert," she whispered.

Now she was embarrassed to be found waiting anxiously in the front yard, so she hurried into the house and settled Herbert on the rag rug in the corner of the kitchen, hovering over him making little dancing motions with his wooden dolls and clucking to him.

"Mama! Mama!" It was Duga who reached her first. "Mama – I fished, I fished!" His grubby little hand held up a string on which dangled a tiny, much-played-with fish and his toothy smile flashed out from under layers of mud and grass.

"Caught that your own self, did you?" she asked. "That's Mama's big boy!" Using her thumb to clean the mud off his forehead, she planted a kiss on the closest thing she found to skin and hauled herself up from the floor.

"Oh, that's a nice mess of fish you got there, all of you." She looked at Jefferson's face, trying hard to read his emotions there but seeing nothing.

The children were hungry, they said – and dirty, *she* said, as she sent them back out to wash up at the pump in the yard. Jefferson went with them, and by the time they came back in, she had the meal on the table, complete with fresh, steaming cinnamon bread and gingered crabapples.

Through the meal, Betsey couldn't decide if Jefferson was silent or if it was just that the children chattered on till there wasn't room for him to talk. She tried not to stare at him, only stealing a glance in his direction from time to time, wishing that she knew what he was thinking.

After the meal, she declared that it was far past time for little girls and boys to be sleeping and amid their protestations she dressed them, then tucked them in and heard their whispered prayers. She expected to find Jefferson in the sewing room, rocking and whittling as he often did in the evening, but he was not there.

With a little jab of fear, she ran outside. There was no light in the barn. Relieved, she hurried to the privy and back again, unable to keep from looking toward the barn once more on the way back. Inside, she crept quietly behind the calico curtain to the bedroom and found Jefferson fast asleep already.

She undressed stealthily and eased herself onto the bed, holding her breath lest she wake him. But he slept on, his breathing deep and regular.

Long into the night she lay listening to him and playing the day's events back in her mind and making herself half sick with worrying what the repercussions of her outburst would be.

She awoke with a still-heavy heart, but as her mind slowly peeled back the layers of sleep, it came first upon the faint, dank smell of earth touched by dew that wafted through her open window. It occurred to her that she used often to dream of the day when, being her own mistress, she could allow herself to lie luxuriously abed until the dawn had fully broken, and she could not help but smile.

"You're a fool, Betsey Anne," she murmured to herself as she swung her feet to the floor. "A'wrestling the night long over things you can't change."

Moving quietly so as not to wake Jefferson or the children, she slipped into her work dress and carried her wash basin out to the pump in the yard. The sun was peeking over the tops of the trees and sparkling in the dew that lay heavily on the grass and wildflowers. Chickens were silently stalking about the chicken yard, their beady eyes darting back and forth, their springy necks jerking up and down or side to side, pecking at the ground with sudden swiftness. Birds of many varieties filled the air with their voices like so many children in a schoolyard. Occasional butterflies appeared as if by magic, lighting briefly on some object or another with a great display of colorful wings as though to bestow the gift of their very being on anyone who chanced to see them there.

Betsey pumped wash water for herself, pushing aside a hovering sense of worry. She unbuttoned the top button of her dress and turned the neckpiece under so it wouldn't get wet. Setting her basin on the top of a stump, she bent over, dipping her soft auburn hair gingerly in the cold water. Even on a warm summer morning, that first contact with water drawn from the cool depths of the well sent a shiver down her back.

She rinsed her hair over and over, then lathered it up with a raw egg and rinsed again before pouring a cup of apple cider vinegar slowly through it. Ringing the extra moisture out of the thick locks first, she sat down on a stump where the sun was already warming and ran her fingers slowly through the curls, smoothing out the tangles.

Perhaps it would be nice, she thought, to be a lady of wealth and leisure, passing the day in pampering one's hair and skin and laboring with intensity over trifling bits of decorative lace.

Duga's sharp cry brought her back to reality with sudden physical impact and she braided her hair quickly into one thick rope and hurried into the house.

She found Jefferson standing by the stove fully dressed, dusting his hat against his thigh. Annie was standing defiantly next to the mat in the corner, engaged in battle with Duga over a corn cob doll. Herbert and Sammy still slept, but were beginning to stir as a result of Duga's strident tones.

Something in Jefferson's face made Betsey feel a sudden sense of shame, of tardiness, perhaps, and selfishness that she had dawdled over her hair instead of putting on the breakfast.

"I can have coffee and eggs in two shakes," she stammered, with a sideways glance at the children. She tucked her head down and hurried over to the stove, jerking the door of it open to poke in a stick. Feeling his eyes upon her, she looked up and found herself engaged in that all-encompassing stare.

He didn't speak but instead settled his hat on his head and stroked his beard while looking deep into her eyes. Then he turned and stumped out the door.

Oh, how she hated that closed mouth of his! Confused, she continued to struggle with the stove, splashing water onto the floor in her haste to get the coffee on. She snatched the screaming Duga from the mat and hurried out to the chicken house to gather eggs, the child's prolonged cries scattering the squawking hens in her path. In spite of all her cajoling and clucking, Duga refused to be silenced. But Betsey hurried on with her cargo of eggs.

Back in the kitchen, she deposited Duga on the floor and the eggs in a crockery bowl. By this time, Herbert was crying in hunger, and Sammy added his voice to the uproar with well-meaning offers of assistance. Only Annie was silent, having obtained the doll of her desire and focused her attention solely on its imaginary needs.

Betsey whipped the eggs so they'd cook more quickly and then hurriedly chopped four potatoes and one onion and deposited them in another skillet. The children grew louder and louder, Sammy beginning to tug at her apron. She began to feel almost desperate in her attempt to get some breakfast on the table, sure that Jefferson would soon appear in the doorway, with horses left hitched to the wagon in the front yard, ready for a trip she wished he would not take.

She didn't really hear anything – couldn't over the noise of the children – but instead caught the motion out of the corner of her eye.

Jefferson. In the wagon. Disappearing over the crest of the hill, down into the valley and away without so much as a word of farewell.

Now her tears joined those of her children as she slumped to the floor in a heap. Drawing them into her arms, she rocked to and fro as much to comfort herself as to quiet them.

CHAPTER FOURTEEN

It was in the dead of night, some three months after he left that the fear gripped her. The icy fingers of an October midnight wrapped around her heart and winter whispered in her ear, *"I'm coming, and you're alone. I'm coming. and you're alone."* The next sensation brought her fully awake and she shook her head as she mumbled to herself, "You're a fool, Betsey Anne, the only thing coming here tonight is the baby, and Jefferson never was any help with that anyhow."

"Sammy! Sammy!" She leaned heavy against the doorpost and called her oldest boy.

"Yes, mama?" He seemed surprisingly alert.

"Get Sarah. Quick as you can."

She struggled through the intermittent pain to arrange the room and gather the things they would need. She stoked the fire up just a little, reminding herself that it would feel warm enough before long. Finally she collapsed on the bed with her eyes shut tight and said out loud, "Please get here!" even though she hardly knew exactly whom she meant.

She guessed it was her mother she wanted the most – but Ma wouldn't arrive until the end of the week. It must be Sarah that she needed, and Sammy had gone to fetch her. Surely they would arrive in a matter of minutes.

Betsey rubbed her face sideways into the rough pillow and tightened her hold against the pain. "Where is Jefferson? Where is Jefferson?" her mind echoed. "Why hasn't he come home? Why? Why?" She went over the history in the circular fashion peculiar to the dark of night, as though thinking it through and through again could somehow change the facts, somehow find the clue she'd missed, somehow change the fact that he was gone. *Gone, gone…*

The letter. The letter from Frances on that horrible blue paper with the little rectangle of unbleached muslin in the folds of it. *Analisa died last week. Died last week. Died last week. I will send you a piece of Analisa's shroud. Analisa's shroud. Analisa's shroud. Shroud. Shroud.* In Betsey's tortured world the muslin tumbled and floated and hung in the air for what seemed like hours, never reaching the floor, and Jefferson's horror-stricken face flashed on and off like bolts of lightning. *Analisa's shroud. Analisa.* His favorite sister. "Baby sister," he said from inside a dark tunnel somewhere.

And then the letter took on a life of its own and began to speak again. *William lost his arm in the thrasher. Arm in the thrasher. Lost his arm in the thrasher. Lost his arm. William. William. William.*

Betsey's own words began to join the dance, sounding strangely harsh and cruel, in a voice she couldn't recognize, couldn't admit to owning. *THEY need your help? Your help? YOUR help? What about us? About US? You've barely kept us from starving! Starving! Starving! Think of your own four children! Children! Children! And a fifth on the way! On the way!*

The bed seemed to rise off the hard packed dirt floor and spin and float like that horrid scrap of muslin. Betsey threw her head back and strained against twisted sheets knotted in her grasp, but try as she might she couldn't slow down the words as they danced around her; couldn't silence the strange mixed-up echo in her head.

Analisa's shroud! Baby sister's shroud! YOUR help? What about us? What about us? William! William? Starving children! Starving children! Arm in the thrasher! Arm in the thrasher! Fifth on the way! Analisa's shroud! Shroud! SHROUD!

In a sudden rushing sense of the absence of pain, Betsey opened her eyes. The room widened around her in a circle of light filled with clamor and smiling faces.

And the cry of a baby that didn't echo at all.

"She has red hair, just like you Betsey Anne."

Betsey thought she might speak but didn't. She pressed her cheek against the forehead of the infant they placed in her arms and wondered how her mother had known to be here now, this day. She smiled and took a deep breath, drinking in the sweet smell of the infant, thinking only how nice it was to have come out into the light of day. Then she drifted off to sleep as a loving mother's hand soothed her brow with a cool, wet cloth.

After Harriet was born, it was decided that Lydia would stay to help Betsey Anne until Jefferson's return from Ohio. Lydia was not particularly happy about the idea, and everyone was aware that helping Betsey Anne was only part of the reason for the decision.

Betsey Anne had heard them talking – Lydia tearful and supplicating, Pa grunting stoically, Ma calmly holding her ground. "You don't need to be around home if he comes a' calling. They're still looking for him – he's a deserter, girl! Besides, your sister's got five children and her husband away – she needs your help."

Later, Pa whispered in Betsey's ear, "Don't let her go spooning – she's too young to know her mind."

Seventeen, Betsey thought. The same age I was when I married Jefferson. She looked over Pa's shoulder at the fair Lydia, soft blond hair and tender pink cheeks glowing in the light from the window. "I won't, Pa," she whispered.

"Watch she don't run about on bare feet or with wet hair," Ma scolded. "Her lungs ain't never been strong and she'll be took by a consumption if you don't watch."

"I'll watch, Ma," Betsey answered. Then she stood shoulder to shoulder with her younger sister and watched the wagon creak away over the rocky hillside.

It was a point of fact that Lydia did not provide much in the way of help. She had indeed been weak and sickly through much of her youth, and as a consequence had been pampered rather than trained.

Betsey would set her to watch the children, and Lydia would drift off to sleep. Betsey would ask her to prepare a meal, and it would invariably be burned, or half-cooked, or otherwise inedible, such as in the case of the crabapple pie to which Lydia added a measure of salt instead of sugar. Betsey would send Lydia out to hang up the laundry,

118

and she would run back in, breathless, exclaiming with the cold, the wet things left in their basket under the clothesline.

And yet it was good to have her. It was hard to be angry with Lydia.

Jefferson's long absence hung heavy on Betsey's heart. She spent long hours replaying that horrible argument in her head – let the lamp in her bedroom burn low night after night while she sat fingering the rectangular reminder of Analisa's shroud, or reading the letter from Frances.

She should have been more understanding – Jefferson had understood when she went home for Granny Wright's burying. But then, Granny was still alive when she set out and it was only half a day's drive, she would offer up as an excuse to herself.

Perhaps she should have gone with him – why indeed had she not thought of that? What was to stop her? She should at least have offered to go, to load up the children and...

It was at this point in her conversation with herself that she would begin the planning, working out the trip to the last detail: how she would have packed and what, how she would have dressed the children, where they would have camped along the way, how she would cook as they traveled, how it would be to meet Jefferson's family, what she would learn about his past. She would sit for long hours into the night, working out the details like that, until finally she would realize that it was futile.

She had not offered to go, and he was already gone. Lord only knew she could not follow.

Harriet put her in mind of Annie as a baby – either eating or sleeping, with few complaints. Other than her red hair, which had no doubt come from Betsey Anne, the infant resembled her father as none of the others had, and Betsey could not so much as look at her without thinking of Jefferson.

And so the nights were sleepless, one after the other, until Betsey began to grow thin and terse, pressing her fingers to her aching temples time and time again after snappishly silencing the children. Apology was always immediate, but she hated herself for her sharp tongue, and added recriminations for it to her list of worries in the night.

It was early December when she stopped, suddenly, in the midst of scraping the burnt remainders of the morning's potato and onion breakfast out of the bottom of the skillet.

"Lydia? Lydia – take that pinwheel quilt from off the bed in there and go hang it out on the clothesline."

"Don't you want me to wash it first?"

"No," she took up the scraping again. "No, it's clean – just hang it out." There was no response. "Please."

Lydia looked out the window and saw the effects of a cold wind. "Can't you pick a warmer day for airing out a clean quilt?"

"It's not about – oh, I'll do it my own self." Betsey wiped her hands on her threadbare apron and in the same motion peeled it off and slapped it on a hook. Grabbing her overcoat, she shrugged into it as she strode toward the bed, pulled it tightly together at the neck as she headed out the front door.

Perhaps she could just go down to see Sarah. She stood for a moment in the front yard gazing with longing at the neat little farm in the valley, with welcoming puffs of smoke rising from its stove pipe. But her next glance was at the road and she knew she did not want to leave. What if this were the day of his return?

So she pegged the time-softened quilt to the line and left it flapping its bright invitation while she hurried back to the dishes and the squabbling children.

"Come on, now, let's get this place tidied up," she puffed as the wind pushed her through the door. "Might be we'll have some company come to call." She replaced her coat on its hook and sidled up to the stove to warm herself, rubbing her hands back and forth together, and stamping her feet up and down.

The prospect of company was welcome to one and all and everyone who was able pitched in on the chores. Lydia went at the sweeping with gusto, and kept with it till it was done, in spite of an overturned workbasket and its consequent thimble search. Duga put all the well-used wooden toys into a basket, and having obtained his mother's thanks, promptly pulled them out again. Annie rolled up her sleeves and scrubbed away ineffectively at the breakfast dishes, soaking the front of her apron and dress. Sammy brought in wood for the fire, three sticks at a time, letting in bursts of cold air with every opening of the door.

Betsey Anne, energized with the prospect of a visit from Sarah, put down the sourdough for the noon meal, finished scraping burnt onions from the skillet, helped Annie with the dishes, re-stacked the firewood, tracked down the last thimble, changed Annie into dry clothes, washed Herbert's face, nursed Harriet, made tea, and set a pot of beans to soak on the back of the stove.

And then, there was Sarah, knocking cheerily at the door as she pushed it open to let herself in out of the cold, the red-and-white quilt draped over her arm.

"Whew! My but it's cold out there this morning!" She was immediately set upon by the children, clamoring all at once in their excitement. "Let me take your coat." "Your nose is red!" "Is you a company?" "Want to stand by the stove?" "Ma made tea and I washed the dishes." "Lydia's here – she burnt the taters." "Ma – didn't you say to hang that quilt on the line?"

Laughing, Sarah did her best to answer each question, giving each child a hug and a kiss on the nose, acknowledging Lydia's blushing presence, and scooping Herbert up from the mat on her round-about journey toward the warmth of the stove. "I believe I will stand by the stove." She smiled a knowing smile as she handed the quilt to Betsey Anne. "I thought I'd bring that in for you, now that it's aired."

"Thank you, Sarah," was the only answer, and the quilt was returned to the bed in a heap. "I have some tea steeping, and there's gingered crabapples if you're hungry."

"That'll be just fine. There now," she held Herbert out in front of her and made a face at him. "Are you warm enough yet?"

To the children, this seemed like the cue to begin their chattering anew, and as Betsey poured the tea and set out the crabapples, they regaled Sarah with a long list of their most recent exploits, from Annie stirring up the cornbread "by my own self" to Sammy "whittling out a block of wood like my Pa does" and Duga claiming to have gone out "hunting for me a **bear**!" Even Lydia added a tale or two of her own, stemming mostly from her popularity with the young men, and her parent's inability to see her maturity.

Sarah listened well, placing her comments and her questions precisely where they were needed to make each child feel the center of her attention, and deftly handing the conversation to the next child just in time. Betsey sipped her tea silently, watching her friend and enjoying the change of pace and the children's joy in it.

And then the morning was gone, the dinner hour upon them. "I best be getting on home," Sarah said, looking directly into Betsey's eyes. "It's mighty cold, too cold for travel if you ask me. A body couldn't go any great ways in this cold."

Betsey Anne picked up Sarah's meaning, lobbed above the heads of the children under the disguise of mere discussion of the weather. Jefferson would not be able to travel in this weather. "You're right, Sarah," she said, feeling sudden tears stinging her eyes. "I reckon it's cold all over."

"Them fool boys of mine still mean to go into town day after tomorrow, in case you got a letter to mail or any errands. I'll send them by here first."

"Oh! I'll go in to town with them!" Lydia was suddenly animated, bursting with excitement. "I'll do the marketing, or whatever, oh, Betsey! Please?"

Betsey Anne and Sarah broke into laughter, and shaking her head, Betsey answered, "I don't mind, Lydia, except we'll have to bundle you up till you can't even budge else Ma'll have my hide."

"Oh, I don't care! I don't care!" Lydia turned on her heel and hurried off to the sewing room where her things were kept as though she would start the bundling process immediately, and the two older women shared another chuckle at her expense.

"Here now, let me wrap that muffler around once more," Betsey said, taking the end of Sarah's knitted neckpiece and winding it around behind. "I guess you'll keep warm enough if you hurry – thank you for coming." And Sarah was out the door, trundling down over the hillside and across the wintry field, looking like a carefree child.

"Well, now," said Betsey Anne, turning back to her brood. "I reckon we better see about our dinner." Harriet chimed in with a cry that told everyone she wanted her dinner first, and with a smile,

Betsey went to her while the rest of the household settled back into its normal activities.

Betsey rocked gently, listening to the creaking of the rocker on the planks of the sewing room floor, gazing at her infant daughter but seeing instead Jefferson's face, and her own, in a parade of memories and regrets, mingled with a new resolve.

There had been no time for a private conversation with Sarah – could be no time for such with a house full of children and too cold to send them out to play. But somehow just seeing her friend, just seeing that Sarah understood...

Well, she knew what Sarah would say.

She touched Harriet's soft cheek with her finger and smoothed down the curly red hair as she nestled the child closer to her breast. "I reckon it's time we told your Pa about you," she whispered.

"I reckon it's time."

CHAPTER FIFTEEN

Betsey Anne spent most of the next morning seated at the kitchen table working on her letter to Jefferson.

There was so much that she wanted to say. She wanted to say that she should have been more understanding – that she should have shown him she cared about his loss. She wanted to say that even so he should not have left that morning without a word. She wanted to say that she wished she had packed up the children and gone to Ohio with him. She wanted to say that he'd been gone far too long, that he was wrong to leave them to face the cold of winter alone.

As Sammy banged in and out, carrying in armloads of sticks he'd gathered in the woods, Betsey thought of the wood stack Jefferson had scarcely begun when he left in July, depleted already, and no good way for two women and five children to chop any more. She thought of the pump in the yard that grew harder and harder to work, of the fence around the chicken yard that had taken her all day long to repair when Duga's climbing brought it down.

And then she heard her own voice echoing in her head, *"You ain't kept us from starving – I've done that my own self. Slaving around here, doing my duty, day in and day out. Washing, and cooking, and cleaning, and **sewing**."* She wanted to write that she was sorry, that she didn't mean to sound that way, that she was just tired. So very tired.

Betsey pressed the heels of her hands into her eyes to stop the flow of tears. Going to the stove she poured herself a cup of thick leftover coffee and set it with a thump on the table. "Annie – let loose of that doll and stop fighting with your brother. Duga, can't you stop that whining? You'll wake the baby." She smiled at Sammy, diligently carrying in another armload of sticks, then glanced at Herbert who lay staring at the sleeping Harriet, and Lydia, bent over a piece of mending with a frown.

"Liddy – it takes less time to do it right at first than to take it back out and do it over," she scolded, instantly sorry, for it caused Lydia to jam the garment back into the workbasket and shove her hands under her thighs.

A glance at the window told Betsey it was almost the dinner hour, and she turned back to the blank scrap of brown paper on the table. With a sigh she picked up her pen and wrote:

Dear Jefferson – I take my pen in hand to write you of the birth of your daughter, Harriet. She was born the 17th of October and has red hair. Save for that, she puts me in mind of her father. The children is all wanting to see you real bad. Duga says he can catch a bear and Sammy is trying to whittle some. We should like to have you home for Christmas. Write and let us know when you can set out. Your wife, Betsey Anne Hawkins

Folding the letter and sealing it inside a tiny brown envelope, she went in search of her treasure-box of letters to dig out Frances Garnier's address. *Thomas Jefferson Hawkins by F.M. Garnier* she penned carefully on the front of the missive. *Royalton, Delta PO, Fulton County Ohio.*

She put the pen away and set the letter up on the mantle, its corner propped behind the lamp, and stoked up the stove to start the dinner.

"Who wants to stir up some cornbread?" she called cheerily.

All afternoon the letter stood there, a visual reminder of Jefferson's absence. It seemed to smirk with its scrawling address, seemed to call out to her, "Thomas Jefferson Hawkins, **Ohio.**" Ohio. Ohio.

Time and time again she forced the thought of it out of her mind with an everyday task or a moment with the children. "Annie, are you learning them dolls to do a good job of work and help their mothers?" "Sammy, come show me that whittling you got there." "I expect I'll send Mrs. Henderson's cloak to town with you tomorrow, Liddy, so I best get to it."

She bent her head over the sewing and turned her mind to it as well, tiny finishing stitches and embellishments taking focus as well as skill.

But when night came, she was haunted again with memories, and doubt, and regret. Surely she could have done something to make him stay — if not that day, then some other. If not one thing, then many.

How many little things had she done wrong, or failed to do, these past years? How many hurts had she handed out? She recounted to herself the many things she should have done, words she wished she'd said — oh, she should have told him that she loved him!

She sat up in bed, suddenly drenched in sweat, her heart pounding, her stomach lurching, her throat dry.

There it was. That was the whole problem — love. Or rather, the lack of it. *"Love's the only plant you can grow without a seed,"* Sarah was always saying. And from time to time, Betsey realized, she had worked diligently to grow that plant.

In Jefferson.

She had tried to make Jefferson love her. But had she tried to make herself love Jefferson?

She turned the quilt back and set her feet out on the cold dirt floor. On tiptoe, careful not to disturb any of the small sleeping forms, she slipped out to the kitchen for a mug of stale, cold coffee and a hard biscuit to settle her stomach. She stood before the letter while she chewed, staring at it in the shadows, remembering rather than reading what the envelope said.

Thomas Jefferson Hawkins by F.M. Garnier, Royalton, Delta PO, Fulton County Ohio.

She set the mug back on the stove and hurried back to the warmth of her bed, as suddenly shivering as she had been feverish.

No, she decided, she had never really tried to love him. She had wanted, even needed, for him to love her, and for him to show her that he did. Images danced in her head — the rocking chair, the plank floor in the sewing room, the toothy smile he so seldom displayed. These things had made her feel that he loved her, and so, had made her — briefly -- happy.

But had she loved him?

Harriet awoke and Betsey Anne sprang from the bed to snatch her up and quiet her quickly, so as not to awaken the other children. Looking down at the infant as she nursed, Betsey's thoughts remained on Jefferson.

Perhaps it was her failure to love him that sent him to Ohio. Perhaps it was.

Perhaps it was not.

She drifted off to sleep with Harriet nestled in the crook of her arm and dreamed of a strange land where there were *two* Jeffersons. There she danced upon clouds, surrounded by singing birds and the fragrance of flowers, her right hand held daintily aloft by the charming Jefferson, dressed in his Sunday best and smiling broadly. Forward and back, forward and back, she stepped, lightly, gracefully, feeling as though she were a great beauty and realizing slowly that she was dressed all in pale yellow silk decorated with little blue nosegays. Placing his hand in the small of her back, the smiling Jefferson swung her gently in a circle, first drawing her close to him, then spinning her away. But when she again turned her face to his, it was no charming smile she saw but instead that flat-lipped grin of his beneath his tattered hat. Gasping, she drew back, but he held her close and she heard John Bernard's hateful laugh, growing slowly louder and louder. "Flowers?" a scornful voice said, and she twisted her head to see who it might be, still held firmly against Jefferson's dusty coat. "That's not flowers that you smell, you fool, it's perfume." The laughter grew louder still and she clapped her hands over her ears, twisting and turning, trying to break free. Suddenly, she was released and began to run, stumbling over stones and stumps that sprang up where clouds had been before. Falling to her knees, she touched her dress of roughest calico, torn and mended many times over. "Perfume, perfume, perfume," echoed the voice. "Ahh, ha ha ha ha!" reverberated the horrid laughter. The ground beneath her gave way and she tumbled through nothingness, seeing now Jefferson's sweet smile, and then his most insolent stare. Over and over she tumbled, round and round she spun.

"Mine," said a plaintive voice. "No, mine!" came the vehement answer.

The indignant cry of an infant brought Betsey's nightmare to a jarring though welcome end. Rubbing her eyes and trying to swallow, she looked first at Annie and then at Duga, playing tug-of-war over her head and having landed the disputed toy in the middle of Harriet.

"Mine," Betsey said in a croaking voice, clamping her left hand over the tiny wooden cow. "Now get."

She stumbled out of the bed and jiggled Harriet back to sleep with a minimum of trouble. Peering out the window she discovered that the day had dawned bright and clear, if not warm.

"Should be a good day for the trip to town, Liddy," she said moments later as she came into the kitchen, tying her apron behind her. "I expect them boys'll be here pretty quick, so we best get some food down you."

Excitement evident on her face, Lydia flashed a wide grin, "I already fetched in the eggs and Sammy's gone down to the cellar for the taters."

In a few minutes, Betsey's practiced hands had set out a wholesome breakfast and the whole family turned to the interesting task of dressing Lydia for the cold trip, buzzing about her like so many bees, laughing and jostling and all talking at once. Betsey Anne wrapped Mrs. Henderson's cloak carefully in brown paper and tied it with a piece of rough twine. She penciled her market list on the back of a note from Flossie Cline which had given instructions for her last sewing order and pressed the list into Lydia's hand while scolding her to be careful.

The Barnes boys came rumbling up into the front yard with a whoop and a holler, and Lydia was half out the door before Betsey Anne remembered the letter. "Oh, my! The letter, Liddy!" she shrieked, hating the nervous sound in her voice. "The letter I wrote for Jefferson, I mean," she said more calmly and picking the letter off the mantle with two fingers. "I want you to post it for me. You'll need a penny for the postage."

Betsey patted her apron as if she might have secreted a penny in its pockets and Lydia said, "I have a penny, Betsey Anne. I'll see to it." She looked directly into Betsey's eyes and for a moment, Betsey thought, "She knows."

Then they were off, Lydia sandwiched neatly between two solid bundles of sixteen-year-old sturdiness, happy laughter rising up and over the hillside as they trotted away.

CHAPTER SIXTEEN

So then began the waiting in earnest. They'd been waiting before, to be sure, since September really, when it was deemed that Jefferson had had time to have checked on his family and started back home. But this was different – since the letter had been sent. This waiting was intense and eager; it woke with them all in the mornings, and lay down beside them at night. It had a deadline – Christmas.

We should like to have you home for Christmas, she'd written. Surely he would come – he would not want to disappoint the children. He would come, rattling up over the hill in his jiggedy way, pulling his team to a straining halt in the front yard. The children would whoop and holler and clamber up on the wheels of the wagon, and he'd laugh and gig them under the arms and tousle their hair. Then he'd pass out the presents he'd brought them – countless wooden toys he would've whittled sitting on his sister's front porch listening to everyone talk of old times.

Then he'd look out at Betsey over the tops of the children's heads, and he'd just look at her for a while, where she'd be standing in the doorway with Herbert beside her and Harriet in her arms. And then he'd flash out that glorious smile of his, the schoolboy so-you'll-dance-with-me smile, and Betsey would know that he loved her, that he'd missed her while he'd been gone.

That he'd forgiven her.

Most likely he'd wait till the last minute to come, but there was no sense in them waiting till the last minute to get ready for him, Betsey thought. So she set the preparations into motion, giving everyone a task. They set to cleaning the house like it was the first day of spring.

Every curtain and cover was taken down and scrubbed, hung out on the line in spite of the cold, and pressed to crisp perfection with cornstarch and hot heavy flatirons. The floors were swept and then swept again, the planks in the sewing room scrubbed till they shone. The windows were washed, the walls were scrubbed, and everyone's clothing was fresh and their countenances glowing.

Over and over again they planned the Christmas menu – and hoarded the better foods for that meal by skimping on their daily fare. Over plates full of bland fried potatoes, they'd talk about how much Pa loved a good onion; sipping plain tea they'd gloat over the amount of sugar they were saving in the jar on the shelf. Smoked fish was set aside and everyone watched the chickens closely – whoever laid the fewest eggs would find herself on the Christmas platter.

Betsey figured and refigured the amount of her credit at Henderson's store – meager enough it was, as Mrs. Henderson had ordered but two garments since July. But she was sure she could get the necessities and still have enough for a nice piece of goods to make a shirt for Jefferson, and she could turn the scraps into delightful dolls for the children, a hankie for Lydia perhaps, and she could get peppermint sticks all around. Yes, this would be a Christmas to remember.

Betsey's eyes began to brighten a little, her appetite began to improve, even for plain potatoes and cornbread and eggs. She told Lydia she'd ride into town with the next neighbor that made the trip.

On several bright mornings the rattle of a wagon was heard, and all the family dropped their chores and grabbed their coats, flying out to the front yard with joyous expectation on their faces only to find that it was not Jefferson at all, but only some customer or another arriving with an order or to stand for a fitting.

"My! What a warm welcome!" they would say.

And Betsey, feeling a blush rising in her cheeks, would answer, "The children are expecting their Pa in time for Christmas and all." Then she'd turn back into the house to hide her disappointment.

One afternoon as Betsey sat stitching, she heard a masculine voice hallooing in the front yard. She started from her chair in a sudden frenzy. Jefferson! And she hadn't heard him – where were the horses, the wagon? What trouble had there been? In some curious way her mind rushed through a dozen possibilities as her feet carried her through the kitchen and out into the yard.

The others had also been startled – Sammy from his whittling, Annie and Duga from their naps – and they followed her into the yard, bewildered.

But Lydia was apparently unsurprised. For they beheld her seated on a stump, smiling up at a handsome lad of about eighteen, with the skirt of her best Sunday dress peeking out from beneath her heavy coat.

It was Duga that intervened. "Aw, auntie, I thought it was Pa!"

"Come on, children, let's get back in the house where it's warm." Betsey guided the three with a firm hand on the backs of their slim young necks, slamming the door against the cold. That girl! Scarcely here two months, still pining away over Owen Wilson as far as Betsey knew, and here she was receiving suitors!

What was it Pa had whispered in her ear? *"Don't let her go spooning – she's too young to know her mind."*

"Oh, I guess she knows her mind alright," Betsey fumed aloud. "And her mind's full of flirting."

But when Lydia came in, her face flushed from masculine attention as much as from the cold, her eyes alight with pleasure, Betsey Anne could not keep her anger from melting into mere concern. "What's the young fellow's name?" she asked.

"Frank." Lydia settled dreamily on the makeshift bed she used in the corner of the sewing room. "Frank Blanchard."

Betsey was silent, pretending to focus on her sewing while puzzling out what to say next. Something had to be done, of course. Pa would never forgive her if she let Lydia...

"You heard anything from Owen, Lid?"

"No!" The sunlight went out of her eyes, a frown enveloped her from head to toe. "No – not a word." There was a pause while Betsey pumped the treadle on her machine. "But I expect he don't even know where I am."

Betsey Anne bit her lip. "I guess you could write to Ma and ask if he's turned up around home looking for you." She took a deep breath.

"I been thinking to ask Charles Barnes if he could take me in to town – tomorrow maybe."

Lydia stared at the ceiling for a while, until Betsey began to wonder if she'd drifted off to sleep. Still, she hesitated to turn around and look. Finally, Lydia spoke. "I expect I'll write."

Betsey didn't answer, but instead went to the kitchen and bundled Sammy up for a trip across the fields to Sarah's warm farm with her request for a ride into town.

Lydia did not emerge from the sewing room to join them for supper, and Betsey fell into an uneasy sleep with an extra worry on her mind that night. But in the morning, there was Lydia, bright and sunny, with rosy cheeks and a ready smile, tickling Herbert under the chin while Betsey set breakfast on the table. Nothing more was said about Owen or Frank until Charles Barnes pulled his wagon up before the door and Lydia slipped her a small brown envelope addressed daintily to Ann Springer, pressing a penny into her palm for the postage.

"Ma'll be awful glad to get a letter from you," said Betsey with a knowing smile. "Now you watch them children close!" She paused for one last glance around the room – Sammy smiling confidently; Annie and Duga engrossed in their play, oblivious to her departure; Herbert looking at her as if he might somehow understand that she was going out; Harriet, fast asleep in the cradle. It occurred to her that she had not been away from them – not since the twins were born. In fact, not since that month that Sammy and Annie had stayed with Ma and she and Jefferson had…

Swallowing hard, she fought back a sudden rush of tears and said, "I'll be back before you know it."

The ride into town beside Charles Barnes might have been a pleasant one, had Betsey not been entirely consumed with her own thoughts. She held Lydia's letter between her mittened hands, staring at the front of it and allowing her mind to wander until she was startled to find that they had arrived in town.

"I'll be quick about my errands, Charles," she said as he helped her down from the seat of the wagon. "I'll be wanting to get back to the children."

She went first into Henderson's and made her purchases, having made out her list with care. She chose a piece of ivory colored linen to make a shirt for Jefferson, and ordered a little extra for dolls for the children, knowing she had plenty of tiny bits of lace in her workbasket to embellish them with. A bit of the same linen would do for a hanky for Lydia, as well. Two peppermint sticks for each child, shortening, corn meal, and a slab of bacon for the homecoming breakfast rounded out her order, and Mr. Henderson promised to see to the loading.

Betsey Anne stepped out the front door onto the wooden sidewalk with a sense of repeating her own history, her mind reverting to the day Jefferson had brought her in to town from Flossie Cline's. She'd gone to post a letter to her ma that day, too, while Mary Jane Crabb had cackled in the back of the store with Jefferson, and they'd loaded her sewing machine in the back of his wagon underneath that old green blanket of his.

What a long time ago it seemed. Betsey opened the door of the tiny post office and paused a moment to let her eyes adjust to the dim, windowless room.

"Oh, Mrs. Hawkins, I've got a letter here for you."

"Perhaps Lydia will get her answer before I even post her letter," Betsey thought, laying Lydia's missive on the smooth-worn counter and placing the penny on top.

"Here it is. All the way from Ohio."

The tiny room seemed suddenly very close and hot. Betsey gasped for air, stripping her mittens off as quickly as she could to free her hands for loosening her muffler and the collar of her coat. "Thank you then," she managed to choke out, spinning around and reaching blindly for the door, a tunnel of darkness closing in around her eyes.

"You're a fool, Betsey Anne," she told herself as she took a deep breath of clear, cold air outside. "You asked him to let you know when he could start out. You should have expected a letter."

But her hands still trembled as she looked at the envelope in her hands. It was blue – Frances Garnier signature blue, Betsey thought. Brown ink. Frances's feathery penmanship. So she'd written it for him – perhaps he'd started back already then. Thick. Very thick. Betsey weighed the letter in her hand as if trying to decide how heavy it was. No telling what fool thing Frances might have stuck inside there, she thought with a shudder, remembering Analisa's shroud.

She cast a glance around her for a place to sit down with it. Her knees were weak, knocking together already. She took another deep breath and sank down on a dirty wooden step to resume staring at the letter. Well, then. She bit her lip and turned the envelope over. Fitting her nail under the edge of the flap, she loosened the glue and let the contents spill into her lap.

The first thing she saw was her own letter, refolded and stuffed back into its envelope. Her heart skipped a beat, but she scolded herself, "It don't mean nothing – it's been read and all. It'll tell something in the other letter." With shaking hands, she picked up the thin sheet of blue paper and began to read.

Dear sister – I take this opportunity to address a few lines to you. We are not very well just now for some of the children is having the ague. There is a good deal of sickness through the country this fall. Your letter came at hand a few days ago. I was glad to hear from you, but was sorry to hear that Thomas is so neglectful of his family. You want I should write and let you know where he is. Well, Betsey, I cannot tell you much about it. Charley Rolph came home three weeks ago today. He said Thomas was working in Fort Wayne and he boarded at Mattison's. Now Betsey, this is all I can tell you about him. He promised to write me when he left here, but he never has written me a line. At least I never have received any from him. It seems strange to me that Thomas would come off here and stay so long and leave you, his family, and you in the condition you was in as you wrote you had a little babe about two months gone, and he does not write to you or send you any means to help yourself with. Now, Betsey, if there is anything wrong between you, write to let me know. Whether there is or not, if I knew where to direct a letter, I would write him. Well, I shall have to close. I feel in hopes when this reaches you Thomas will be at home. Write to me as soon as you get this, and let me know whether you have heard from him or not. Hoping this will find you all well, I must bid you good bye. F.M. Garnier to Betsey A. Hawkins.

"Oh, oh no! oh no!" Betsey's breath came hard and fast, her tongue seemed swollen larger than her mouth. "Jefferson, Jefferson, oh! Jefferson!" she whispered to herself as the words swam before her eyes.

She could not think what Frances meant – Jefferson working in Fort Wayne? Wasn't that in Indiana? How long since he'd left his family in Ohio? Why hadn't he come home? Oh, surely Frances didn't think…

Betsey looked down at her lap as she absently folded the letter and noticed for the first time a small piece of white paper, folded once. She pressed it open against the calico of her skirt and squinted at the faint penciled note.

Dear Mother, brothers and sister

I now take my pen in hand to tell you with pleasure how glad I was to see Pa. I was overjoyed to see him. I shall enjoy the -----

There was a smudge here that Betsey could not read, and she stared at it some minutes, trying to puzzle it out, before telling herself it didn't matter and reading on.

I shall enjoy the ----- he brought me. You must not worry or get lonely. We are having fine weather and I think it will be a good time for traveling. We are all going up to Uncle Walt's this evening. I can't think of much to write so I will close for present. So good by for a while, Alice

PS take notice -- write soon

Alice.

Betsey closed her hand around all three letters and shoved them deep inside the pocket of her coat. In her head, she was hearing harsh laughter, watching a frightened sow run for cover in the woods.

The pig had been from Alice's mother. "As a token of her esteem," she imagined she heard Bernard's grating voice repeat. Laughter, more laughter now, not just from Bernard but from George Cline and Flossie and Jefferson, echoing in her memory. *"Shows just what she thinks of you, Tom J!"*

Dear Mother, brothers and sister.

That's what the letter said. *How glad I was to see Pa.*

Betsey was walking, almost running, one foot in front of the other, pounding, heavy footsteps, her fingers clenched around the letters in her pocket, tears streaming unheeded down her face.

How glad I was to see Pa… Alice.

She pushed open the heavy front door of the hotel and pressed forward to the desk, ignoring someone who was already standing there talking to the proprietor.

For a moment she couldn't find her voice, only stared open mouthed as the two men stared back at her. Slowly, mechanically, she lifted her arm and swiped the rough sleeve of her coat across her eyes and nose, though the tears kept coming.

"Prudie Richy," she whispered. "Prudie Richy – is she here?"

CHAPTER SEVENTEEN

Duty.

She had bent under the weight of it; now she sheltered beneath it. She had carried it like a cross; now she wore it like a warm mantle. She had borne it with loathing and sacrifice; now she treasured it, sought it.

Duty.

She had plodded forward through its monotony, day into day, week into week, month into month; now she looked to its familiarity for solace, safety. She had laid aside her dreams for its reality; now she hid from reality within its false walls.

Duty. Precious duty.

There had been a strange sort of relief in the fact that Prudie Richy was at her chores that day. Betsey Anne had stood, for a long moment at the top of the hotel landing, mouth open, tongue still, fingers curled around the wadded letters in her pocket. Prudie Richy had stared back, one hand holding a bucket of filthy water, the other clutching a bundle of soiled bed linens.

Then Betsey closed her mouth and retreated, down the stairs and out the door, wiping the traces of tears from her face, determined to regain her self control before she climbed back into Charles Barnes's wagon.

She retraced her steps to the Post Office, retrieved Lydia's letter home and scribbled on the back of the envelope, *"The children hope you'll come for Christmas. Me and Lydia, too, so come on."* She paid out another precious penny for a new envelope and a third for a stamp, smoothed her letter between her hands and redirected it to *"Thomas Jefferson Hawkins, Fort Wayne, Indiana."*

Somehow she had managed to look normal, to speak from time to time of inconsequential things on the ride back home. And at the door of her own little tumble-down shack, she picked up the work and wrapped it around her soul like a soft woolen blanket.

There was little enough sewing to do that paid anything, what with winter and the war combined. But she dispatched what there was with skill and with zeal, and then set to work on things for her own family, feverishly, as though they'd all go naked if she dared to stop. She fashioned a shirt for Sammy out of this remnant, trousers for Duga out of that, a doll for Herbert, a quilted bunting for Harriet, a tiny apron pieced together from dozens of lacy scraps for Annie.

The new piece of linen lay untouched in its brown paper wrapping, tucked out of sight at the bottom of the workbasket.

She cleaned and re-cleaned what was already sparkling, labored over an effort to turn the standbys of the cellar into interesting meals, insisted that Lydia "shirk a bit" from the work, and sent Sammy, bundled tightly and laughing loudly, down over the hill and across the field to ask if there'd been any mail, more often than Charles Barnes went into town.

Duty.

She worked with purpose, with dogged determination, focusing all her waking thoughts on her children. Well she remembered Ma's admonition to "speak softly and pleasantly" to the children, and to this she added a tinge of worry for the hurt they must be suffering with Jefferson's continued absence.

But her dreams were haunted now by three Jeffersons. One, the smiling, laughing, charming father of her children, whose tearful, lonesome faces floated longingly behind him. In and out of her dreams he moved, and she was always drawn to him, reaching out with work-scarred hands to touch the roughness of his jacket. Pulling him close she would look up into his face and she would cry out in dismay when she saw his second self, the smirking Jefferson with that insolent glint in his eyes, staring silently at her until his expression slowly changed into one of horror and betrayal. Down in front of his face would float a three-inch scrap of linen shroud-cloth and he would turn and walk away. This was the third Jefferson – walking away, shoulders bent beneath the harsh words she'd hurled at him. She tried to stop him, opened her mouth to call after him, but when she tried to speak, out floated words from Frances's letters to follow him like a wake behind a boat.

Sorry to hear Thomas is so neglectful of his family. Betsey, if there is anything wrong between you… He does not write to you or send you any means… Thomas so neglectful… Fort Wayne... Little babe two months gone…

She would awaken with a start, sweat causing her bed linens to cling to her arms and legs, terror pounding in her heart. **Thomas,** she would say to herself. Not Jefferson. **Thomas.** Thomas was Alice's father, and Alice's mother then, was – what? No more than Prudie Richy was to Jefferson.

Jefferson had indeed left Prudie Richy – still sloshing out chamber pots in the hotel. But he had not left Betsey Anne and the children. Surely not. Most likely he had worried, all the time he was visiting his family, about how hard Betsey had worked all these years, about all she'd said about supporting them, supporting him, and that was why he'd taken work in Fort Wayne. Besides, there was a war on. He was needed at the docks, most likely, because the younger men would all be off putting down the rebellion.

Well, he'd get her letter now, and he'd know about Harriet, and he'd know that she wanted him to come back home.

And he'd come. Yes, he'd come.

"Your pa's gone to work a while, on account of the war," Betsey told the children. "So I had to redirect the letter, but I'm sure he'll still get it in plenty of time."

One day Sammy came skipping home over the hard packed snow to announce with glee that there had indeed been mail for them. Betsey's heart pounded loudly in her ears. But it was only from Ma, saying that they'd be there for Christmas.

They arrived late on Christmas Eve, their arms bundled full of packages, their faces shining red from the cold. There was time only for hugs and kisses and cups of steaming tea before everyone was ready to sleep, in such temporary arrangements as could be made in the tiny house.

But Christmas morning, long before the light, the hustle and bustle and chatter of the long-awaited day was in full bloom. The breakfast was simple and quick, the chores parceled out and polished off with unfamiliar swiftness. And then everyone gathered around in a circle while Ransom helped Sammy pass out the gifts, and they took turns opening the gifts one by one, taking their time exclaiming over each.

All Ma's presents were practical: a slab of salt beef for Betsey, a sack of flour for Lydia, a pound of real sugar for Sammy, a tin of currants for Annie, and carefully folded paper packets of vegetable seeds for the rest of the children, with licorice sticks to adorn the outsides. Pa had fashioned stick-and-corn-husk dolls for all the children, and carved wooden roses on leather thong necklaces for Betsey Anne and Lydia. Betsey took her tears to the stove a dozen times, pretending to check the contents of her pots to hide her emotions.

The boys brought practical presents, too: axes and saws for chopping wood, hammers and nails for repairing the chicken house. Betsey watched them through the kitchen window and turned to her pa with a frown. "Don't seem quite right, somehow, them working that hard on a Christmas Day."

"It ain't work really," Pa answered, putting his arm around her shoulder, "They're just giving of what they've got, such as it is, and glad to have somewhat to give."

She leaned her head against his shoulder and tightened her arm around his waist for just the slightest second, then quickly turned back to her meal, her cloak of pretense drawn close beneath her chin.

The day flew by, all too short. They suppered on the remains of the special noon meal, planned so long in the hope of Jefferson's return. They packed away the few morsels that were left into paper packets for the next day's long drive through the cold. Betsey steeped a new pot of tea and set out sourdough for morning while Lydia and Ma tucked the children into their comforts for the night, and Pa and the boys saw to the chickens and carried in wood and water.

Reluctant to see the day close, they gathered around the stove and Pa began to sing. Betsey sipped her tea and listened, her fingers gripped tightly around her warm cup, fighting back tears that kept trying to betray her.

"You're a fool, Betsey Anne," she thought to herself. "A fool — spending such a sweet Christmas Day wallowing in self-pity."

Rousing, she thumped her tea cup on the table. "Sing something funny, Pa," she said brightly.

Immediately the others called out their favorites and young Adam won out by starting in to sing his, and they laughed and sang until Ransom fell asleep with his head in Ma's lap. Adam poked him and led him off to his pallet in the corner and they all drifted off to their beds.

You never knew about the mail, Betsey thought as she listened to Lydia's even breathing beside her. Probably Jefferson hadn't got her letter yet, what with the war on and all, and him working so hard at the docks these days. Must be cold work...

It was two weeks into 1865 when Sammy's trip down to Sarah's warm kitchen next brought home a letter. This time, Betsey Anne's heart stood still when she saw it -—her own letter to Jefferson, come back to haunt her a second time, "Unknown" scrawled boldly across his name in an unfamiliar script.

Her hands shook as she shoved it deep into her apron pocket, and her voice trembled as she said, "Oh, I expect I made some mistake directing that letter to your Pa. I'll get down to the Post Office soon as I can and sort it all out."

Her answer satisfied the children, but didn't relieve their disappointment in thinking there was a letter to read when there was none. They fought and fussed all afternoon, and Betsey Anne snapped at them and scolded Lydia, poked her finger with a needle, and burned her other hand on the stove. She finally ended the day by sending them all to bed early after a supper of dry bread. Retreating to her room with a dimly burning lamp, she settled on top of the bed to write another letter, this time to Frances.

There were a thousand things she would like to ask Frances, but she was unwilling to admit them even to her own thinking more than briefly. So quickly, with a firm hand, she wrote:

Dear Sister — We are all fine and hope this letter finds you well and your family also. The children ain't even had the usual sickness this winter, and for that I am grateful. Sorry to hear your children had the ague and all. You asked was there anything wrong between Jefferson and me, and there is not, except he has not written me since he left for your place. I am at a loss to know why he has not or where he could be. I directed my letter to Fort Wayne as you said he was working the docks there, but it came back and the postmaster marked unknown. I wish you would tell me how to direct it so I can send it again. And if you hear from him, tell him for me about his daughter, born October, and that we look for him to come home any day now.

Betsey Anne paused, biting her lip, then resolutely wrote again.

Give Alice love from all her brothers and sisters, and write as soon as you get this. Your sister, B. A. Hawkins

She slept and dreamed she was Alice's mother, giving the horrible J.H. Bernard a sow to deliver to "Ol' Tom J."

CHAPTER EIGHTEEN

Royalton, April the 5 1865

Dear Sister — I received your kind letter. I was glad to hear from you and hear you was all enjoying tolerable good health. We are all well at present. The children have been having the ague some, but they are all quite well now. I should have answered your letter sooner if I could have had time. I have been very busy even the last week. I was making soap and boiling cider and spinning. I was sorry to hear you had not heard from Thomas. It is strange to me why he does as he has. When he left here, he promised to write to me, but I have never received a line from him since he left here. I heard from him about four weeks ago by a man that came right from Mattison's to here. He said Thomas was there in Fort Wayne and he boarded at Mattison's. I told him to tell Thomas I had got a letter from you and you felt very uneasy about him — that you had written to him and your letters had come back to you. I told him to tell Thomas for me if he thought anything of his family to go to them or else write to them. If I had thought of it, I would have given him your letter to carry to Thomas. I did not have a hand to talk with him more than two minutes, so did not think of half what I wanted to. I think if I could see him about ten minutes I could rouse him for a little while at least. When he left here, he said he was going to look around and find a place that suited him and then he should send or go fetch his family out here. Why he has not done so I cannot tell. Feel in hopes when this letter reaches you it will find him at home. Do not make yourself miserable a borrowing trouble about him. Write and let me know how you are getting along to live. Did you raise anything on your farm last summer? Write to Jefferson and direct to Mr. Johnny O'Neal, Fort Wayne, Indiana. Mr. O'Neal told me when he was here that was all was needed.

Arthur has not got home yet and I do not know when he will, but we feel in hopes he will be at home before a great while. Well, I had better close by hoping this will find you and the children well and Thomas at home. Write soon. Yours truly, F.M. Garnier to Betsey A. Hawkins

Royalton, June 26 1865

Dear Sister – I received your letter a few days ago and I will try to answer it. I was surprised to hear you had not heard from Thomas when you wrote to me first, for he started for home as much as six weeks before you wrote to me. Betsey, there is something wrong somewhere, but what I cannot tell. I hardly think there has anything happened to him, at least I hope not. I feel quite anxious to know his whereabouts. I wish you lived near where I could assist you. I could help you in many ways if you was near where I could. But keep up good spirits and do the best you can. Trust in the all wise Providence and everything may come out all right yet. I got a letter from Elisabeth a few days ago. She said they was all well and Mother was coming up soon. You may be assured I am your friend and I will not keep anything from you in respect to your husband. I will send you some money to pay for postage and a sheet of paper, for I would like you to write to me as soon as you get this. We are all well and hoping this may find you all well. I will bid you good bye, F.M. Garnier to Betsey A. Hawkins

Royalton, December 26 1865

Dear Sister – I will try to answer your letter of the 12th. It came at hand in due time. I was surprised to hear you had not heard from Thomas when you wrote. William and Audrey was here when I got your letter. They was as much surprised as I was. William says Thomas started for home about the middle of October. John Elles, one of our old neighbors, saw him when he went through Toledo and talked with him. He told him to tell Mother he had started for home. William says he got the pay for his horses and wagon for he had sold them and was to take the rails. Betsey, I have written you all I know in respect to him, but I certainly think he started to go home. I am afraid there has something happened to him, for I cannot think he would desert his family without giving them some warning of it. You said you had heard he had been to the Rapids. Can't you write to someone there or take some way of finding out for certain whether he has been there or not? William has written to Mattison to see if he has heard or knows anything about him. You may expect to hear from William as soon as he hears from Mattison. I would think he would write to you or send you some means to help yourself and family if he had gone to work anywhere. I was glad to hear you was well as is your sister. I wish I could see you all, then we could tell one another's doubts and fears much better than we can write them. Mother has not got around here yet. I have not seen her since she left here last fall. Arthur got home one week ago last Saturday evening. He is well and has escaped unharmed. He has been engaged in ten hard fights since he went away this last time. We are all well and hoping this few lines will find you all well and in better spirits and Thomas at home. I shall have to close. Write as soon as you get this for I feel anxious to hear from you. Yours truly, sister and friend, F.M. Garnier to Betsey Anne Hawkins

Royalton, March 18, 1866

Dear Sister – I will take this opportunity to write a few lines to you, although it is with a heavy heart that I cannot write any cheering news to you. Your letter came at hand a few days ago. I was glad to hear you was all well. I do not know what to think in respect to Thomas. I fear we shall never know any more the reason of his absence than we do now. I felt in hopes Mattison would know something that would solve the mystery, but he does not know anything more than we do. When Mattison got your letter, he wrote to Elisabeth. He said he was not very well and was feeling very sad. He said he had just got a letter from you and you did not know where Thomas was. He said he told him he was going home and would write to him as soon as he got home. William wrote to him to know if he could tell him anything, why Thomas had not gone home, and Mattison said he supposed he had gone home until he got your letter. He said he collected all was due him and he had between four and five hundred dollars. I do not think Mattison knows anything more than we do. If he did, I think he would have told William so and he would not manifest so much uneasiness about him now. Betsey, I do not believe that Thomas would have deserted us all without giving us some reason for doing so. Mother thinks we will never hear anything more from him, but I feel in hopes we will, although it seems very doubtful. I feel very much troubled for you and the children, how you

are going to keep your family together. I wish you was near to me. If you was, I could help you in many ways. But this is poor consolation to anyone in trouble and in need. I feel in hopes when this reaches you Thomas will be at home. I wish I could know just where he is, whether he is dead or alive. It would be a great consolation to me. Mother is here now and will spend the summer up here. She sent you two dollars of this money. Well, I shall have to close by hoping this will find you in better spirits. We are all well. Write as soon as you can. F.M. Garnier to Betsey A. Hawkins
PS William's address is Richfield, Lucas County Ohio, Ford's Post Office

"I'll say one more time, Betsey Anne, we just got to stop worrying about old Thomas Jefferson Hawkins and put our hand to making a living on this place." It was Lydia who broke the silence after the reading of the latest letter from Frances.

Betsey looked up from the letter and searched her sister's face. What she saw was a far cry from the dreamy sixteen-year-old who had first come to live with her, pining for a Union deserter she felt was the love of her life. Just a few months past eighteen, but doubtless a grown woman, Lydia was strong, competent, resolute.

Betsey thought of the first days of Lydia's coming to live in her home: the hours she spent rocking in the rocking chair, staring straight ahead, the simple tasks she failed to complete, the meals she ruined, the scoldings she earned. Now, a scant year and a half later, it was she who managed the household, who scraped together nourishing meals from an almost-empty larder, who coaxed the stitches from Betsey's needle one by one, who mothered the children.

And it was Betsey Anne who sat for hours listening to the scrape of the rocking chair on the unfinished wood floor in the sewing room; Betsey who ironed out the paper from packages of coffee or tea and cut them into neat squares of make-shift stationery; Betsey who sat day after day in her room writing letters to people she had never seen; Betsey who slept each night clutching a bundle of letters addressed to Thomas Jefferson Hawkins, each having gone out into the world to receive its scrawling epitaph: *Unknown.*

"Did you hear what I said, Betsey Anne?"

Betsey shook herself and blinked, seeing suddenly that Sammy, Annie and Duga were peering at her over their aunt's shoulders. They'd heard the letter, too, she realized. There was no secret any longer. Everyone must know by now – that Jefferson was gone. What were they thinking? Did the children remember her harsh words to him before he left? Did they remember his faults, or just their love for him? And not just the children, but everyone in town and all the neighbors. How about Ma and Pa? Oh, what could they be thinking, how must they be worrying, with Pa right down in bed with that aching back of his...

"Well, you can sit there and pine till your hands is so stiff you can't sew no more, if that's what you want to do!" Lydia pushed the bench back with a scrape and stood up in exasperation. She was tall and strong, Betsey thought. With her billowing blond hair and her cherry colored lips she looked like the china dolls in Henderson's store window. "You can sit there till your hair turns gray and you can act like an old granny though you're only twenty-four, but me and the children ain't setting here to watch it."

Lydia went into the sewing room while Betsey looked again at Frances' letter. *I fear we shall never know any more the reason of his absence than we do now. I wish I could know just where he is, whether he is dead or alive.*

"Annie, get your sister, and Sammy see if Herbert'll be alright on the mat there – you can all go along with me down to Barnes's." She stood for a moment looking down at Betsey Anne, small and thin, her unruly red hair excessively bright against her pallor. "What we really need around here is a man, and I'm certain I don't know where to find mine any more'n you know where to find yours. But I do know where to find a job, now that Prudie Richy's gone and married old Briscoe and his eight squalling children, and then at least we can have a decent meal."

Then they were out the door with all of the bustle and chatter that follows four children around like a cloud of dust at their feet and Betsey was left sitting with her hands in her lap, staring at the letter on the table, seeing nothing. Day fell into a shadowy dusk, dusk into deepening darkness before she stirred. Woodenly, automatically, she shuffled into the bedroom and placed the letter in the little box that held all the others – a history of her life in little pieces and parts.

I write you of the death of Analisa Laughton. She died the 4ᵗʰ of July. She had the consumption on the lungs... I will send you a piece of Analisa's shroud... May God help you to do right, Betsey Anne... Betsey, now do try to speak pleasant and kind to your children. If you feel cross yourself, never try to govern them until you feel good natured...

She snapped the lid down sharply, as if to trap the voices of her past. Feeling suddenly cold and hot at once, she wrapped her arms tightly about herself and hurried from the room. Going to the mat where Herbert lay sleeping his unfettered sleep, she wedged herself into the corner beside him. Drawing his chunky form close to her thin one, she breathed in the sweet, still babyish smell of his hair.

"You're a fool, Betsey Anne," she murmured, and slept.

CHAPTER NINETEEN

It was early afternoon the next day before Sarah Barnes climbed the hill with Harriet on her hip and the other three children chattering happily as they skipped along behind her, their clothes neatly pressed, their faces recently scrubbed, their hair smoothly in place. They found Betsey Anne sitting on a stump in the front yard, wrestling with a wet tangle of wild red hair, and Herbert at her feet playing happily with a twisted twig.

Sarah set Harriet on her feet and tucked her little pink hand into Sammy's strong brown one, leaning close to whisper an instruction into his ear. She stood for a moment watching them skip happily off toward the stream, bright, thin March sunlight glinting off the tops of their heads.

With a smile, she turned to Betsey and Herbert. "How's my sweet baby boy?" she crooned, chucking the round little boy under the chin, even though he didn't notice. "And how's his sweet little mother?" she said in a softened tone, setting down the paper-wrapped package she had tucked under her arm, taking the comb from Betsey's hand and beginning to work on the tangle.

"I expect I let myself get out of hand a bit, Sarah," Betsey whispered.

Nothing more was said for a few moments as Sarah carefully separated a strand of hair and worked the comb gently through it. "Seems to me like March is playing us for fools with all this sunshine and warm weather," Sarah said as she selected another matted section of hair.

"That's for certain," came the answer. "It'll be cold and rainy again before we know it."

"Ah ba ba ba ba!" shrieked Herbert, losing his grasp on his twig momentarily. Betsey reached out the toe of her worn boot to push it closer to his hand.

"Yep, cold and rainy."

"And not a thing we can do about it, one way or another," said Sarah. "Except trust in the Lord and take what He gives us."

"Whatever He gives us," echoed Betsey Anne without taking her eyes off Herbert.

Sarah flipped a smooth strand of hair forward and carved out another, working quickly but tenderly. "This section ain't so bad," she said, and flipped another strand forward.

"I guess my hair's like everything else," Betsey said with half a laugh. "Some's good and some's bad, but it's all red!"

Sarah laughed, too. "Some things you just can't change."

"Some things you just can't change," Betsey whispered, as Sarah removed the last of the tangles and combed the entire mass of hair back and away from Betsey's face, twisting it expertly into a tight bun at the nape of her neck.

"I've got a job of work for you, Betsey," she said, patting the younger woman on the shoulder and reaching for the paper package.

Betsey smiled at her friend. "Somehow I knew you would, Sarah. I'll get some tea." She picked Herbert up and moved him to his soft rag rug in the corner of the kitchen, which was ripe with the fragrance of a simmering vegetable stew and rising sourdough bread. The two women were companionably silent while Betsey rattled around at the stove, heating water, pinching out tea leaves, setting out cups and spoons and hard ginger cookies.

"Beth is expecting her first young'un long about August," Sarah offered once the tea had been poured. "She's got more than enough work to do on her place, feeding three hired hands, and her hand garden's twice the size of mine."

"Twice the size!" Betsey exclaimed, dipping a cookie into her tea.

"I brought some goods for making up some baby things," Sarah went on. "Her husband can likely get you some chickens, or even a goat if you want milk and all."

"Or I imagine a garden that size'll put out more than enough squash and pumpkins to go around," mused Betsey.

"Charles picked up the goods at Henderson's this morning, real nice gingham, but the muslin's a bit rough."

"That's all you can get anymore. I expect it's still on account of the war, even though it's over a while now."

"No doubt." They sipped a while and smiled over Herbert when he snored loudly, having drifted off to sleep.

"Lydia said to tell you she'll be home on Saturday afternoons. MacGregor says he'll see that she can ride with someone or else he'll bring her on himself."

"She's got the job then?"

"Oh, Charles said there wasn't no question. Glad to have her, MacGregor was."

"It's hard work, I guess."

"Oh, not too bad. She'll do fine. You've taught her a lot these couple years."

"I guess she's right, and all. It'll help, steady pay and that."

"She's to have her room and board and three dollars a week, Charles said."

"Three dollars a week?" Betsey did some quick figuring in her head. "I guess that'll buy some groceries alright. And maybe more folks can order some sewing done, now that..." she broke off.

"Now that winter's near over," Sarah offered.

Betsey carried her cup to the sideboard. "And now that I'm feeling better," she finished.

The children came tumbling up through the yard, shouting and laughing, with Sammy carrying a string of fish he'd managed to yank out of the stream. He spun a happy yarn full of the details of each catch, augmented with knowing corrections from Annie – no, Duga found the grub under a fallen log, not a rock; actually, it was the *second* fish that swam up under the bank twice. Betsey listened and laughed while she cleaned the fish with interested assistance from Duga and numerous slaps of Harriet's curious hand, and Sarah took her leave, but not before promising to tell Uncle Charles what a good fisherman Sammy had become.

When the fire had been banked down and everyone tucked in beneath their blankets, Betsey told them all a short version of the famous battle between David and Goliath, and then because of protests by Annie that it was a story meant for boys, she followed it up with a quick retelling of the little slave girl who helped Namaan get cured of his leprosy.

Then she went into her room and shoved her little wooden box of letters far up under the head of her bed and wedged it behind the bedpost. "Out of sight, out of mind," she told it, before climbing under her own red and white pinwheel quilt. Sinking into the soft warmth of the feather ticking, she whispered the Lord's Prayer, but fell asleep before she'd quite finished saying, "Lead us not into temptation."

The children were glad enough to accept that their mother had returned to herself. They never questioned her once, though she did think from time to time that Sammy had grown quite mature for his age, almost overnight it seemed. And it was easy enough to settle back down into the routine that had governed the little house for most of its existence.

Betsey was up before dawn, breakfast on the table and sourdough rising by the time the sun shone red or gold beyond the horizon. After breakfast, faces were washed in icy water at the pump outside, hair was combed, shoes were dusted, blankets were folded, with almost military precision. Then the chores were parceled out with a minimum of grumbling, as a grumbler ended by receiving the worst of the tasks without fail.

All save Herbert bustled about their assigned duties until every dish was clean and in its place, the chickens were fed, the eggs were gathered, the wood was stacked, the floor was swept, and lunch was simmering on the stove. Sammy and Annie would walk down over the hill to the Jensen farm for lessons when Olga was offering them, and the others would troop out to the garden for whatever work was needed there – in March it was digging, weeding, clearing away rocks and sticks.

After the noon meal, Betsey tidied up the kitchen while Harriet, Duga, and Herbert lay down for their naps. Later, Duga occupied

Harriet while Betsey once again plied her lifelong trade, with Herbert on a mat beside her. She found to her surprise and relief that there was still genuine joy in producing a well-made garment.

Everyone looked forward to Saturday afternoons with relish. Who would bring Lydia home this time? The tinker with his rattling wagon? The Jensens with their fourteen children? Flossie Cline with another piece of sprigged silk to fashion a dainty dress for the haughty Little Florence – thereby providing hours of entertainment through the fact of Annie's able imitation? Or MacGregor himself with his rolling Scottish brogue and his pockets full of lemon drops covered in lint?

Once they'd seen her conveyance and heard her tale of how she came to be riding upon it, they turned their attention to what she had bought at Henderson's with her hard-earned wages. Lydia was a thrifty one, she was, and would find many ways to stretch her three dollars every week, perhaps by choosing a greasy leg of mutton instead of a beef roast, or by bringing only a slab of salt pork and four kinds of beans. One week she brought home a sack of flour that had been spilled and swept up off the bed of the delivery wagon, necessitating hours of picking out little bits of straw.

But nobody minded Lydia's marketing strategies, really, for it was her very stinginess that made sure she was able to stretch that three dollars to include something special each week: sticks of peppermint candy or cakes of barley sugar, a tin of store-bought cookies, a shiny painted top to spin and make Herbert laugh, a bright new thimble for Betsey Anne, a storybook full of colorful drawings of princesses and fairies and trolls.

It was always after the children were asleep that Lydia slipped Betsey the mail, if there was any, and they sat by the fire in the sewing room to read it.

Betsey Anne – I have got some bleached dress lining for two shimeys, and it cost me thirteen shillings and six pence, but it was all I could get. We don't know yet as we shall go in to the woods. We shan't unless old Cornell will furnish. He is now across the lake, and when he comes back they will go and see him. Then we shall know what we shall do. Everything is so dear it takes a hundred dollars to get nothing. Atwood took two of our hogs to fatten and fed them three or four weeks, then had nothing to feed them. So we had to kill them. They were edible – better than no meat. But we thought he was going to fatten them when he took them to fatten. Fannie says if she had any chance to come home again she would come and see you. If I could see the baby I would give him a hugging and kissing and all the children. How I wish I had something to send you and the children, but I haven't. Maybe I will have next time. Your father says tell you he wants to come up and see you but he can't very well. He has been sick a good deal and we are pretty hard up. All the same, send me word if you or any of you are sick and don't lay there and die and not let me know, for if you are sick I will come to you if you send for me. From your mother.

Despite the somber mood of the letter, they laughed until the tears came when they read the postscript: *Well, Betsey the roosters has just crowed and here I set a writing yet I hardly know what I write. Tell me all the news and Lydia must write too. I don't know as Lydia wants to see me, but I want to see her. But don't let her run around anywhere. Keep her to home and I want you to write. Both of you write often and tell me how you all get along.*

But they did not laugh when Ma wrote, *Betsey Anne, you must forgive me if I have wrote anything wrong. I have not an angry feeling towards Jefferson, but I have disagreeable unhappy feelings to think he will treat you as he does and us too. What is it for? Is it because we have given him one that was dear to our hearts?*

"You'll hear from Jefferson soon, Betsey Anne," Lydia said, standing up to set her tea cup on the mantle.

"I expect," said Betsey without conviction. "And you'll hear from Owen…"

"No," Lydia broke in, with her back turned. "No. I won't be hearing from that louse, nor want to I guess. Anyway, a man that would desert his country would probably…" She stopped, realizing what she was about to say.

"Goodnight, Lid," Betsey said, as brightly as she could, turning her head to hide the swift, unbidden tears.

"Goodnight."

Sunday mornings, there were always pancakes for breakfast, with molasses and coffee, even for the children if they wanted it.

Lydia would liven up the meal so that they would linger over it, fascinated by her tales of the people she'd cleaned up after in the hotel in town.

A professional singer with "more lace on her corset than most girls use their whole life!" and who carried out her own chamber pot in the morning. A minister and his wife with kind faces and over-proper speech, both of which they seemed to leave behind at the front desk, turning into sharp-tongued complainers by the time they reached the top of the stairs. Regular peddlers and tinkers, traveling salesmen, government officials and sharp businessmen, families out in the world looking for a new place to call home. Once even a freed slave all the way from Georgia, alone, with an accent that made it impossible to communicate with him and a pocket full of money "every one was puzzling over where he might of got."

It was October when Mary Jane Podinsky's husband resumed calling on Mr. Henderson, with a new line of goods from his company in Detroit. "He looks some worse for the wear since the war," Lydia said. "Skinny and sallow, and slow of step."

"How's Mary Jane?" asked Betsey, a vision of her cousin standing on a bench wearing yards and yards of pale yellow silk hovering behind her eyes.

"I asked him that when I carried up some hot water for shaving, and he looked all strange like and says *'Mary Jane?'* as if he'd never heard of her. And I says *'She's a cousin of ours.'* and all he says is *'Thank you for the water.'* And then he shuts the door flat, with me still standing right there!"

"He always was a might strange, really, I thought."

"Well, I'd say you thought right! *'Thank you for the water,'*" she mimicked, shaking her head side to side, with her chin tucked down into her neck, pretending to pinch a pair of glasses farther up onto her nose.

After the pancakes, there was always a bustle to get Lydia's things ready for another week – her apron and two work dresses washed and starched, her hair washed and combed, her boots cleaned, and was there any mending needed to her clothes? "Seems a shame to make you work on the Sabbath," she would always say to Betsey. "We don't mind," would always be the answer.

Then over the supper of Lydia's choosing, they would begin to speculate as to who would come by in the morning to take her back into town for another week of scrubbing and washing and picking up behind whatever interesting strangers might come into town.

Lydia's last question would always be the same, on Monday mornings when the two sisters stood shoulder to shoulder in the yard with the old carpet bag packed and sitting at their feet, waiting for the sound of wagon wheels up the rocky hill. "Should I post a letter for you, Betsey Anne?"

"No," would come the answer. "I ain't got much time for writing letters these days."

Lydia would smile, relieved, and squeeze her sister's hand. "I'll write a word or two to Ma."

CHAPTER TWENTY

Royalton, November 25, 1866

  Dear Sister -- It has been a long time since I wrote to you. The reason I have not written is I was waiting to hear from you, whether you was all well or had heard anything from Thomas yet. I was down to William's a few days ago. He said he had made up his mind Thomas was murdered in Toledo. Mr. Elles says Thomas had to take the cars at one o'clock at night. He says Thomas was at his house all the evening till nine o'clock, then he went with Thomas part way down to the depot. They stopped at a saloon. He says there was twelve or fifteen sailors drinking and fighting. He says he went home and supposed Thomas went on to the depot. The woman that kept the saloon said to Mr. Elles the next morning that man that was here with you last night got in a fight with them sailors after you left and he whipped them all out. He says he thought no more about it until several months after he heard Thomas had not got home and we had heard nothing from him. He says he believes Thomas was murdered there that night. He thinks if we could have known about it in time and had the woman arrested we might have found out something about him. The woman was gone, no one knew where. Mr. Elles is one of Thomas's old playmates and is a reliable man. Now, Betsey, in all probability this is all we shall ever know in respect to him, and I would rather this be true than to think he would be cruel enough to desert his family, which I cannot think he would do. I think of him to be a truer hearted man than that. I commenced writing to you yesterday, and I got so nervous I had to stop writing. I do not know as you can read it or not. I should like to send all of you some stockings or yarn to make some if I could. If you was near by I could help you in many ways, but as it is I cannot help you any to speak of. I will send you a dollar, but that will not buy much now days. Keep up good courage as you can. I should like to come and see you all if I could. Kiss the children for me. Hoping this will find you all well, I will bid you good bye. Write soon. Remember and direct your letter to Delta, Fulton County, Ohio. Your sister, F.M. Garnier to Betsey A. Hawkins.

Together they stared a long time into the fire, Lydia afraid to speak, and Betsey thinking thoughts both of far away and of long ago.

"So then," Betsey finally said.

"So then," echoed Lydia. "What'll you do, now?"

There was another period of silence while Betsey considered. Harriet cried out in the other room, and both women turned their heads, tilted a little on the side, waiting to see if she would waken fully. When all continued quiet, Betsey said, "I expect I'll go down into town and file a death certificate."

"Stop the tongue's a'wagging."

"Yes, stop the tongue's a'wagging. And I guess get the farm in my own name."

"You'll have to fix a date."

Betsey looked at the letter again. "I wish Frances had of fixed it."

"She doesn't say, does she?"

The flames crackled. Betsey rocked back and forth in silence. Lydia tiptoed into the kitchen and returned with the teapot, half full of now-tepid tea. Without asking, she poured Betsey another cup and stirred in a spoonful of molasses.

"Toledo," Betsey said, picking up the conversation casually, as though there had been no lapse. "He'd have taken the cars from Toledo if he was heading home straightaway, like when he left his Ma's. In '64."

"Straightaway," Lydia agreed.

"And sailors being in the saloon, musta been during the war."

They sipped a while, listening to the night sounds; Herbert snoring, the hoot of an owl, the wind high in the tops of the trees. The fire began to fade, and Betsey stood up to add a log and stir the flames until they lapped around it.

"I'll fix the date in '64," she said. "October."

"Just after Harriet was born?"

"Right about then. Frances wrote that he went through Toledo about the middle of October."

"Ah," Lydia said, as if that clinched it.

"Toledo in '64." It sounded final. Lydia took the tea cups into the kitchen, returned for the pot and the jar of molasses. Betsey didn't get up.

"Betsey Anne?"

Betsey looked, rather than spoke, her permission for Lydia to go on.

"Didn't Frances say – before -- Jefferson was working in Fort Wayne, on the docks?"

"Must have been mistaken," Betsey said, meeting her sister's eyes. "That would explain why my letters all came back, and all."

Lydia nodded. "That would explain it."

"Toledo. In '64." Betsey repeated. She stood and walked slowly to the door, pulling it behind her as she went through. Turning back, she whispered, careful of waking the children, "Still, it's hard to figure – Jefferson never was much of a fighting man."

It snowed in the night, but Sunday morning was clear and still. After pancakes and stories, Lydia suggested that the children play outside. Betsey looked out at the white expanse of yard and hesitated. But that was all the children needed – they used her silence to clamor, "Please Ma, please!" and "We'll be alright!" and in the end she agreed. Working together, Lydia and Betsey Anne bundled the four of them in every warm garment they could find, taking care to cover ears and noses and to pull heavy woolen mittens on to every pair of hands.

While they washed up the dishes, they could hear the children whooping and hollering as they jumped and ran and rolled in the fresh-fallen snow. Betsey Anne smiled over at Herbert, content with a wooden doll carved long ago by Jefferson. Lydia followed her glance.

"Did you think he'd come back?" she asked. "All this time, I mean."

"I don't know," Betsey answered, immersing her hands again in the sudsy water. "He has a daughter you know."

"Well, all the children –," Lydia squinted over at her sister. "He probably never knew about Harriet, you mean?"

"I don't mean Harriet, nor Annie." Betsey opened the front door and tossed the coffee grounds out. "You warm enough?" she called, closing the door without waiting to hear the children shout "yes".

"I mean Alice."

"Alice?"

"I got a letter from her. Once. Two years ago. Said how glad she was to see her Pa. Called me mother, and called the children brothers and sisters."

"And her ma?"

"I don't know. Once a man came here – Bernard was his name. As oily as a snake and filthy as Lucifer himself. Brought Jefferson a big old sow and said it was the last he'd hear from Alice's mother." She scrubbed fiercely at the heavy cast-iron griddle, though it was already clean.

"What did you do?"

"When?"

"With the sow – about Alice."

"Well, at the time, I guess I thought Alice was maybe a girl he'd known – maybe he should have married her or something. And maybe her mother – well, I guess there were other things I thought more about in them days." She handed Lydia the griddle. "I never even asked him who she was. I made him kill the sow, and then I couldn't bear to eat the meat and he put it in a bear trap and forgot it."

"The whole thing?" Lydia was horrified at the waste, almost figured the cost of such an extravagance in her mind.

"I didn't know who Alice was until I got the letter from her – after Jefferson was gone to Ohio. I still don't know nothing about her mother."

"Were they married, do you think?"

"I don't know." She tossed the dishwater out the door and called again, "Are you warm enough?" Giving an involuntary shiver as she slammed the door behind her, she said, "If they were married, then no. No. I wasn't expecting him to come back."

She filled the kettle with water from the reservoir at the side of the stove and set it on the burner to heat.

"If he left one wife, he'd leave another," she concluded. "And I was – I was hard on him."

That last was hard to say out loud, though she'd long since admitted it to herself.

Lydia placed the last of the dishes in their places on the sideboard shelves, and pulled out the wash tub, setting it near the stove. She went into the other room for the dress and aprons that needed washing. "No mending this week," she said, as she tossed them down. Betsey picked up a bucket of cold water from near the door and filled the reservoir, then poured the rest over the clothing, and Lydia began to scrub.

"Sammy, can you fetch me a pail of water?" Betsey called from the door, setting the two buckets out.

"I used to think Owen would come back," said Lydia.

"Don't you think so any more?"

"No."

Betsey added the hot water to the tub and put some more on to heat before squatting down to help with the scrubbing.

"Nor care, I expect." Lydia wrung out a brown calico apron, refolded it, and twisted it again. "Shall we hang these outside today?"

"They'll smell fresher that way, and if they don't dry we'll stoke the fire a little hotter come night and move them in." Betsey twisted another apron and stacked it on top of the one Lydia had finished.

"Fannie wrote me last week. She said Owen's ma says Owen's out peddlin' somewhere. Says he married him a wife and there's a baby on the way."

"Do you care?" Betsey's voice was soft.

Lydia's answer was matter-of fact. "No. Not really. I don't know as I ever loved him. I just wanted him to love me."

"It was the same for me."

They continued scrubbing in silence, each lost in thoughts of her own past. When the last garment was wrung, Betsey threw the water out the front door, and Lydia piled the finished garments back in the tub to carry outside to the clothesline. Betsey gathered Herbert up in her arms, clucking softly to him. "Lydia?" she said just before her sister closed the door.

Lydia looked back over her shoulder and smiled sadly. "Toledo," she said, as if she read Betsey's mind.

"In '64," Betsey answered.

1867

CHAPTER TWENTY-ONE

"Murdered in Toledo in October of '64," said Betsey Anne to Hattie in the Post Office, filling out the form to apply for the death certificate.

"Murdered?" asked Hattie when she saw Lydia at the hotel.

"After a fight with some sailors," Lydia confirmed. "Just before he was to get on the cars to come home, about the time that Harriet was born."

"I thought he was working in Fort Wayne on the docks?"

"Them folks that told his sister that must have been mistaken," said Lydia.

"Rushing home to be with poor Betsey Anne in case she had another hard delivery," said Hattie to Mrs. Henderson in the general store. "And Betsey and poor Jefferson's family thinking he were working on the docks down in Fort Wayne all along, saving money to make some improvements on that run down farm of theirs, or buy a new section over in Indiana, maybe."

"Ambushed by thieving sailors, poor Jefferson Hawkins," said Mrs. Henderson to Mr. Henderson over supper that night. "And they took his money and made out that he was working alongside them at the docks in Fort Wayne."

"Seems he had a job promised to him, at the docks in Fort Wayne," said Mr. Henderson to Amos when he came in for Flossie Cline's order. "Was heading home to collect poor Betsey Anne and all the little ones when these sailors robbed him and left him for dead."

"Robbed and left for dead by sailors that done deserted from the war," said Amos to Cline's hired girl, Sadie. "In Toledo, with a fine job promised and a coming to take Betsey and them children to a fine new home he'd spoken for in Fort Wayne."

"Thieving deserters robbed him and took his name and his job in Fort Wayne, and poor Betsey never knowing till now," said Sadie to Flossie while she pounded down the sourdough.

"Deserters my eye," said Flossie to George as she blew out the lamp that night. "Has something to do with old John Bernard, or that Althea that run off with Lorne Rugles and left Tom J' pining and poor Alice to be raised by her grandmother, if you ask me."
"Where'd they say it happened?" asked George.
"Toledo," Flossie said. "Toledo, in '64."

"Your Pa was killed by some sailors down in Toledo," said Betsey Anne to her children, softly.

"Aunt Frances said Pa was working in Fort Wayne," said Annie.

"She was mistaken," said Betsey, stroking Annie's hair and hugging Duga closer, but looking in Sammy's eyes. "He was killed in Toledo, catching the cars to come home, clear back in '64, just before Harriet was born."

"My Pa was killed by some sailors in Toledo," whispered Sammy to Hans Jensen, taking lessons at Olga's kitchen table. "A long time ago – during the war."

"Killed in the war," said Hans to his father as he mucked out the barn that night. "And all the time them thinking he was just working on the docks."

"My Pa's dead," whispered Annie to Jane Henderson behind her slate. "And my aunt Frances told Ma by mistake he was working at the docks in Fort Wayne."

"And Miz Hawkins thought he was working in Fort Wayne," Jane announced over supper.

"Had a job promised to him," said Mr. Henderson.

"Those thieves probably worked out that lie so as to collect his pay," said Mrs. Henderson.

"Murdered him and hid his body and kept it a secret, so they could be collecting his pay from the docks," Jane said to Annie next day. "And all the while your poor Ma waiting for him to come home."

"Poor Ma," agreed Annie, shaking her brown curls from side to side. "Poor Ma."

"Likely murdered by some sailors after a fight in a saloon," said Betsey Anne to Sarah Barnes. "Said he was in Toledo, catching the cars late one night."

"Sailors?" asked Sarah. "During the war?"

"During the war. Toledo, anyway. Toledo's where he was going for the train. He was heading home straightaway."

"Straightaway? From his ma's place?"

"In '64."

"Sounds as if he was heading home straightaway from his Ma's place, instead a working on the docks in Fort Wayne like she's been a thinking from his sister's letters," said Sarah to Charles in the quiet of their bed.

"She must have been mistaken, someway, the sister I mean," said Charles.

"Someway."

...think it likely Jefferson was murdered in Toledo a way back in October of 1864. They said he was to take the cars late that night, planning to be home before Harriet was to be born though he had no way of knowing it was a girl nor never knew. I thought it was hard to think why he would a be working way off in Fort Wayne and not write me nor send for me or the children or at least send on part of his pay. That was harder even than to know that he's dead these two years, and murdered besides... Betsey wrote to her ma and pa.

"Might be we were mistaken about Jefferson Hawkins, someway," said Ann Springer as she fixed a poultice on her husband's aching back.

"Might be," he said.

"Sorry to hear that your husband was killed," said Mable Thompson, handing her new dress, firmly wrapped in brown paper and tied with twine, to her near-grown son, before tying on her fur-lined hat in Betsey's kitchen.

"Yes, thank you," murmured Betsey Anne, shivering in the cold blast as the boy opened the door and went out.

"In Toledo they say?"

"Toledo," Betsey answered. "In '64."

The door was slammed from the outside by the pull of the wind and Betsey leaned against it with her eyes closed. Eight weeks and more it had been since that letter from Frances. And still these conversations.

She walked to the stove, rubbing her hand across the top of Duga's close-cut head as she passed him. "Are you ready for some dinner, Duga?" His quick smile was his only answer. "Bring me in another stick or two, then," she said.

She filled the tea kettle with already-warm water from the reservoir, and lifted the lid to the pot of soup that had been simmering on the back burner all morning. "Toledo," she said to herself, wondering how long it would take to convince everyone.

"Toledo. In October of 1864," she repeated, wondering how long it would take to believe it.

It was then that Lydia burst in through the door with a great billowing of skirts and cape, and a great gust of cold wind, her face reddened, her hair wild.

"Betsey Anne!"

Betsey turned to look at her.

"Betsey Anne – I've gotten married!"

"Married!" Betsey fairly shrieked the word, fear gripping her heart with its icy hand.

But Lydia hadn't stopped talking. "...so handsome, and riding along there this morning on his big horse, looking for all the world like a Prince or a knight in shining armor..."

Betsey's consciousness faded. She sank down on the bench, her wooden spoon falling with a soup-laden thud from her limp fingers. Married. Lydia, married. To a man she'd only met that morning! Why was she talking so fast? Who was she trying to convince?

"…and the Methodist preacher was standing right there…"

Lydia's excited narrative carried right on without Betsey, as though she hadn't noticed her sister's discomfiture. As though there were nothing wrong. Nothing wrong! Oh, this was so wrong! What would Ma say — or worse yet, Pa? Why was that fool Methodist always marrying people too young to know their own minds? Why didn't he even check to see if they had their majority?

"…all the way out here on the back of his horse, flying like the wind…"

Here? He was here? What sort of man must he be, to have married a young girl on so short an acquaintance?

"…horse in the barn. And he'll be right in, Betsey Anne, oh, wait till you meet him!"

A man like Jefferson? Betsey turned wild eyes on her sister, ran a stiff tongue over stiffer lips and tried to swallow. She retrieved the spoon from the floor and dropped it in the dishpan, taking her apron off with the other hand. She smoothed her work dress and as she put her hands to her unruly hair, the man in question appeared in the doorway.

"Betsey, this is James Boon," Lydia was saying breathlessly. Did it sound rehearsed? "James — my sister, Betsey Anne Hawkins."

CHAPTER TWENTY-TWO

Betsey could not speak. Her throat constricted and she stood staring, open-mouthed, at the man.

Her first impression was that he was the most handsome man she'd ever seen, but the longer she stared at him, the harder it was to work out just **why** she had thought that. His back was straight, his shoulders broad and square, but he was not exactly tall. His eyes were green, wide set and large, but his nose was dominant and seemed to run headlong into his forehead, between his pencil-thin eyebrows, as straight as if it were chiseled from stone. His suit was not particularly well tailored, but the fabric was sturdy and serviceable; his shirtfront and collar were white and stiff, but a trifle tight. "Ma'am," he said, and doffed his hat to reveal hair of the blackest black, thick, and wavy, combed straight back from his forehead.

"Ah ba ba ba ba!" shrieked Herbert from the corner.

James Boon looked toward the child with a smile that quickly softened as he looked upon the boy, nearly five years old but no more advanced than an infant. He twirled his hat in large, hard-working hands, and turned back to look at Betsey Anne.

"Are you alright?" he asked.

Betsey closed her mouth and swallowed hard, looking from one to the other. Lydia was silent, waiting to hear Betsey's congratulations. Boon seemed curiously still, waiting calmly through Betsey's hesitation. "Oh, oh my," she said finally. "My – **married**. Sudden, don't you think? I mean…"

"Oh, Betsey Anne, don't you see? Some things you just **know**!"

Lydia turned her back, busied herself with hanging her woolens on the hooks near the door.

"Liddy's only eighteen," Betsey blurted out, her voice seeming too loud even to her own ears. "How old are **you**, Mr. Boon?"

"Twenty-five," they answered in unison.

"Twenty-five," Betsey repeated with emphasis, as though the number proved something. "Twenty-five. And do you have a place? A farm? A job?"

"I've just come down from Canada," he answered, turning an even gaze toward Betsey, who had slumped down onto the kitchen bench for the second time in half an hour. "Rode into town this morning…"

"And I looked down from the second floor and saw him riding along there…"

"And when I went in, she was right there, at the top of the stairs, looking at me as if she'd been expecting me."

"Just as if…"

"And the Methodist was standing right there, too, as if he'd been sent…"

"By God, I think, sent by God to marry us…" Did they practice this speech?

"Right then and there."

"Right then and there."

"Right then and there?"

Lydia reached out to touch Betsey's shoulder. "I told James you need our help here what with the children all so young, and Jefferson --" there was a pause.

"Oh, dear Lord!" shrilled Betsey. "Is that why you married him?"

"Murdered, in '64," Lydia continued, ignoring Betsey's outburst. "So you needn't worry that we'll run off and leave you on your own. We'll stay right here on this farm."

"What?" Confusion overtook her in a feverish wave and she fanned herself with the apron she was still clutching in a wad. "What?" she repeated.

"I'm more than willing to stay on here," said Boon, "As long as you need me."

"What?" Betsey Anne shouted, jumping to her feet and stepping in close to Lydia, her face only inches from her sister's. "Did you think this would fix things? *Did* you? Think that you could just up and marry the first man as come along and grinned at you and all of a sudden things would work out like you dreamed?" She plowed on, her words coming hard and fast, her face stained with unnoticed tears, her shaking hands gripping Lydia's shoulders. "Well it don't work, and I'm living proof of that! Look at me! Look at this place! I was tired of working in another woman's house, and tired of caring for another woman's children, cooking and cleaning all day long and the other woman getting the good out of it and along come Jefferson and I thought here's the man what'll get me the things I want out of life. But he didn't, did he? *Did he?*"

She was screaming now and let go her hold on Lydia's shoulders to open her arms and wave them wildly at their surroundings. "*This* is what I got for marrying Thomas Jefferson Hawkins! A house that was barely more than a shack when it first went up and ain't no better now, with *dirt* for a floor, and a rocky hill full of stumps that grow back into trees before anybody gets around to pulling them out!"

Betsey wiped the streaming tears from her face with her wadded-up apron and stood looking down at Herbert, blissfully unaware of the turmoil around him, and Harriet fast asleep on her quilt. Turning, she caught sight of Duga, standing just inside the door with an armful of wood and a look on his face that she'd seen all too often. "This is what I got for marrying Old Tom J," she said, her voice suddenly calm and quiet. "A house full of children as don't even know their pa, and me feeding them on crabapples and the sweat off my little sister's back."

Lydia waited long enough to be sure the tirade was over before she spoke. She put her hand in Boon's big hand and squeezed it just a little before she said, "Betsey Anne, I didn't marry Old Tom J. This man is..."

"Different?" Betsey broke in, sarcastically. "Different?" She walked back toward them and stood toe to toe with Boon, looking deep into his eyes. "What makes you think he's different?"

"I prayed!" It was out without a thought, and once said seemed startling and cold. "I mean, I always pray," Lydia tried again. "Today I **prayed** that God would show me…"

"I prayed," said Boon. "That God would show me, give me peace."

"Peace?" It was foreign-sounding to Betsey. Not something she'd ever thought to get from God, really. **Help**, she'd longed for; **hope**, she'd clung to. But peace?

"Peace," said Lydia, softly.

"And?" Betsey whispered the question, tears once again pouring down her cheeks.

"There is peace."

"Well then," said Betsey, with a sudden surge of determination. Wiping her tears once more with the sodden apron, she gave it a shake and tied it back around her waist, smoothing it down with her hands as though it were fresh off the line. "Well then. I expect we'd best settle some things around here. I'll move my things into the sewing room and you can have that room to yourselves that way. At least until you can put up a house of your own."

While she talked, she dealt soup bowls onto the table, and spoons and mugs, swiftly, with a practiced hand, and flung a pad to the center of it to receive the pot of boiling stew. "Duga! Show your Uncle Boon where he can wash up, and wash yourself while you're at it!"

Betsey Anne kept up a steady prattle throughout the short meal, as much to keep herself from thinking about the situation as to convince the others that she had accepted it. "I don't believe I've ever seen a man with hair as pretty as yours, Mr. Boon. Did I let these potatoes get too soft? Lydia meets all kinds of folks up there at MacGregor's Hotel." Did she see Lydia exchange a nervous glance with Boon?

She continued her own nervous prattling. "Or at least I guess she used to meet them, but now of course she'll be staying to home here. Poor MacGregor, that's two hard working girls he's lost, and not that long between them. What part of Canada did you say you're from? Duga, give your brother a hand there with his soup. Harriet! You're too big a girl to make such a mess. How many children in your family, did you say Mr. Boon?"

There wasn't really time allowed between her questions for the others to answer, but they inserted brief syllables and agreeable nods, exchanging knowing smiles from time to time. In truth, no one dawdled over the meal, and the dishes were washed and stacked on the shelf in record time.

James Boon emerged from behind the faded brown calico curtain that had been the only bedroom door for nine years, looking a trifle embarrassed about no-one-knew-what and dressed for work. "Well, I'll get out and see what needs doing on the place," he said. "How about some help, young man?" This last was addressed to Duga, who beamed his agreement.

In spite of the earlier tensions, the two women fell into the comfortable camaraderie of work, side by side, throughout the afternoon. It took only minutes, really, to move Betsey's things from the front bedroom to the sewing room. It took a single private moment, when Lydia had been sent to fetch in water for washing, for Betsey to retrieve the little wooden box of letters from its hiding place under the bed.

She wiped the dust from its hand-hewn lid with a corner of her apron and considered opening it, touched by a passing sensation that she was somehow leaving behind the last vestige of her married life by moving out of her bedroom. But she heard Lydia thump the water bucket against the front door and swiftly she set the box under the edge of the narrow cot that would now be her bed, giving it a shove with the toe of her boot before returning to the kitchen.

The sheets for the big bed were washed and hung on the line until nearly dry before Lydia pressed out every wrinkle with hot, heavy flatirons that would have blistered her hands a few months before. The mattress was turned, the dirt floor swept and swept again. The oil lamps were filled, the window and walls washed with hot water and vinegar.

Annie and Sammy came chattering in, having been introduced to their new Uncle Boon by a condescending Duga. Annie was immediately set to watch Harriet and Herbert, while Sammy was sent out in search of the man of the hour.

"Tell your Uncle Boon I want him to move this wooden door off the sewing room and hang me a curtain instead," Betsey said, turning toward the stove. "So's I can hear if any of you children need me in the night."

Then the women turned their attention to the evening meal, both wanting it to be special, but perhaps for different reasons. Lydia punched the sourdough bread down for the last time and put the loaves into the oven, while Betsey marshaled all her skill to liven up an otherwise unremarkable cut of beef with a smothering of onions and a jar from her never-ending supply of gingered crab apples. She sliced potatoes thinly and added them to the brimming skillet along with a spoonful of bacon drippings and a generous pinch of salt.

"Smells good," approved Boon, coming through the door with a handful of tools, two grinning boys close on his heels.

"We're helping, Ma," shouted Duga. "Both of us!"

By the time the door and the calico curtain occupied their new places, the supper was on the table, a rice pudding was waiting on the sideboard, all the women of the house had washed their faces, combed their hair, and donned their clean dresses, and even Herbert was looking shiny and sitting up straight in the special chair his Old Pa had made for him. Lydia fidgeted while Boon and the boys cleaned up for supper, first putting the cups to the right of the plates, then moving them to the left, and back again, putting an apron on and taking it off again, and flicking away invisible specks of dust from the top of the table.

But the meal was pronounced a success and the children filled the air with chattering and clamoring, piling one and all into Uncle Boon's lap to beg for a story or a song while the women tidied up the kitchen, filled the water reservoir for morning and set out the sourdough starter for the next day's bread.

"Well, that's enough now, and you've got lessons in the morning and plenty of chores to go around," said Betsey, hanging her apron on its hook by the front door as Lydia disappeared into the bedroom. Though excited, the children protested little and were soon finished with their trips to the privy and warmly tucked beneath their quilts with mother's warm kisses melting on their foreheads.

"Goodnight," Betsey said, turning the last oil lamp down to a faint glow and blowing the last of its light out with a quick puff. She stepped behind the calico curtain and stood looking around the room, so familiar by day, so unfamiliar as a place to pass the night, feeling desperately alone.

"You're a fool, Betsey Anne," she muttered under her breath taking her nightgown out from under the pillow. "It ain't as if you've left Jefferson off there in the other room. He's dead. Dead, more than two years gone."

"Betsey?" The faint whisper startled her.

"Lid!" She clutched the front of her dress, drawing it closed as though embarrassed for her sister to see her camisole. "What is it?"

"Betsey, I forgot there was a letter for you, came in yesterday's post." She held the missive out and Betsey took it in a trembling hand.

"Thank you."

"Goodnight." Lydia pushed back the curtain. "Betsey?"

"Yes?"

"It's for the best, you have to believe me – and there **is** peace."

"I know, Lid, I know."

The curtain swung into place and quivered again when the wooden door closed on the bedroom before Betsey turned her attention to the fine parchment envelope in her hand.

Sylvana February the 12 1867

Absent sister – I suppose you have come to the conclusion that I do not care anything about you. I cannot blame you if you do. I have waited and hoped to hear something from Thomas for I hardly know what to write, but I write now hoping you will forgive my long silence. How do you get along? Let me know. I will try and see if there can't be something done for you. It isn't but little that I can do for you. We have found out that Thomas is living. He was in Ingnau, Michigan last winter and all summer before this. Last summer, there was a man by the name of Watson that married my niece – he used to know him when he was young. Thomas worked for his father before he was ever married the first time. We saw him and had a long talk with him. He thinks there is no mystery about it. Thomas was on a boat that ran out of the harbor to meet the vessels so they could unload. Watson said he ate a good many meals with him. William was up there but could not find anything of him. Heard of a Hawkins but could not tell whether it was him or not. This is all I can tell you about it. I shall be glad to hear from you. I will enclose 50 cents for you to buy paper and an envelope. Will try to send you more next time. Keep up good courage and trust in God for the rest and all will be well. Will bid you good bye for the present. Kiss the children for me. Tell them to be good boys and girls and grow as fast as they can so they can help their mother. From your sister and friend, Elisabeth Rolph.

PS Frances Maria was here last week and said she was a going to write to you soon. They are all well.

The paper slipped from Betsey's fingers and lay unheeded in her lap as she stared into the dying fire, the rocking chair clicking over a seam in the smooth plank floor. *Oh God...Our Help...Oh God...Our Help* it sang, on and on, while Betsey's heart searched for the words her mind was not willing to hear: *Our Hope for years to come.*

She did not want to hope any longer. It was better to have moved on.

"Murdered in Toledo, in '64," she whispered, and wondered if it counted as a prayer and if it was it evil to pretend her own husband was dead, just so she wouldn't have to face the truth.

CHAPTER TWENTY-THREE

Royalton April 13 1867
Dear Sister — It has been a long time since I wrote to you. I do not know but
you think I had forgotten you. As you see, I have not. I hope you will excuse
me for my neglect. I have had a great deal to do this winter. I have been
spinning for a piece of cloth, so I find it keeps me pretty busy with the rest of
my work. Lucinda has been gone away from home a good deal this winter
and I find I miss her help very much. I was at Sylvana last week. Elisabeth
has been very sick this winter, but is quite well now. Mother's health is good.
She is staying at William's this spring. His wife, Audrey, is very sick. They
think she has got the consumption. Elisabeth says she does not think she can
live a great while. They have one child, a little girl. We have had a very
dry winter. People have been bothered to get water for their stock. I do not
think I ever knew so dry a season since I can remember. Lucinda and her Pa
has gone to meeting and the children are out to play as it has turned warm.
I will try to finish my letter. Arthur is on the cars and Bradford is out in
your country somewhere. If he has been at your house, I would like for you
to write and let me know. Betsey, I have thought of you a great many times
that I would like to know how you and your little ones are getting along. If
you was where I could assist you, it would be a great pleasure to me. I have
not heard from Alice since I heard from you. We are all well and hoping
these few lines will find you all the same. I shall have to bid you good bye.
Kiss the children for me. Write as soon as you get this and I will do the
same. From your sister, F.M. Garnier, to Betsey A. Hawkins.

"Well, that's a nice chatty letter and all," said Lydia as Betsey lay
down Frances's trademark sheet of blue writing paper. "What else
does she send?"

Betsey checked the envelope. "A dollar, no -- two. A measure of tatting work, and a square of linen with a bit of feather stitching along the edge. And here's another letter, looks like." She unfolded the small sheet of thin white paper and glanced down it. "Children, this letter's for you, from your cousin Lucinda on your Pa's side." She began again to read aloud.

Royalton April 13th 1867

Dear Cousins,

As Mother is writing to Aunty I will scribble a few lines to you cousins so you may know that I have not forgotten you yet. How I should like to see you all. How I should like to know...

Betsey suddenly choked and put a quick hand to cover her mouth, then managed to splutter out "know you better," and continue with the letter.

Samuel I suppose you are almost a man. Emory and Watson think that they know as much as Pa does about farming. They are getting to be large boys. Annie, I suppose you do most all the house work now. Janey thinks she can do lots towards it. She will fly around sometimes like a hen with her head cut off. Elta May says she 'hasn't a going to work till she dits bid nuf' then she is going to 'hep Mudder'. She is a little mischief and fat as a little pig. Janey knit two pair of socks this winter. She goes to school when there is any. She can read and spell like a house-a-fire. Elta can read in the A-B-C. I don't expect anything else but what they will go ahead of me. There is no use of my trying to keep ahead of them.

Aunt Lib is coming up here next week and she is a going to bring Emmy Lou and Jimmy with her. She has got Uncle William's little girl, and she will come of course. If you could come, what a pleasant time you could have! There will not be a tree in three miles around that they will not climb and swing till their heads will swim. Samuel, what are you a doing now days? Emory and Watson is helping Pa. Now, Cousins, you will write to me, will you not? See what a nice sheet I have wrote to you. I don't know whether you can read it or not. My pen is a poor string. If I could send you a great big apple I would do it. I will close for this time. Annie, I will send you a little of my work. There will be enough to put on a pair of panties for yourself. And Samuel, I will send you a book mark. I cannot send you anything that will do you any good this time but will try and do better next time. I will bid you good bye this time – to Annie and Samuel, farewell, Lucinda Garnier.

"Didn't she send **me** nothing?"

"Don't she think I can tat my own work? I can tat better than this!"

"What ever would I want with a book mark anyhow?"

"How come she don't write to Harriet and brother and me?"

"Children! You sound so ungrateful!" Betsey shook her head, folded the letter hurriedly and stuffed it back into the envelope, then pushed her end of the bench back from the table. "At least brother here ain't got no complaints!" She ruffled Herbert's hair as she passed his chair. "I expect you'll have to use one of them dollars to buy these naughty children some sweets when you go in to town, Aunt Liddy, just to shut them up!"

This remark, as planned, caused enough of a clamor around Lydia to allow Betsey to slip unheeded into the shelter of her own room. Once the door – built and hung by James Boon -- was closed behind her, she fumbled in the envelope until she produced the small white sheet with the cramped writing. Perhaps she had just read it wrong. Her eyes scanned the opening sentences.

How I should like to know where your father is.

Shaking, Betsey stumbled over to the cot in the corner and, leaning down, felt blindly for the wooden letter box. Slipping the latest missive under the lid without opening it properly, she gave the box a quick shove to lodge it firmly against the wall under the cot, and sank down with her legs curled beneath her and her face buried in her arms where they lay folded on her pinwheel quilt.

"You're a fool, Betsey Anne," she whispered. "This don't really change nothing, no more did Elisabeth's letter change anything either."

Perhaps that was true. What did it really change anyway? Jefferson was either dead or he wasn't; in either case he was gone. She began to cry softly. Oh, but she was tired of wondering, and worrying, and waiting. And how peaceful it had been those few short weeks to believe that he had died in the very act of coming home to her. Or at least to pretend to believe it.

She sat back and wiped her face with the corner of her apron.

This wouldn't do – crying in the middle of the day. At any moment one of the children might open the door, might come bouncing in with more remonstrance for poor Lucinda or detailed plans for a dollar's worth of sweets. Or perhaps Lydia would come in and stand there in silence, seeing the tears and guessing the truth.

And the truth, if truth it were, would only ruin and destroy, would only hurt and distress. No, she would keep it to herself. She would let the others believe in Toledo and have some peace at least. Why should the pursuit of truth override peace?

She looked at the door – in itself a testimony to the new reality since the marriage of Lydia and James Boon. She looked down at the brown calico apron she wore, one last practical use for the sturdy fabric that had served as a bedroom door for all her married life. It had hung over the entrance to the sewing room for only a few weeks before Boon had replaced it with a strong, solid door made of the wood of trees that should have been cut years ago.

The truth will set you free. She'd heard that somewhere – the Scripture maybe? Set you free. No. Not when the truth was that nobody knew the answer; not when the truth was an endless mystery. Not when the best the truth could be was that a father had deserted his children – first one child, and then five more.

She checked her face in her little round mirror, looking deep into the hazel eyes of a woman who wished that the truth about her husband might be that he were dead. Somewhere behind those eyes a door closed, locking away the secret and its pain. She licked her dry lips and tucked a few stray hairs behind her ears before slipping back into the kitchen to fuss busily at the sideboard as though she had never left the room.

"Now, children, let your Aunt Liddy be," she said without turning around. "It's certain she's got better things to do than listen to your wheedling."

"Now that's a fact," came the deep, warm voice of James Boon in reply. "Like getting some dinner for me!"

This having the effect of transferring all the children's clamoring to Uncle Boon, Lydia got stiffly up from the table and joined Betsey at the sideboard, reaching for the bowls and spoons for the noon meal.

Betsey squinted at her sister. "You're moving a might slow, Lid."

"Aw, it's just the ride to town and all. Tires me out some."

"Lydia looks tired," Betsey said to Sarah later that afternoon, after she had walked down over the hill and across Charles Barnes's field, newly turned under and smelling faintly alive as only God's rich soil can do. She set a basket of warm sourdough biscuits on Sarah's red-and-white gingham tablecloth. "Gray, somehow."

"You think she's taking ill?"

"I'm afraid of it – I expect I'll send to Ma for some of her tea or a tonic of some kind."

There was silence for a moment or two while Sarah poured out some coffee and offered a small pitcher of maple syrup to sweeten it.

"She's happy, at least," Betsey Anne finally said. "Which is more than I thought she'd have when she up and married Boon so fast that way."

"He seems a nice fellow, what I've talked to him." Sarah cut into the still-steaming biscuit on her plate and spread it thickly with fresh butter. "Charles likes him."

"Charles has helped him, and all of us, for that matter. And things has certain changed up to our place since Boon come along."

"Is the coffee too strong?" It was not a question meant to be answered, really, and Betsey Anne recognized it for what it was – an open door, an invitation to talk.

"I keep wondering what kind of man marries a girl but eighteen years old nigh the minute he lays an eye on her. And every time I wonder it, I answer myself it's the kind of man like Jefferson is – was. Then I look for the bad in Boon and I almost hate that I can't find it."

"You can't?"

"I keep thinking it has to be there. But he just keeps on smiling and playing with my children and working on my farm doing all the things Jefferson never did." Betsey bit into a biscuit covered with Sarah's thick, sweet pear preserves and chewed thoughtfully before wiping her mouth on a soft calico napkin. "We'll likely have a cellar full of vegetables from the garden this year, now all the stumps are gone. There's a field taking shape out the back, and he says we'll grow enough wheat on it for a credit down at Henderson's. The boys are learning to work…" her voice trailed off.

"Lydia make the biscuits?" Sarah selected another and cut it in two. "Did you see my napkins? I wore that dress for best two years, for work another, and finally had to cut it down to four napkins and a new apron last week."

"Serves you well if you buy a good strong piece of goods." Betsey sipped her coffee, using the interval of small talk to work her mind around what she wanted to say. "Annie made the biscuits. She's getting big, that one."

Sarah stepped away from the table to stir through a bubbling pot of beans with a long-handled wooden spoon. She kept her back turned overlong thinking perhaps Betsey Anne could talk better to the knot of hair on the back of her neck than she might to her face.

"Jefferson ain't dead." The sentence was whispered, barely audible to Sarah, but it hung in the room like a heavy black cloud hangs before the sun, bringing a sudden chill and an inescapable darkness.

"Not dead? I thought…"

"So did I. Sometimes I still do. Frances said…" Betsey folded her napkin then shook it out and folded it again while Sarah sank back into the chair on the other side of the table. "But Elisabeth, his other sister, she says it ain't true. Says there's no mystery to it, he's working on a boat, right here in Michigan and all."

Looking up to catch Sarah's concerned gaze, Betsey smiled a little half smile, punctuated by a grunted laugh. "I got that letter in February, and I ain't said nothing. Not to the children, not to nobody, even you. And this morning there's another letter from Frances, and she says nothing about him, and I'm thinking maybe what she said before is more true than what Elisabeth said – then Frances's girl, Lucinda, sticks in a note to the children and says 'how I should like to know where your father is'."

Betsey blinked back tears, looking hard at Sarah's stove, and beyond it into the field. Minutes passed while she labored with her own thoughts.

"I almost read it to the children," she said then. "Only I saw just it in time and stopped. And I cried and cried and tried to think why it should upset me if my husband is alive!" This time she sobbed, openly, putting a clinched fist to her mouth, then covering her nose with Sarah's "new" napkin.

Sarah silently removed the biscuits and plates from the table, then poured half a cup more of hot coffee into Betsey's earthenware mug and her own.

Betsey drew a deep breath before continuing. "Here all this time I been wondering what kind of man Liddy married, and all the time what's worse is what type of woman her sister is." She continued, staring at the toe of her boot and speaking in a monotone. "The kind of woman what wishes her husband were dead, just so's she could know he won't never come back and ruin what's good."

She turned to Sarah and smiled ruefully while the tears flowed anew. "Sarah, James Boon is a good man no matter how hard I try to pretend that he ain't and Jefferson's a rounder, through and through!" She mopped ineffectually at her face, plunging on in a torrent of words as violent as the flood of tears. "And I don't want Jefferson to come back and chase Boon off the place! I don't! I don't want him back!"

Her voice had risen to a hysterical pitch, and Sarah had pulled Betsey's head down onto her own shoulder, softly stroking the curly mop of hair twisted and pinned into a ladylike bun but still managing to look unruly.

"Sarah, I wish I'd have married James Boon." It was a whisper, choked out between swollen lips, and followed by a shaking, lung-racking sob. "I mean, I'm happy for Liddy, I really am – but I wish I'd have married James Boon, or someone like him."

It was some time later before Sarah offered any opinion on the subject at hand. She had helped Betsey to wash her face, to recapture the wildest of her free-ranging hair. She had led Betsey out the front door into the crisp April dusk to walk and to admire the lingering light and the preparations for spring that existed on the Barnes farm, even taking time to point out a new coat of red paint on the north side of the barn.

Finally, tying a string around a bundle of calico scraps with instructions for Betsey to present them to Annie for a few lessons in sewing, she ventured a hypothesis. "It don't matter really, Betsey, whether he lives or not. He ain't coming back. He may as well have died clear back – in '64 – for all the difference it makes."

"I expect you're right."

"And who wouldn't wish to have married a better man, after all you've been through these years. Just think on what's good from it all – them children of yours, I mean – and chalk up your mistakes – and Jefferson's too -- and get on with it."

Betsey walked to the door, tying her bonnet under her chin and reaching for the parcel of scraps. As she stepped out into the near dark, she turned back. "Sarah?"

"Yes?"

"Peace – they keep saying there's peace in it all – Liddy and James Boon, I mean."

"That's good."

"Sarah, how do you find peace? How?"

"Pray, Betsey. Pray and believe. Pray with your eyes shut, and then open them up and look around you till you begin to see the hand of God."

"What if the hand of God don't never show up?"

"It's here already, Betsey Anne."

Sarah watched Betsey's back as she made her way back across the darkening field, looking tired and aged far beyond her years.

"It's here already," she whispered again, her heart filled with prayer.

CHAPTER TWENTY-FOUR

In truth there had been peace, at least outwardly, on the Hawkins farm, though in Betsey's heart and soul there still lingered a deep and tortured mystery and doubt. Her waking thoughts were nagged by it, coming up on her from behind, a fleeting spot of darkness that came and went like a pesky fly disturbing a pleasant picnic or a tranquil nap.

And her dreams were haunted by it. No matter if she dreamed of canning, and sweet steam rising from pots of simmering fruit, if she dreamed of the children, precious faces upturned to her kisses, or even if she dreamed of sewing as though she watched her own fingers ply the needle and a golden thread through silk as fine as butterfly wings, there would always come a vision of Jefferson. Superimposed over the moving picture in her mind's eye he would come – faint at first, then sharper of image and deeper of color until it seemed to her that she had awakened and the other dream was only a memory.

He would stare at her, silently and sternly, his disembodied face floating back and forth, now so close that she could smell the liquor on his breath, and then so distant that she was almost uncertain it was Jefferson at all. "Betsey!" he would whisper, and his voice would send a chill down her spine. "Betsey Anne!" And then he would begin to laugh, a loud and jarring sound that somehow turned into the plinking sound of a saloon piano and Jefferson would begin to dance, slowly, almost tenderly, with a tall and slender woman who always seemed to be wearing a dress that Betsey had made once upon a time. Just as they would swing around till Jefferson's back was turned and Betsey was almost able to see the woman's face, the music would turn again into laughter filled with the sound of insanity and Betsey would sit upright in her narrow bed and gasp for air.

She would give a push and a punch and a shake to the feather pillow and turn the side that always seemed wet down toward the ticking, then ease herself back onto it, screwing her eyes shut and wishing for merciful sleep that never returned. "Toledo – he was killed in Toledo – in '64 – October – October of '64 in Toledo," she whispered, over and over again like a prayer learned by rote.

Night after night, no matter how peacefully her sleep began, the minutes just before the dawn were marked by the same hideous end, and Betsey would emerge from her seclusion worn and a trifle irritated, looking around at the other members of the family with a slightly puzzled expression, as though she were unsure why they had not seen what she had seen.

But they had not. If they had dreamed at all, they had dreamed of peace, of plenty, or perhaps only of the satisfaction that grows from the accomplishment of work.

Work abounded on the farm now – though not with the same sense of toil and drudgery that it had always before held. Instead it was simply a constant bustle of purpose, a natural state of occupation.

In the house, Lydia seemed to be suddenly more in charge than Betsey – or rather, she was the pipeline for suggestions from James Boon, who had slipped quietly and undemandingly into the role of household head. "James says the fish are biting, down on the creek," Lydia might say. Or "James was wondering should he haul the bedding out for us, so we can beat it out good today?" Annie was part of the women's circle in the family, quite big enough now to truly lend a hand with cooking, cleaning, washing, and supervision of Harriet. Even Harriet was able to accept numerous small tasks, under her big sister's watchful eye.

Boon had fixed a little wagon for Herbert and had removed him from the kitchen, where he had spent all of his five years beneath his mother's swishing skirts. The boys would drag the smiling child in his padded wooden wagon wherever they would go. And when they were at lessons, James Boon himself would lift Herbert to his shoulders and march out the door with him, making a sing-song repetition about "women do the women's work, but we are men, men,

men!" And Betsey would smile and listen almost wistfully to the child's consistent, loud and happy reply of "Ah ba ba ba ba!" heard all the way from the barn.

The barn had been repaired and even painted, and now housed not only Boon's own horse, but another slightly aged beast with strongly muscled hind quarters that had been bought to help with plowing and the pulling of stumps. A young cow was being raised in a pen behind the barn, called by the name of Maudy and the promise of her future issue of milk was an expectation that gave rise to many heated conversations around the supper table. In spite of Betsey Anne's hatred of swine, which she had never truly explained to any of them, a yearling pig had been bought and butchered immediately and the meat salted down and cured.

A wheat field was indeed taking shape behind the house. Small section by small section the trees were girdled and then cut, revealing a view of neighbors that Betsey had almost forgotten existed. And then the stumps were wrested from the ground by hours of sweaty labor – which strangely proved to be one of the favorite activities for the boys. The first section had been gotten ready in time to plant a small crop. A row of real cherry trees, no more than two feet high, and braced on both sides with sturdy sticks lashed together with twine, had been placed along the back border of the field.

The chicken coop had been torn right down and rebuilt from the ground up, and the addition of a new rooster had brought a bumper crop of baby chicks and increased egg production as well.

Boon felt the outhouse had seen a better day. A new hole was dug and a new building constructed to cover it, with yet another day's labor devoted to smoothing out a gently sloping path from the house to its door. The old structure was hauled down, the depths beneath it filled in firmly with the soil from the new hole and its timbers burned into tiny ash.

Even the little house, which had so long stood looking poor and unfinished, received its share of the workmen's attention. Cracks and crevices in the walls were chinked with mud, rotted boards were pulled out and replaced. White paint was applied to the walls, inside and out. The bedroom was endowed with another window to allow for a cross-draft, and the kitchen likewise received more of the outdoor light. In the height of the summer, the roof was torn down, and when it went back up it was higher, allowing room for a sleeping loft with a round-runged ladder made especially for Sammy and Duga to enjoy.

Soon, Boon had said, the lumber would come back from the sawmill – lumber from their own trees, cut to open up the field – and when it came, there would be planks applied to the kitchen and bedroom floors. Betsey's heart had leapt when she heard the promise, and she mentally ticked the days off the calendar, especially in the mornings when she plied her swift broom to the hated hard-packed floor.

There were still sewing clients, though not as many as before, and the stitch work again brought a feeling of pleasant restfulness to Betsey Anne. Annie would sit beside her, watching and learning, and from time to time be given a small piece of hand work. "Anything worth doing is worth doing right," Betsey told her, remembering how her own mother had insisted on neat, straight stitches even from a four year old so many years ago.

Everyone laughed a lot, and chattered, full of boastful pride in their accomplishments, and hopeful plans for the future. "I near cut down a whole tree myself, Ma!" or "I always catch the most fish, don't I?" And then "I'll have Maudy's first milk and make a buttermilk cake for Sunday dinner!" or "When I get big, I dunna marry Unca Boon!" This regularly-repeated claim from Harriet would always produce a round of laughter and shouts of "You can't do that!" from her brothers and sisters, but the uncle in question would merely wink at her and say, softly, "That's my best girl!"

Harnesses were dredged up from the cool recesses of the barn, repaired and cleaned and put into use after lying idle for so long. The moving parts of the water pump were tightened and oiled, eliminating the grinding squeak that had cried out from it for some two years gone.

The garden – in which Betsey Anne had fought with rotting stumps and their continual offspring of new tree shoots all her married life – was cleared and turned under and marked out in rows as neat and straight as any seam Betsey had ever sewn. Later, the beans were provided with stakes and twine to grow on, the dirt was all heaped in perfect little mounds, ready to receive the seeds, to accept the touch of the rain, and to drain the moisture so as not to drown the sprouting plants. Weeds were vigilantly removed, by hand or by hoe, and when required, water was carried in buckets and carefully directed to trickle down the trenches between the rows of healthy plants. By fall, Betsey was sure, a harvest of squash and beans and cucumbers and onions and potatoes would be laid away in the darkness of the cellar, layered in with straw or tightly sealed in barrels, hanging in loose-weave baskets or standing in jars neatly sorted, the pickled cucumbers together, the boiled green beans next, gingered crabapples and raspberry preserves beside those.

Everyone worked and was happy at it. Side by side they labored on, with satisfaction in their accomplishment and in their provision for the coming winter, each one except Harriet and Herbert with a clear memory in their minds of other, colder, hungrier seasons. Side by side they labored on, untiringly it seemed, with purpose and expectation, with agreement and cooperation, but without the hot and harried, hair-in-the-eyes, sweat-on-the-brow, pain-in-the-limbs strain that had always accompanied their work in the past.

All this change was engineered and directed, driven and sustained, by James Boon. He arose before daylight with a smile on his face and kindness in his voice and took on the tasks one by one – working hardest himself, but never failing to include the others, to instruct them, and to share with them his plans. Still he found time to fashion toys from straw or pine needles; to cut fishing poles and supply them with twine and with hooks and bait; to supervise Sammy's whittling, or Duga's carpentry; to walk backwards holding both of Herbert's trusting hands, urging him step by wavering step though the child could not take a step on his own. Always, Boon found time to walk hand-in-hand with Lydia to a secret spot along the creek and watch while the moon cast its golden reflection over the rippling water or the purity of the dark settled over them like a soft blanket of black velvet.

It seemed to Betsey as if James Boon never rested, nor did he ever seem to exhaust himself, or to bring himself to a point of frustration and irritability. He never sulked or shouted. He never left the farm without taking Lydia and sometimes Betsey, or at least one or two of the boys. One sunshiny day, he even rode down off the hill with Herbert nestled in front of him, clinging to the horn of the saddle with a look half of fright and half of ecstasy shining from his eyes.

Betsey looked for fault, but found none, and daily found herself comparing Boon to Jefferson. And while she was most likely the only one in the household thinking this way, she was certainly not the only one in the surrounding community to think, or even say, "That Boon is doing a good job out there at Widow Hawkins's place," or "Nice of that young couple to stay on a helping the sister and all her brood of children."

But it was not until the weeks that followed her tearful visit to Sarah Barnes that Betsey partook freely of the simple joys that abounded in her family. The sense of foreboding that hovered behind her waking thoughts was pushed back farther and farther, until it lightened and became more and more infrequent. And even a night or two was passed without the appearance of Jefferson in her dreams.

It was late in June when she awoke for the third morning in a row, calmly, and with her pillow dry beneath her head, and no conscious recollection of her dreams, only a vague sense of pleasantness. It occurred to her that at last Thomas Jefferson Hawkins was truly dead.

"Newaygo," she whispered, replacing the oft-repeated chant of "Toledo in '64."

"Newaygo," she said again, sleepily, voicing her new hope that Jefferson would never again consume her sleep with his presence or his absence. "Newaygo, June of '67." Dead or alive. She did not know. Perhaps she would never know. Perhaps she would still wonder — occasionally, or often even. But she had crossed over some imaginary line in her heart; she had emerged from her slavery to his betrayal.

CHAPTER TWENTY-FIVE

Betsey settled the sleeping infant into the cradle, tucking soft blankets closely around her, then sank onto her cot and put her hands over her tear-swollen eyes, pressing her fingers into her temples in hopes of relieving the ache that pounded there. The events of the last few months marched through her head again, one behind the other, heel to toe like soldiers on parade.

Why hadn't she been able to see sooner that Lydia was expecting? Perhaps she had seen it, and just refused to admit it – too soon after Lydia's wedding and all. Why didn't she at least insist that Lydia rest, looking so gray like she had?

But no, they found out soon enough what condition she was in – they found out soon enough, they made her rest. It was just her lungs, her lungs had never been strong since she was just a girl. Ma said her lungs had never been strong. The doctor, the doctor said the same when they took her to see the doctor. Oh, why had they taken her all that long way, all that rough way in the wagon to see the doctor, only to learn what they already knew? She was so tired after that, so listless and colorless, lying in the bed all those long weeks.

But no, that was good for her, all that bed rest, it was just what she needed, the best they could do. Yes, that was the best thing, the long rest in bed, with the tonic from the doctor and the poultice from Ma. If anything would have helped. Maybe it still would have helped, if she'd had a little longer, a little more rest before her time came, like she should have had.

And the baby was so big and strong. Ma kept her own counsel on the size of that baby and the shortness of the time since that sudden wedding. She only said it was a wonder there wasn't anything wrong with the babe. So big and strong.

But if she hadn't been so big, maybe Liddy could have gotten through it. A smaller baby would have to be easier to bring into the world. Oh, God, why couldn't the baby have been a little smaller! Why? Ma said they had to be thankful, that a baby so big would do fine on cow's milk, a baby so strong would do fine.

"You did a good job, Liddy sweet," Ma had said. "A right fine job, little mother."

"You'll take care of her, Betsey? You'll love her anyway, James, you'll love her like you promised?" Lydia was whispering hoarsely. "It ain't her fault, James, and I'm sorry."

"Sh, sh, sh," James had been on his knees beside the bed, smoothing damp blond curls away from her eyes. "Sh, sh, sh. Everything will be alright, everything will be alright."

Betsey opened her eyes, sitting straight up, fighting and kicking back the thin sheet that covered her, desperate to get up out of the bed, to shake off the relentless memories, the endless march, march, march in her head. Peering out the window, she could see the faintest outline of light along the horizon and decided it was near enough daylight that no one would fault her for rising.

She slipped out of her nightgown and into her work dress as noiselessly as possible, not wanting to risk waking the two-week-old infant in the cradle beside her bed. Tiptoeing through the kitchen she took a moment to lay a mother's loving glance across each sleeping face, Annie, Herbert, Harriet on their pallets in the corners, Duga and Sammy only visible as lumps in the loft, their young uncle Charles a larger lump between them. She listened intently by the bedroom door, enough to know that Ma and Pa were soundly if not peacefully asleep in the big bed – Boon couldn't face it he'd said, he'd rather sleep in the barn.

She stepped out into the slowly graying stillness, closing the door softly behind her. She pulled her shawl tightly around her shoulders, but somehow the cool air felt refreshing on her skin, on her hair. She stood motionless, just breathing, breathing, feeling the caress of the morning dew, smelling the damp richness of earth and the fragrance of fallen leaves and pungent trees, listening to the symphony of bird songs punctuated by distant roosters' cries and occasional barking dogs, allowing her thoughts to focus only on her outward senses.

"Easy, easy." The deep, rumbling tone of James Boon's voice so readily seemed at home among the other sounds of early morn that she nearly missed it, and only after a moment opened her eyes and realized what she'd heard. "That's the way."

Still walking on tiptoe as though her footfall on the moist grasses would awaken the household, Betsey reached the corner of the house and looked down into the field where Boon was already at work with the old bay horse and a contraption of leather straps, battling a stump that had stubbornly defied him for months.

"Hard work heals a heavy heart," she thought to herself as she watched him applying the pain of his loss to a great physical effort. Unaware of the passing moments she stood, watching, until the sun had sufficient time to pop its red brow boldly up and send its first strong rays shooting across the tops of the neatly planted rows of wheat to illuminate the scene she watched, setting James Boon in glowing relief against the green backdrop of the forest. Could she see the beads of sweat upon his nose and forehead, or did she just imagine that? Could she see the muscles working in his jaw, or the brightness of determined focus in his eyes? Could she see a wall of hardness forming around the pain in his heart, picked out by the fingers of the glinting sun?

Or did she just imagine it was there?

Suddenly aware that he might look up and find her there, surveying him body and soul, she shrank back against the wall of the house letting her breath out between pursed lips. Work. She needed work. "Hard work heals a heavy heart," she said again to the listener in her head, and holding the hem of her skirt above the wet grass she made her way to the garden where the feel of the soil and the pursuit of weeds and insects would supply her needs.

She did not know how long she knelt there, pulling up the tiniest weeds, patting little mounds of soil around the sturdy vegetables, and pinching out the harmful insects one by one. She did not know; she did not care. She did not allow her mind to reach for any fact beyond the work at hand.

But she was not surprised when she was finished to find that the rest of the family was up and about, the children clothed and washed, their chores underway, and breakfast sizzling in a cast-iron skillet on the stove.

Nor was she particularly surprised to see that another farmer had tied his team to the post beside the barn and left them dozing in the sun, hind legs cocked, while he leaned against the side of the barn to visit with James Boon. In fact, she was sure she could predict the conversation almost to a word.

"So sorry to hear about your wife, so young and all."

"Thank you, it has been hard."

"Thanks to the good Lord the young'un is alright."

"Yes, and she is a wonder, and looks so much like her mother."

"I see you've been a working down there in the field – it's so good to see this place coming around now days."

"Yes, and it's good to work."

Here the farmer would pause, no doubt, and squint toward the house, perhaps place a gnarled hand on Boon's rigid shoulder and give him a shake or a pat. And then he would ask *the question*.

They all asked it. Every farmer or clergyman or businessman. Every neighbor or gossip or friend. Every bringer of condolence or casserole. They all asked James Boon the question.

While they were looking at Betsey Anne.

She turned aside from the scene at the barn and slapped briskly at the mud on the front of her dress while she walked toward the pump to clean up for breakfast. But her heart could not turn aside so easily as her face could. Her heart still heard the question, though her ears had not heard a word.

"What'll you do now, James Boon?"

What'll you do now?

And this was probably the day the question would be answered. For this was the day the Springers would head home. It had been long enough, Pa felt, for young Adam and Ransom to keep the farm alone. It had been long enough to mourn their terrible loss. It was time to pick up their lives.

Betsey Anne got through breakfast by thinking only about the eggs, the onions, and the potatoes. "No," she answered shortly to each person who asked her if she wanted some bacon.

She got through the cleaning-up by chattering like a small girl about the minute details of the trip. "It'll no doubt be getting chilly before you get home today. I wish you could've started a little earlier maybe. I'll get an extra skin bag and put water in. Well, there's plenty of biscuits left over, and jerky you can eat along the way."

But when Ma said she would feed the infant Lydia one last time before she went home and carried the little bundle to the rocker in the sewing room, Betsey had to bite her lip. And after the child had been fed on Maudy's milk and laid sleeping into her cradle, when Ma came silently back into the kitchen, Betsey was sobbing, try as she might to hold it in.

"Now then, Betsey sweet, that's enough now. That's enough."

"How can you say that, Ma? How *can* you? Liddy, pretty Liddy – gone, and her baby without a ma, and you say I've cried enough?" Betsey turned a hostile back toward her mother and sobbed afresh into her apron, drawing a deep breath with a jagged edge.

"Set down here a minute, sweet, and have a talk with your Ma." Betsey sat, for she always would, no matter how old she was, obey her mother's command. There was silence for a moment or two, while Betsey worked to control her weeping and Ma silently stroked her daughter's wayward curls, waiting it seemed for the right words to arrive from somewhere outside herself.

"Betsey Anne, if you go on like you have, you'll be old before your time, and you'll live and die in sorrow like your Granny Wright. It's true she'd had a lot of hard in her life. And it's true she'd had a lot of good. But when it came to remembering, when she closed her eyes alone in the night, why she opened up the box what held the bad, and that's what she combed through with her weary fingers." Again there was a pause, Ann's eyes closed as if listening.

"Now your Granny, she knew God and that's certain. But she never knew **peace**, the kind of peace that comes from God. And that's on account of she was always looking in the wrong box. God layers His peace in amongst the good that He alone gives us, daughter, and I look there for it every day. Now, the Good Lord allows that other box in a body's life, too, and He lets it get plumb filled up sometimes. But He don't hide His peace in there. What He layers in with our troubles is the **need** for peace, so's we'll go a looking to the foot of the Cross."

The Springer wagon had rattled up before the front door while she was talking and they had seen Boon helping Pa down, while young Charles held the team. The two women sat in silence, except for an occasional jerking sigh from Betsey, watching as the two carpet bags and a paper bundle of the things Lydia wanted her Ma to have were loaded into the wagon bed.

Ma smiled up at the men as they came in. Pa returned her smile, then searched Betsey Anne's face with eyes that could always see right through her, and finally turned his gaze to James Boon, stoic in his bereavement. "What'll you do now, Boon?" he asked.

"We'll marry," said Boon, without hesitation, looking straight at Betsey Anne.

Betsey gasped and looked around the circle of three, all eyes on hers, holding her gaze longest on Boon's strong, intent visage. "We'll marry?" she said, fighting an almost hysterical urge to laugh right out loud with relief and surprise and even joy mingled with her grief.

"We'll marry," said James Boon, never taking his eyes from hers. "We could all ride as far as town together and see if we can get that job done today."

"Seems to me that Methodist is always ready to hand for marrying folks!" cried Ann Springer, giving Betsey a squeeze around the shoulders, pressing her graying temple to Betsey's red one and starting the fit of healing laughter that overtook them all.

CHAPTER TWENTY-SIX

The itinerant Methodist was indeed found lodged at the hotel and was indeed willing to perform a marriage ceremony for the appropriate fee, although he did seem a trifle nonplussed when he realized the situation.

Clearing his throat and looking from face to face, he said, "Well, it seems to me this is a great deal like..." He thumbed through his soft, well-used Bible. "Here it is, Deuteronomy 25:5, If brethren dwell together, and one of them die, and have no child, the wife of the dead shall not marry without unto a stranger: her husband's brother shall go in unto her, and take her to him to wife, and perform the duty of an husband's brother unto her," he intoned. "No, no that's not quite it. Let me see..."

Betsey stood fidgeting, wiping sweaty palms on her dress, clinching the sides of it up into a ball, then remembering herself and letting it go. She stared at the minister's homely face with its three-day stubble and crooked nose and tried unsuccessfully to focus on his words.

"Here it is, James 1:27, Pure religion and undefiled before God and the Father is this, To visit the fatherless and widows in their affliction, and to keep himself unspotted from the world." He read with a sort of stentorian emotion, starting in a loud and ponderous tone and building to a pitch that spoke either of doom and destruction or the glory of God, pointing his left index finger into the air for emphasis. This time it was not until the reverberations of his voice had dwindled to silence that he realized this passage, too, was short of what he was looking for.

He flipped the pages of his Bible back and forth with a thumb moistened by his tongue, running a gnarled finger down the columns and mumbling under his breath. "Psalms, Psalms, 145, 146, here it is, The LORD preserveth the strangers; He relieveth the fatherless and widow: but the way of the wicked he turneth upside down. No, no, no. Maybe I want the water into wine…"

Looking up suddenly with his mouth hanging open and an air of having been caught daydreaming in school, he chuckled a little and his listeners chuckled back. Betsey felt a surge of relief and realized she'd been holding her breath, as though she suspected he might decide not to marry them after all.

"Now then," said the minister, tucking his scripture under his black-robed arm. "I guess you get my sense, whatever the passage." Raising his right hand above their heads, he began again, and still Betsey found it impossible to understand his words, though she was pretty sure he had included some form of "Wilt thou have this man?" or "Do you take this woman?" Somehow she managed a word of assent at the right moment, and heard James Boon do the same.

And then it was done. Betsey hugged her Ma and her Pa, shakily patted her brother Charles on the shoulder, and made affectionate gestures toward her children, all with a smile she held on her face until her teeth dried out and she had to lick them with her tongue to get her lips to close.

She was married. Again. To a man she knew but little.

Suddenly it seemed too similar to her marriage to Thomas Jefferson Hawkins. A decision made on the fly, with circumstance and need, or at least desire, entirely unrelated to the man himself, driving her choice. Was she even free to marry? She felt queasy and hot and cast about the room searching for a chair or a bench or a stool — anything to sit down on, anything at all. The room began to darken, the air within it to thicken. There was a hand under her elbow then, a strong arm across her back, and from somewhere she heard the Methodist's voice ring out the benediction with all his usual dramatic flair.

"The Lord bless you and keep you, the Lord make His face to shine down upon you and be gracious unto you. The Lord lift up His countenance upon you and give you peace!"

They were out the door then, standing on the hotel's wooden porch with a bright October day going its ordinary way around them. Children were playing, mothers were scolding, farmers were loading wagons, horses were trotting past. It seemed odd to Betsey Anne that they did not stop, all of them, and turn to stare. Didn't they know? Couldn't they see that something important had happened? Where were the questioners now with their incessant *"What'll you do now?"*

Herbert was the first to be settled into the wagon, shrieking happily with his customary enjoyment of anything out of the ordinary. His brothers and sisters piled in on top of one another, jostling for position and chattering as though *nothing* was out of the ordinary. Betsey found herself on the wagon seat with no recollection of climbing there, and Ma handed up the infant Lydia with a wistful smile.

"*Peace*, he said, Ma, *peace* from God."

"Yes, child, peace," said Ma, patting Betsey on the knee. "And all you need to do is receive it."

Betsey turned to look at Boon, taking his seat beside her and picking up the reins. He smiled at her, a little formally perhaps, and briefly, before his eyes drifted downward to his own sleeping daughter in her arms, and then across her to Ma and Pa and Charles. "Lord bless you," he said, and started the mismatched horses toward home with a "tch" and a gentle flick of leather on their shiny backs.

Peace. In some ways she felt peaceful. It was right and good, surely, this marriage to James Boon. She knew at least enough to know that he loved the children, one and all, and that he could work. He would feed them; he would make the farm feed them all. And she would care for them – and for him. It would not matter that he didn't love her as he'd loved Lydia, surely.

It did not matter.

Peace. Peace. *The Lord bless you and keep you, the Lord make His face to shine down upon you and be gracious unto you. The Lord lift up His countenance upon you and give you peace.* She said the words over and over again in her head, clinging to them, gathering them together in a bundle so to speak, and holding them close to her heart. Receive it, Ma had said. She could not think of a better way to receive a gift from God than to memorize the promise of it.

And peace somehow began to grow within her breast.

It started simply as the mere absence of panic as they drove home. Later it was the absence of tears as she fed and changed her sister's namesake; still later it was the realization that this child was now her own. Peace was the happy laughter of the children at their play. Peace was the aroma of nourishing stew that arose from the pot Ma had buried in the fire pit before they left that morning.

Peace was James Boon swinging off down to the barn with Herbert calling out "Ah ba ba ba ba!" atop his stout shoulders. Peace was that old sense of pleasure in fabric and thread and the firm fit of her smooth-worn thimble.

Peace was the calm in Annie's voice when she laid seven plates on the supper table, leaving one alone on the sideboard, and said, "I do miss Aunt Liddy, Ma, but I expect she likes it up in Heaven." Peace was Sammy and Duga with baskets full of freshly-caught fish and faces shining through dirty smudges.

Peace was the swiftness with which the household returned to a normal routine, comfortable if not easy; made hard only by work, not by strife. It was just like before really, Betsey thought, when Liddy was there. James Boon had a way of thinking about the farm that never ceased to amaze her; it was like he could see some grand picture in his head of what their farm would be like two or three years down the road and then parcel out what would have to be done each day and each month in between in order to get there. He always managed to dispense with a few chores before breakfast and to be heard washing up at the pump outside just as Betsey laid the food on the table.

"Lord we thank Thee for the many blessings which Thou hast bestowed upon us and for the bounty we see before us, Amen," he would say, every day, just as he had before Lydia died. Just as sincerely one day as the last. "Very fine breakfast, Betsey Anne," he would say when he had eaten his food and wiped his mouth with a faded calico napkin. Then placing his hands on the side of the table, ready to push back the bench and rise, he would look around at eager faces and assign the tasks, always ending with, "Well, men…" which the boys took as their cue to get started, fighting to be first out the door.

Peace was the very bounty James Boon mentioned in his prayers. Food enough to feed the family and even to reach out a helping hand to another family from time to time through all the severe winter months. Six healthy, happy children were growing strong from good food and hard work, including the sturdy Lydia. Blessed with her mother's fair looks and her father's robust build, she grew swiftly and learned quickly, proving to them all that she had not suffered in the difficult delivery.

Before a year had passed, baby Lydia was riding with Herbert in his little cart and entertaining him all day with her antics, burrowing in the fertile soil, patting up little mounds as though ready for planting, pursuing unfortunate worms and grubs. She babbled on to him for hours at a time, in a language all her own, with expressive rise and fall of inflection and funny little bobs of her head. Herbert seemed somehow to understand every syllable she uttered, always answering her when she paused.

"Ah ba!" he exclaimed during one of her soliloquies at the dinner table one noon. "Ah ba!" he repeated, pointing a butter-covered finger at her.

"No!" she cried, striking at his finger with a sourdough biscuit to extend her reach and pointing a finger back at him. "Ah**ba**!" She brought the pointing finger in and patted herself on the chest with a loud thump. "Iddy! Iddy!" she shouted insistently.

"Id!" he said, triumphantly, producing instant silence around the table, the entire family awestruck at his pronunciation of a new word. He looked around the table, satisfied with his command of their complete attention. "Id!" he said again, pointing the same oily finger at the rosy toddler, and widening his mouth into a happy grin.

"Iddy," said Annie.

"Iddy," said Sammy.

"Iddy," said Duga, himself the author of his own nickname.

"Iddy," said Harriet. "I guess she wants to be called Iddy."

"Iddy," whispered Betsey Anne, her eyes locking with Boon's eyes, knowing that he, too, was unable to decide which child to be more proud of. There was such a look of tenderness there, such sweet love for his daughter, for all the children, and for an instant she imagined she saw something else. But she looked away, her eyes sweeping across the six happy eaters around her well-filled table.

Peace was James Boon reading to the children about David and Goliath or Samson and Delilah before kissing them all around and shooing them off to their beds promising them a hard day's work on the morrow. Peace was exchanging a smile with him as they stood ready to leave the kitchen, each with a hand on their respective doorknobs, each having cast one last loving glance around the room.

"The Lord bless you and keep you, the Lord make His face to shine down upon you and be gracious to you. The Lord lift up His countenance upon you and give you peace," Betsey whispered to Iddy, fast asleep in the cradle beside her bed. "You'll be a growing out of that cradle soon enough, Iddy girl, soon enough."

She lay for a long time with her eyes open, until they adjusted to the dim moonlight that filtered through the window. She looked around the familiar room, her eyes lingering on the objects she had long ago so endowed with meaning. The sewing machine, the rocking chair, even the plank floor -- all had been to her some form of desperately-needed proof that Jefferson loved her.

She twisted her mouth a little – half a frown, half a wistful smile. Jefferson had tried to love her, she thought now, or at least he had wanted to love her, though he never knew how. And the fault, if fault there was, had been her own. *Love's the only plant you can grow without a seed.* Sarah had said it to her, over and over. She had repeated it to herself like the chant of a prayer.

And indeed she had watered love faithfully, had tended the imaginary plant with care and patience, daily checking to see if love had grown.

But she had tried to grow it in the wrong heart. She knew that now. She had tried to grow the love in **Jefferson's** heart, and not her own.

Betsey turned to her other side, giving her pillow a push and a shove and drawing a light cover up under her chin. It did not matter that James Boon did not love her.

Closing her eyes, she smiled and drifted off to sleep.
Peace.
Peace was just knowing that she loved James Boon.

CHAPTER TWENTY-SEVEN

It was a year, almost to the day, after Lydia's passing, that Betsey Anne awoke with a heavy heart and a dull ache in the back of her head, despite pleasant, temperate weather.

"You're a fool, Betsey Anne," she muttered to herself. "You haven't a thing to be a crying about."

She hung her gown on its peg and gave her work dress a shake before pulling it on over her head. Almost automatically, she tweaked the sleeve of her new "meeting" dress, hanging in its place. Made from a deep, rich green silk, its bodice was fitted to glove-like smoothness, its *a la corde* sleeves measured her arm to perfection. The gored skirt flared out fully to accommodate the new hoops that Boon had picked out and carried home in the back of the wagon; he'd lost his nerve by the time he pulled up in the front yard, she remembered, and called out to her that there was "something here in the wagon for you" before hurrying off to the barn. The hem was puffed all around with soft black velvet, which also trimmed the sleeves and collar.

To Betsey, the dress looked like one fit for royalty, especially hanging next to her sturdy black alpaca and her other calico work dress – even with a work-softened old apron draped over its shoulders to keep it clean. She had sewn every stitch carefully and lovingly, feeling at odd moments a sense of guilt for any stitch she had ever placed hurriedly in someone else's gown. She had never had a garment that was anything but practical, never had a second "meeting" dress.

Each morning since the fabric had been purchased, a single

glance at it had been enough to put a thrill of joy in her heart. But not this morning.

There was a dark sense of something amiss hovering behind her eyes, though she could not pinpoint its source.

The children were already stirring when she entered the kitchen. Betsey tied on her apron and called out her orders; there was no need for quiet, since Boon was no doubt already down at the chicken coop tossing out the grain.

"Annie, stir up some cornbread quick-like and then get Herbert washed up and help him with his shirt. Harriet, you can set the table this time and get up some cider. Duga, your turn to fetch in the water, and bring around my wash bucket while you're at it. Sammy, you can gather the eggs and if Uncle Boon has the milk ready, haul it on up."

She pulled open the door and saw that Boon had already set the fire in the pit, and placed the iron stew pot on its rack nearby, knowing she would bury the dinner early on wash day. She paused on the doorstep, surveying all she could see. Was anything wrong?

Her eyes took in the tidy garden, the recently-harvested field, the bright barn. Duga was pumping water swiftly into the second bucket; Sammy was opening the gate to the chicken house and laughing with Boon, who was banging on the bottom of the scratch pan to empty it completely. The chickens were busily scratching and pecking, their jerky motions making them look almost frantic. Maudy was munching hay, placidly watching the chickens while she chewed and chewed and chewed. The barn door stood open, showing that the horses had already received their morning rations. A group of tools stood ready against the barn wall, a sign of Boon's ever-present planning.

"You're a fool, Betsey Anne," she scolded herself for the second time in half an hour. "Duga, don't forget to fill the reservoir," she reminded, patting the golden head as he trundled by with the sloshing buckets.

The bacon was quick to fry over the hot center of the fire, and she was glad, for the smell of it turned her stomach. She cut potatoes and onions in her hand with a sharp paring knife and dropped them into the pan of bacon drippings, giving them a quick stir. Then she quartered some more and plopped them into the stew pot, along with some carrots and a sprig of sage. She carried the heavy pot over to the pump and added a good portion of water.

"Uncle said to give you these two chickens for the stew, Ma," said Sammy, holding out the two birds, dangling by their three-toed feet.

"Thank you, Sammy," she said, taking them, thinking to herself, "That man don't forget a thing."

By the time Boon came up to wash at the pump, the stew was buried, the children all had shining faces, and the cornbread was cut into golden-yellow squares and piled on a plate in the center of the kitchen table, surrounded by plates of bacon, potatoes, and scrambled eggs. Glasses of cold cider were beside each plate, and fresh milk was on the sideboard. Betsey carried in the coffee and filled a mug for herself and another for Boon while the others were shuffling into their places.

And still, Betsey was looking around for something amiss. The ache in her head had reached down her back until it lodged between her shoulder blades, and had filled her head till it seemed her temples must be visibly pounding.

"Annie, could you bring me up a ginger root for some tea?" she asked, unable to eat the food on her plate.

"Sure, Ma," came the bright answer, and Annie was up and out the door, headed for the cellar.

"Something troubling you?" Boon reached a hand to touch hers, bent his head to look into her down-turned eyes.

"Oh, just an ache in my head," she half-lied, not wanting to try to explain something she could not explain to herself. "A cup of ginger tea'll fix that, no doubt."

He smiled at her, the same way he smiled at Harriet or Iddy when they showed him their skinned knees or slivers in their fingers, then wiped his mouth and said, "Well it's a fine breakfast, even so, Betsey Anne." Looking around the table at the expectant faces, and turning to find Annie framed in the doorway, he got a twinkle in his eye.

"Now then," he said, drawing out the suspense for them all. "Now then, I'll tell you what – if you can do up your chores and help your Ma finish the wash before noon, you can all go fishing today!"

There were cheers all around, both from those who understood and from those who merely knew there was some excitement afoot, followed by a hurried conference and a self-assigning of the necessary tasks among the children. Boon stood up from the table and walked straight into the sewing room, much to Betsey's surprise, returning with her rocking chair and carrying it out into the yard to station it beside the wash basin.

Sticking his head back in through the open front door, he smiled gently at Betsey where she sat waiting for the tea to steep. "You shirk a little today, Betsey Anne, and let the younguns do the work. Too much work'll not do your head any good."

Then he was gone, whistling, and pulling the babbling Iddy and Herbert in their wagon behind him.

And still the incessant sense of foreboding hung over her like a storm cloud. Perhaps she was taking a fever. She downed a spoonful of her mother's worst-tasting tonic and carried her ginger tea out into the yard where Annie was filling the wash pot and Harriet was piling up the clothes to be scrubbed. Betsey Anne sank gratefully into the rocker and sipped at the hot liquid, now and then fanning herself with her apron.

"It's a warm day, ain't it?" she said aimlessly to the girls, not expecting an answer and squinting over their heads at the boys working furiously in the garden. When her tea was finished, she handed the mug off to Harriet, who took it to the kitchen without stopping to ask what or why, then she leaned her head back against the smooth wood of the rocker and pressed her fingertips to her temples.

It was luxury, really, she thought to herself, to be able to sit idly in a chair in the shade while all the work of a busy farm went smoothly on without her. These were fine boys and girls she had raised, all of them knowing what to do and doing it without complaint. A cool breeze floated past her face and played with the tendrils of hair that always escaped her pins, cooling her face and neck. The tonic and the tea began to have their effect and her headache slowly receded.

But still she could not shake the sense that something was wrong somewhere.

Petitioned by breathless children all in a row before her with the sun high above their heads, she agreed that bread and jerky would suffice for their noon meal and the stew would be just as good come suppertime. She helped them pack up the picnic and smiled at their backs as they hopped and skipped down over the meadow, with the little wagon rumbling behind them and Boon calling out "Who can catch the most fish today?" in a cheerful voice.

Left to her own devices, she decided once again that impending illness might still have been the cause of her unhappy attitude and that rest was the best weapon against illness. She unbuttoned the front of her dress part way down and rolled the sleeves above her elbows, then took off her boots and lay down on top of the faded pinwheel quilt Sarah had made so long ago.

Closing her eyes in the dim coolness of the room, she slept, but lightly, and for the first time in a long time she dreamed of Jefferson. She could not see him, really, in her dream, but only a shadow of him, a shape of him somehow. She heard his voice, but not his words. She felt his touch, but could not touch him. She felt the heat of his breath on her skin and smelled the liquor on it. The shadow wrapped itself around her like heavy smoke from a green fire, circling around her feet first, then her knees, her waist, her arms, her head, where it choked her with a sickly-sweet smell of perfume before it was blown away by a strong wind that knocked her down and left her with a pounding in her head. Pounding, pounding, pounding, like a builder's hammer or a soldier's drum. Knocking, knocking, knocking, like a woodpecker high in a tree.

She awoke feeling flushed and sweaty, her heart pounding along with her head. Her first sense was that the headache was back, so real was the pounding even after sleep had fled. But after a moment she realized that instead the pounding was real – someone was pounding on the door, and beginning to shout.

"Miz Boon? Miz Boon!"

Betsey struggled up groggily from the bed, dimly aware that she must have been asleep for hours, that the sun was hovering at half-mast to the west. "I'm coming!" she called out, reaching for the doorknob and pulling open the sturdy door, letting in a flood of light.

Her mouth hanging open, her heart pounding, she gripped the

knob until the knuckles on her hand turned white. Never had she expected to see Prudie Richy – Prudie Briscoe – standing at her front door.

Somehow Betsey managed to garner enough good manners to invite the visitor in, to seat her at the table, to offer her a cup of tea, though she was grateful it was refused. She sank down on the bench opposite the guest and swallowed hard, unable to think of anything to say.

"I know what you must think," Prudie began, working the crumpled ribbons of her bonnet between stubby fingers, studying them carefully as though checking them for defects. "I mean, I know what she told you, and all, and that's why I come. I didn't want, I don't want…" She broke off and looked up for the first time, searching Betsey's face with surprisingly sharp, black eyes that peered out in a bird-like way beneath heavy eyebrows. "It's certain you know a woman like me is right lucky to have a man take her in, and whatever you think, I love them children."

Betsey was irritated, in no small degree due to the cloying fragrance of Prudie's perfumed soap, filling every inch of the warm air in the kitchen. It was the very perfume in her dream, the perfume that had always accompanied Jefferson's absences and his drinking.

Her first instinct was to say, "What in the world are you talking about?" and force the poor woman to put it in plain words. But she knew the instant she thought it that such a question would only serve to extend the interview; it was obvious that while Prudie was offering explanations for her marriage to old Briscoe, she was really talking about Jefferson. About Jefferson coming home smelling of Prudie Richy's distinctive perfumed soap.

"Anybody can see that you love them children," Betsey said, too sharply.

Taking heart, Prudie looked back into her lap, vigorously smoothing the bonnet ribbons as though she were trying to read notes inscribed among the wrinkles. At last she spoke. "I've had a letter from her…"

Betsey broke in, "Who?"

"Mary Jane Crabb."

"Oh. A letter." Betsey said. "I might've known," she was thinking to herself. "I might've known, it seems there's always a letter when it comes to bad news and Jefferson."

And she was certain the shabby, distraught woman before her had not come bearing good news.

"I've had a letter from her," Prudie continued with effort. "And she says she wished she had it all to do over and she could do different."

Betsey was feeling hot all over and the room was getting dark. "Different?" She forced the word out with what little breath was left in her lungs.

"I used to let them have my room, was all, Miz Boon," Prudie blurted suddenly. "I know what she told you, but I didn't never..." she reddened.

"Ride the old stag's back?" Betsey blurted out.

"No." Prudie reddened further.

"It was Mary Jane? All along?" Betsey's mouth and throat were dry as cotton, her head was spinning. She was vaguely conscious of Boon's presence in the room, his hand on her shoulder, but she couldn't have told where he came from or when. "All along..."

"They got some kind of sick, up there in Ignau..."

"Ignau!" The word was like a blast from a gun, bringing Betsey back into sharp focus. "Ignau?"

"The two of them," Prudie's black eyes darted from Betsey's face to Boon's, and she took a deep breath. "Both of them took sick. Jefferson's dead already and I expect by this time she's gone, too, judging by what she said in her letter, and no doubt that's why she's sorry of a sudden for all she done."

"Mary Jane and Jefferson..."

"Dead."

"In Ignau..."

"They took sick, somehow, and she wanted me to know what she told you..."

"All along..."

"She said she wished she hadn't of told you that, said she wished she hadn't of ever laid eyes on your man."

"Me too."

"Ma'am?"

"Me too." Betsey was hearing Mary Jane's own voice across the years – *"Oh, you wicked thing!"* she had laughed out, ringing and reverberating throughout Henderson's store. "Me too," she repeated woodenly.

"I brung you the letter," Prudie whispered, placing a crumpled envelope on the table and sliding it across to Betsey.

She had to read it, of course; she had to know the whole thing. Her fingers shook as she unfolded the letter and began to read.

Ingnau, October 5, 1868

It is with a weak and repentant heart that I take my pen in hand to try and make things right between us as these is my last days upon this old earth. I done you a wrong more than you know and fear it may still linger on and cause you trouble that you did not earn. I know you remember those days in which I used to meet Jefferson Hawkins in town and ply you with a coin I knew you could ill afford to turn away to coax you to give us your room, but you likely do not know that was the least of it, for I told his wife that you were the one he made to ride the old stag's back. How I wish I had never laid eyes upon the man and set out on such a course of action, let alone to cover my own sin by a telling lies on you. I doubt that you will care but feel the need as I lay here a dying to tell you the rest of what I done and you may tell his wife if you've a mind to and if she is around there still. I did try to leave him and went on and married Podinsky as I thought he would provide for me in style as I was a-wanting. Then the war made money tight and he upped and took a payment from the man he worked for to go and fight instead of him on account of the draft. I ran through the money quick enough and ended up a-working behind the bar in a dirty saloon in Toledo, when who should I see there but Hawkins and just like that we fell in together again. But hard living done caught up with us now and the fever taken him and I can tell I ain't so far behind. So forgive me now if you can find it on your heart to do so and I expect I will have to take my chances with the Almighty but hope to get some mercy if there's such a thing to be had after all I done. Mary Jane Crabb to Prudie Richy

Betsey wrapped her arms tightly around herself and stared at the table with glazed eyes, rocking herself back and forth unaware that she had begun to moan. Boon nodded to the guest and gestured toward the door. Only too glad to comply with his silent request, Prudie Briscoe hastily pulled her bonnet down over her ears and nodded to Boon as she hurried out the door, leaving the heavy scent of her too-fragrant soap behind her as surely as if it were sitting bodily on the bench.

There was some clanking and banging, some going in and out, some conferencing in hushed tones. Betsey was vaguely aware that the children disappeared over the rim of the hill, no doubt headed for Sarah's. A bowl of steaming chicken stew was set before her, and another cup of ginger tea, with two heaping spoonfuls of brown sugar stirred in.

Still she sat staring, rocking, moaning.

"Eat, Betsey Anne," Boon's voice was soft and mellow. "Eat the stew, it's good, it'll do you good."

She picked up her spoon, but didn't put it in the bowl. Mary Jane. Mary Jane Crabb and Jefferson. Sweaty and tangled in Prudie Richy's strong-smelling sheets. Mary Jane Crabb and Jefferson. In Ingnau. All along. All this time.

All this time.

Tears began to drift down her cheeks, silently but swiftly. "It's all a lie, Boon," she whispered finally. "I lied to you."

She was aware that he stopped eating, wiped his mouth, turned to face her. Still she didn't look at him. She took a deep, shuddering breath. "I knew he wasn't dead. At least I think I knew. I had letters, Frances, she thought he was dead, or pretended to think so. Toledo in '64. A fight – sailors – saloon." Her breath was short, her words were clipped, tumbling out one on top of the other.

"But Elisabeth and William knew, they knew he was in Ingnau, and I guess I knew that too. But, oh Boon! I wanted him to be dead! I know it's awful, and sinful, but I wanted him to be dead so I could stop wondering, so I could stop looking for him and trying to figure out what I'd done wrong and how I could fix it!" She buried her face in her apron and sobbed out loud.

"I wanted him to be dead, Boon, so I lied and I said he was dead, and I kept on saying it even when I found out it weren't true, so's you could stay here and we could all have food on the table and a pump that works and some planks on top of that hateful dirt floor!"

Boon was silent for a few minutes, and it seemed to her that he was calmly sipping his cider while she poured out her heart, while years of pain were wrenched from the depths of her soul. His calm began to reach toward her somehow, and her sobbing subsided. She dried her face with her apron, and thinking how unladylike it was, even blew her nose on a corner of it, then she straightened a little and picked up her spoon again, pretending she was going to eat.

Still she could not look at Boon.

Finally he spoke. "Maybe you had to marry me, Betsey Anne. Maybe you did. But I didn't have to marry you. I didn't have to stay. But from the first time I saw you, well, I cared for you. Like I'd always know you, or should have.

"I guess as long as we're having a confession here, I might as well tell you that I lied to you, too – we both did, Lydia and me. She was in trouble, if you take my meaning, and when she told him, he hit her with the back of his hand. I saw him do it and without thinking I showed him the quick way down the stairs, and there she was, crying, and not knowing what to do. So we talked, and we prayed, and there was this peace – this peace that you could almost touch it was so strong. So we married and we kept that secret till this very minute."

He had gotten up from the table and was standing by the door looking down at her. "I'm not going anywhere, Betsey Anne. Even if he's not dead still. Even if you don't love me, now nor ever. I'm not going anywhere. I'm not Jefferson. And I love you."

There was a pause. "I love you, Betsey Anne. And I thought, I hoped, you…well, I guess I was wrong. But I meant what I said in front of God and your folks. And I'm not going anywhere unless you tell me to go."

She sat for a long time without moving, her hands tightly gripping the edge of the table, hearing his step and the bang of the door long after the actual sound had died down. He had known, he had hoped all along that she loved him. Only now he was beginning to doubt it, and there was only her own foolishness to blame. She was making a mess of things again, and this time she was most certainly doing it all herself.

Giving herself a little shake, she left the kitchen and shut the sewing-room door behind her. She washed her face, shed her work dress, and climbed into all her best undergarments – her whitest chemise, her corset, her Spencer. She wrestled with her hoops and slipped on her lacy petticoat, the one she'd made especially for the green silk dress. Almost holding her breath, she took the apron off the shoulders of the shining garment and felt the silk rustle against her skin as she slipped it over her head.

She brushed her hair out and wound it back up in a tight bun, then thought better of it and brushed it down again, feeling like a giddy schoolgirl. She wiped the day's dust off the toes of her boots, and pushed her feet into them with some effort, wishing she had put them back on before she donned the wiry hoops. Smoothing the front of her dress, she started out for the barn, rehearsing her speech under her breath.

She had only to step out into the October sunshine before she saw him. Freshly washed, hair glistening, leaning against the side of the barn like he had nothing better to do, chewing on a piece of straw.

Waiting for her.

Somehow her feet carried her the rest of the way down the path till she stood toe to toe with him, her head tipped forward against his shoulder, the sweet, true smell of him filling her nostrils.

"James..." she began.

But there was nothing she had to say, not really.

He had known all along.

THE END

LaVergne, TN USA
14 November 2010
204786LV00004B/5/P